SERIES RECAP

CW01500376

Tattered Huntress

Daisy Carter is a low elf living in Edinburgh, eking out a living as a delivery driver. She is dispatched to Neidpath Castle to deliver a parcel to Hugo Pemberville, a celebrated high elf who is famous for treasure hunting. When she hands him his parcel and waits for his signature, he recognises the silver ring in her eyes that indicates she is a user of spider's silk, a dangerously addictive drug that Daisy takes to control the wild magic inside her. Hugo's demeanour changes instantly and, with considerable rudeness, he tells Daisy to leave. Before she does, she spots some notes about the location of a special, long-lost locket necklace.

Upset at Hugo's attitude, Daisy suggests to a belligerent troll named Duchess that she leaves her current habitat in favour of a more pleasant one under the bridge at Hugo's ancestral home. When Hugo discovers that Duchess has taken up residence there, he calls Daisy's boss and ensures she is fired because of her drug addiction. To retaliate, Daisy uses the information from the notes to find the necklace before Hugo does.

Daisy takes it to a man called Sir Nigel. Impressed that she found it, he offers her a place in a treasure-hunting competition to find some chests of Jacobean gold. Daisy later realises that the locket on the necklace was enchanted; having opened it before she handed it over, she is now supposedly the boss of two very annoying brownies, Hester and Otis.

Daisy and the brownies join Sir Nigel's treasure hunt to find three parts to a magical key which, when combined, will reveal the location of the treasure chests. There are numerous other competitors, including Humphrey and Eleanor, a friendly couple who are somewhat lackadaisical about the hunt.

The first key part is located in northern England. Daisy would have found it first, but she is delayed when another team is attacked by a giant snake. She saves them, but in the meantime Hugo and his team of Primes find the key part. Hugo initially thinks Daisy engineered the snake attack in a deliberate attempt to harm her competitors, but he soon realises the truth.

The second key part is located in the north of Scotland, in a concealed chamber behind an underground cavern called Smoo Cave. The entrance to the chamber is unlocked by another competitor, Gordon, a sorcerer who appears to have an uncomfortable relationship with Hugo.

Daisy discovers she is claustrophobic and panics when she is underground. Unable to continue searching for the key part, she falls through the ground in the cave and is knocked unconscious. When she awakes, she is challenged to a fight to the death by a one-eyed creature known as the Fachan. The Fachan eventually decides that she is not a worthy opponent, but he gifts her a sentient sword called Gladys and shows her the way out of the cave.

Suffering from spider's silk withdrawal, Daisy starts hallucinating. Hugo finds her and helps her recover, and his attitude towards her softens considerably. She re-joins the treasure hunt

SKULLDUGGERY

BOOK THREE

THE THRILL OF THE HUNT

HELEN HARPER

for the third key part, which is located in one of many houses owned by a rich man known for his unpleasant behaviour. With the help of Hester and Otis, Daisy discovers that the man has been keeping magical creatures captive. She releases them, sneaks into the house and finds the key part. Before she can retrieve it, though, Humphrey appears and takes it.

With no key part, Daisy can no longer participate in the treasure hunt, and only Humphrey and Hugo remain in the competition. She is suspicious about Humphrey and spies when all three key parts are put together and the location of the treasure chests is revealed. They are on the tidal island of Cramond, near Edinburgh, and Daisy quickly heads there to wait.

She witnesses Humphrey attack Hugo with a terrible power known as blood magic and steps in to save him. Humphrey escapes, while Hugo and Daisy are trapped on the island as the tide comes in. They are forced to shelter there for hours, during which time Hugo reveals that his best friend died as a result of a spider's silk addiction and Daisy confesses that she takes the drugs because otherwise her magic will overwhelm her.

Eventually they make it safely back to the mainland where they recover the treasure and ensure that Humphrey is arrested. Daisy is offered her old job as a delivery driver – but she decides to become a full-time treasure hunter instead.

Fiendish Delights

Daisy is working as a freelance treasure hunter, but most of her commissions so far have involved little more than lost-and-found searches. That changes when a young girl, Sophia, manipulates her into searching for a doll she had recently lost. Daisy tracks the lost doll to a witch called Mud McAlpine, but he will only return it if she gives him a freshly cut toenail from a troll.

Daisy, Hester and Otis travel to Pemberville Castle where Duchess the troll is living. Daisy reconnects with Hugo and he agrees to help her retrieve the doll. With one of Duchess's toenails in their possession, they return to Mud McAlpine. Starstruck by Hugo, he breaks the ward on his flat so they can enter.

Once they are inside, he conjures up a magic scroll that will lead to one of the mythical thirteen treasures of Great Britain. Almost as soon as the scroll appears, Sophia shows up and reveals herself as a fiend called Zashtum. Daisy learns that fiends are evil beings created through the misuse of blood magic whose ultimate goal is to gain more power for themselves. They cannot be killed, only banished by powerful witches.

Zashtum fights Mud, Daisy and Hugo for the scroll. Eventually Mud manages to banish her, but he is critically injured and the scroll is destroyed. However, Daisy saw enough of the words on it before it burned to start hunting for the treasure.

Daisy, together with Hugo and his group of treasure-hunting Primes, travel to a rural cemetery in Wales where they believe the treasure is buried – but they uncover nothing more than an old dragon's tooth.

Daisy manages to interpret more of what she saw on the magic scroll and they return to Wales with the sorcerer Gordon Mackenzie, who agrees to help them. Gordon and Hugo have a long-standing disagreement resulting from Gordon's search for Lady Rose, a high elf who vanished thirty years earlier. The elvish community has long suspected that Hugo's parents had something to do with Rose's disappearance.

The team locate the treasure, a gold and silver chess set, but before they can remove it from the cemetery a dragon appears and snatches it away. Aware that the dragon could be in danger from fiends that are still hunting for the chess set, Daisy and Hugo resolve to retrieve it.

When they travel to a nearby town to find the dragon's lair, they are confronted by a fiend, Baltar, who seems to think he's met Daisy before. He has the opportunity to kill Daisy but chooses not to, and Daisy does not understand why.

Daisy and Hugo discover several potential locations for the dragon's lair. Their relationship is deepening, but Daisy is losing control of her magic and having to take more and more of spider's silk to stop her powers from spilling out. Because of this, she chooses not to act upon her feelings for Hugo; however, she does agree that once the chess set is safe, she will spend three months with Hugo and his team to learn to control her magic properly. Once she has achieved that, she can start weaning herself off her addiction.

There is no dragon at the first lair. Daisy is separated from Hugo and the brownies and meets the Fachan again. They are attacked by three fiends, including Baltar. Using Gladys, the sword that the Fachan gave to her when they first met, Daisy kills Baltar. She assumes that Gladys has special powers that forced Baltar to die.

At the next lair, Daisy reconnects with Hester, Otis and Hugo and they find the dragon who took the chess set. Daisy realises that a fiend has used magic to impersonate Hugo and fights him. The fiend reveals that he is Athair, the most powerful one in the country. He could easily kill Daisy but he lets her go, whispering to her that she is his daughter.

Hugo and Daisy turn the chess set over to Sir Nigel at the British Museum. He tells them that it is possible for a fiend to kill another fiend; as Daisy killed Baltar, she starts to believe that what Athair told her might be true.

CHAPTER
ONE

I was sure that somebody somewhere enjoyed posh parties with dainty canapés, fizzing champagne and the delicate strains of Mozart in the background. Unfortunately, I was not that person – especially when all I really wanted to do was curl up in a corner and quietly die.

'Would madam care for a sourdough buckwheat blini garnished with oak-smoked salmon, beluga caviar, beetroot foam and gold leaf?'

Madam would much rather have had a greasy burger, a hot bath and twelve hours of uninterrupted sleep. However, I managed to smile at the young tuxedoed waiter and decline politely with a shake of my head. He was clearly a low elf, and to be a low elf in this room you were either friendly with someone like Hugo Pemberville or you'd been drafted in as staff to serve the highfalutin' elite of the magical world.

I'd scanned the hundreds of well-dressed guests and there wasn't a single one who was a low elf like me and the wait staff. Then again, it was possible that I wasn't a low elf either. I grimaced and tossed back my glass of champagne before snagging another one.

'I'm bored,' Hester complained in my ear. 'This is a very dull party.'

'It's a cultured, civilised affair, Hes,' Otis told her.

'I don't want to be civilised or cultured.' She sniffed. 'I want to have some fun. This is the first night we've been away from Pemberville Castle in six weeks. I'm wearing my best dress – and I'm about to collapse from boredom.'

She wasn't the only one on the verge of collapse, though my woes were physical. I could feel myself swaying with exhaustion, every muscle in my body ached and my eyelids were heavy. Even lifting the glass of champagne to my lips felt like an effort. If I wasn't careful, I'd probably pitch face first into the nearest punch bowl.

My fingers strayed to my clutch bag, inside which nestled three pills of purest spider's silk. Swallowing one would keep me awake and alert for another couple of hours, but it was only five hours since my last hit; bone tired or not, I had to hold out for longer between doses. I *had* to. I was bitterly aware that my fatigue and aching body weren't solely the result of my recent training regime; my addiction to spider's silk was taking its toll in more ways than one.

Otis buzzed anxiously, 'Daisy? Are you alright?'

'Of course she's not alright!' Hester snapped. 'Hugo is on the other side of the room flirting with a very attractive woman in a revealing dress, while Daisy is here propping up the wall.' She nudged me. 'You should get out there and find someone of your own to flirt with. Then Hugo will get jealous, dash over here in a manly fashion and whisk us all away from this shitty, shitty party.'

I ground my teeth. 'I'm not twelve, Hester, and this is not a school disco. And Hugo would not whisk anyone away in a fit of preposterous jealousy.' I looked over at him. He was indeed deep in conversation with a stunning brunette whose glossy hair and sparkling jewels made her look as if she'd stepped off a catwalk. She kept touching his arm and leaning in to whisper in his ear, and my stomach kept clenching in annoyance.

I looked away. I had no claim on Hugo, not really. 'Besides,' I continued, 'as you well know, we're not here to enjoy a party or to flirt. This is business.'

Otis flapped his wings worriedly. 'There's no sign of Sir Nigel. Maybe he changed his mind at the last minute and he's not coming.'

'Yeah,' Hester agreed. 'He probably decided to do something more interesting with his time.' Her tiny bottom lip jutted out. 'Like fold his collection of bow ties into origami shapes. Or watch paint dry.'

'He said he'd be here and that he'd tell me everything he's found out about the fiends. Why don't the two of you see if you can spot him?' I suggested. 'Ask around.'

'And what will you be up to if we do that?' Hester asked suspiciously.

Ideally I'd be resting my eyes and playing the role of professional wallflower.

I spotted a familiar figure heading towards me. 'The same,' I said. 'Last one to find Sir Nigel is a rotten egg.'

'That's you,' Hester told her brother. 'You're a rotten egg.'

'No, *you're* a rotten egg.'

Lacking the energy to deal with their bickering, I waved them off then forced my mouth to curve into a smile as I greeted Gordon Mackenzie, the accomplished sorcerer and occasional nemesis of Hugo. 'Hi, Gordon.'

He ran a shaky hand through his hair and gave me a quick grin. 'Good evening, Daisy. I was hoping to bump into you.'

'Really?'

His cheeks turned pink. 'Really.' He coughed and shuffled his feet. 'I hate these sorts of things,' he said. 'Parties like this are full of people trying too hard to impress their peers. I'm not well suited to them.'

'You should talk to Hester. She's not impressed either.'

Gordon gave a surprised laugh. 'At least I'm not alone, then.'

'Definitely not.' This time I smiled more genuinely. 'How have you been?'

'Good. Busy.' He twitched awkwardly. 'How have you been?'

'Much the same.'

There were a few beats of silence, then Gordon dropped his eyes. 'I'm not very good at small talk either,' he admitted.

'To be fair, neither of us is a glittering raconteur at the moment.'

'I'm not surprised. You don't look very well, Daisy,' he said, then winced. 'I apologise. I didn't mean to be rude.'

I patted his arm. 'You're not being rude, Gordon, just honest. Never apologise for that. I'm tired. I've been training with Hugo and the Primes for the last month and a half and it's hard.' I swallowed. 'Really hard.'

Then I flexed my biceps. 'But look! I've got more muscles. I can swing my sword with greater control and I can empty my mind of thoughts for a whole nine minutes while I meditate. It's progress. Of sorts.' I shrugged then immediately regretted the action when a wave of pain rippled down my spine.

Wild magic flared deep in my belly, threatening to spring out from my fingertips. I hastily tamped it down; boring or not, the last thing this soirée needed was for me to set the room on fire because my magic was out of control.

Gordon understood what had nearly happened and he reached towards me. At least he didn't run away screaming. 'Are you okay?' he asked.

'I'm fine.' I swallowed hard. 'Honest. I'm doing okay. It's harder to control my powers when I'm tired, but I've got this.'

'Are you sure?'

'Positive.' I took another sip of champagne and tried to act as if nothing were wrong. Unfortunately, I didn't fool either of us – especially when the long-stemmed glass trembled in my traitorous hands. 'Have you seen Sir Nigel?' I asked. 'I need to pick his brains about something.'

'I'm afraid not. I think he's been delayed in Glasgow.'

Cumbubbling bollocks. My dismay must have shown on my face because Gordon leaned in closer. 'Is there anything I can do to help?'

I sighed. 'Not unless you're an expert on fiends as well as being a world-renowned sorcerer, and you can tell me what the likelihood is that a fiend would have sired a child and that child would be me, and if that's true whether I'll turn evil or die from my spider's silk addiction before that happens, and if my inability to control my own magic is because I'm at least fifty-percent fiend with the capacity to become a psychopathic murderer with no regard for anyone's wellbeing other than my own.' I took a breath.

Gordon stared at me.

I glanced down at my empty glass. 'I should stop drinking champagne,' I added. I put the glass down on a nearby table before I inadvertently dropped it and smashed it to smithereens.

He continued to stare at me.

'I won't hold it against you if you run away, Gordon,' I said.

He didn't move. Maybe my tirade had made him freeze with terror.

Finally, he met my eyes. 'Fiends are made, Daisy, not born. Yes, they embody evil, but that's not you. You are not a bad person, and you're certainly no more likely to become a psycho-pathic murderer than I am. I can't speak for the spider's silk problem because that's outside my area of expertise, but if Hugo is training you to help you beat your addiction, you're in the best possible hands. I don't know if you'll die from your addiction, but I do know that you're a good person and that's what counts, not who your parents are.'

Now it was my turn to stare. Gordon had spoken with quiet conviction; he wasn't afraid of me, he didn't patronise me, and he didn't tell me everything would be alright. He simply spoke the truth as he saw it, and that meant more than he would ever realise.

'You know what, Gordon?' I said softly. 'You're a good person too.'

He blushed deeply, fiddled with his cuffs, bowed and started to back away. 'I'll leave you in peace.'

Exhausted or not, I couldn't let him off that easily. 'Wait! You said that you were hoping to bump into me. Is there something I can help *you* with?'

He gave an almost imperceptible shake of his head. 'You've got a lot on your plate. Don't worry.'

I folded my arms. 'I'm not worried, but I'm here to listen.' I offered him a mock hard stare. 'Frankly, Gordon, I could do with the distraction, especially if Sir Nigel isn't going to show up. You came to our rescue in Wales at New Year. The least I can do is listen to you now. What's going on?'

He started to gnaw his bottom lip, then cast a glance first over his right shoulder then over his left before shuffling closer to me. Despite his nervousness, I couldn't mistake the flash of hope in his eyes. He really did want my help.

'You know that I'm looking into the disappearance of Lady Rose Assigney.' He was talking about the high elf who hadn't been seen for decades and whose disappearance was often blamed on Hugo's absent parents.

'Yep.'

'And you know that I've not had any success in discovering what happened to her.'

'She vanished without a trace thirty years ago, Gordon.'

He nodded. 'The last time anyone saw her was the thirtieth of May 1994. The anniversary is coming up soon.'

I did my best to reassure him. 'I'm sure you've done your absolute best, but even you can't work miracles.'

'I've exhausted almost every option,' he admitted.

I raised an eyebrow. '*Almost* every option?'

Gordon swallowed. 'There's an object that might help me get to the bottom of what happened to her. I've seen it mentioned in several books. It's a magical object that...' His voice trailed off and he seemed embarrassed. 'Well, let me just say that it's a magical object that might provide the answers.'

I no longer felt quite so tired. 'What is it?'

He reached into his breast pocket and took out a folded piece of paper. When I opened it up, I was confronted by a small hand-drawn diagram of a skull. My brow furrowed.

'It's not a real skull,' Gordon said hastily. 'It's made of gold and the drawing is to scale.'

If that were true, it was only three inches high. 'Okay.' I was reasonably certain what he was going to say next, and for once the frisson of anticipation that ran through my veins was nothing to do with drugs. This was exactly what I needed to keep my mind off my health problems.

'My skills lie in old books and ancient runes,' he said. 'I'm not a treasure hunter – I don't have any experience in that field, and I suspect that I'd be useless if I tried.'

My excitement got the better of me. 'You want me to speak to Hugo and persuade him to hunt for this magical skull. With my help, of course.'

Gordon blinked. 'Uh ... no. I was rather hoping that you'd agree to hunt for it on your own.'

I was so taken aback that I jerked and narrowly avoided colliding with yet another waiter hoisting aloft a silver platter with more elaborate but unappetising canapés. Everyone always asked for Hugo; *he* was the celebrated treasure hunter and *I* was the inexperienced upstart who rarely got a look in. 'Me?'

'Yes, you. You're smart, resourceful and powerful. You're the perfect person to search for the skull.'

Before I started to preen at his gushing praise, I tilted my head and gave him a narrow-eyed look. My earlier excitement was fading away. 'How many other treasure hunters have you spoken to before me?'

'One or two.'

At least he didn't try to deny it. 'One or two?'

Gordon shifted his weight. 'Okay,' he admitted. 'Maybe it's more like six.'

'Let me guess,' I said wryly. 'The others declined because they don't want to annoy Hugo. And you won't ask Hugo because he'll definitely say no.'

'See? I said you were smart.' Gordon's gaze was nervous but earnest. 'We both know that Hugo will only say no because he's scared.'

I felt a twitch of discomfort at discussing Hugo behind his back and I glanced over at him. The beautiful brunette was still by his side but he wasn't looking at her: he was looking at me, his expression inscrutable.

I nodded. 'Hugo is scared that your investigation will prove his parents' culpability in Lady Rose's disappearance.' And likely her murder, too. 'But they might have had nothing to do with it. Your investigation means that speculation about their involvement will never stop.'

'But my investigation could also prove that they weren't involved and clear their names!' Gordon protested.

I drew in a deep breath. 'Do you think they were involved?'

'Honestly?' He shrugged. 'I have no idea. There is circumstantial evidence but nothing concrete.' He didn't take his eyes from me. 'Lady Rose had a family too, Daisy, and they deserve closure. But the simple fact is that I'm running out of avenues to explore. If this magical skull doesn't provide any answers, I'm prepared to put my investigation to rest for good and tell Lady Rose's great-aunt, Grace Assigney, that we'll never know what happened.'

I rubbed the back of my neck. Everything about Lady Rose's disappearance all those years ago was complicated, and I didn't want to get involved if it would hurt Hugo. I cared about him too much. Gordon was right: Lady Rose should be found so her remains could be taken care of properly and her family had answers – but those answers might never *be* found. Life wasn't fair, no matter how much we wanted to believe otherwise.

In any case, this wasn't the place or the time to be making any sort of decision. I needed a fresh head to consider everything – and I needed to talk to Hugo. 'Send me what you have on the skull and I'll think about it. But,' I added hastily before Gordon's delight became too obvious, 'I'm not making any promises.'

He reached for my hands and squeezed them. 'Thank you, Daisy. Thank you so much.'

'Don't thank me yet,' I grunted. I glanced towards Hugo again, but this time he wasn't there.

TWO

Inhale.

I adjusted my grip on Gladius Acutissimus Gloriae Et Sanguinis – Gladys for short – and spun, slicing the air in front of me.

Exhale.

I ducked, jabbing the tip of her blade forward forcefully.

Inhale.

I side-stepped at speed, raising her up in a blocking motion.

Exhale.

I pivoted to my right, stumbled – and planted my entire body face-first in the soft ground. The tinnitus that had been my frequent companion for weeks flared up, whining out of pitch, while my whole body shivered. Cumbubbling bollocks.

I cursed aloud. 'Fuck.'

A shadow fell in front of me as I struggled to raise my head and forced the rest of my body upwards until I was standing once more.

'You lost concentration again,' Miriam chided. 'But at least this time you remembered to breathe.'

I hissed with frustration. 'I'm tired.' It sounded like a petty excuse but it was the truth.

Her response was both quiet and kind. 'I know. You've been training for twelve hours a day for six weeks, Daisy, and it's bound to take its toll. Your late night can't have helped, but it's the training regime that you and Hugo set up which is causing the real problems. If I could grade you for effort you'd be top of the class, but you must learn when to give yourself a break. You've been pushing too hard. You didn't even take a day off last week when it was your birthday.'

I'd had birthdays before and I'd have birthdays again – if I could beat this and succeed. I met her eyes. 'This is the best opportunity I'll have to bring my magic under control. If I can't, I'll never be in a position to wean myself off spider's silk.'

I was already running out of time; as my trembling hands attested, the side-effects of my long-term drug use were getting worse. I had magic lessons with Hugo, sword lessons with Miriam and meditation lessons with several of the Primes who resided at Pemberville Castle – but I still didn't have control.

'You're doing too much.'

'I promised Hugo. This was the favour he asked of me.'

'*He's* asking too much.'

I sighed and wiped away the sweat and mud from my face. 'We all know what the alternative is.' My magic would grow wilder and I'd take more spider's silk to try and control it. As a result, I'd end up dead. I knew that was still the most likely outcome, no matter how hard I tried.

'Are you training for yourself, Daisy?' Miriam asked. 'Or for Hugo?'

I didn't reply. To be honest, I didn't know the answer.

Her mouth puckered in disapproval. 'The pair of you are both too stubborn for your own good. Don't think I don't know about all those late nights you're spending on fiend research.

Athair could have been lying about his relationship to you, but even if he was telling the truth, none of us care about who your birth father was.'

They'd care if I turned into a fiend, though I didn't say that. Instead, I slid Gladys into her sheath at my side and bent down to pick up my water bottle. After taking several long glugs, I faced Miriam again. 'Where is Hugo, anyway? I've not seen him since last night.'

Despite my best efforts not to, I'd fallen asleep in the car on the way back to Pemberville Castle after the party. Hugo and I had not spoken at any length, and the matter of Gordon's magical golden skull was itching at me – plus, I'd missed Hugo's company at breakfast.

The more time I spent with him, the more comfortable his presence made me feel – and there was always the underlying lusty simmer between us that we'd agreed not to act on until I'd sorted myself out. Even I had to admit that was part of the reason I was pushing myself so hard.

'He headed out at dawn muttering something about some business he had to attend to,' Miriam said. 'I don't know what.'

I frowned. Since the time I'd sneaked into Pemberville Castle to steal his old dragon's egg, while he'd been planning to slip away with it for the same reason as me, we'd made a point of not keeping secrets from each other. That was why I'd told him and the rest of the Primes what Athair had revealed about my heritage.

'I'm sure he'll be back soon,' Miriam reassured me.

I hoped so. 'I'll find him when he returns.'

'Go for a nap. I'll make sure someone wakes you up when he arrives.'

Sleep was incredibly tempting. I glanced towards the towering turrets of Pemberville Castle then looked away again. 'I'll go for a run first.'

Miriam's eyes narrowed. 'Daisy—'

'Only to clear my head,' I said quickly. 'I won't overdo it and I won't go far.'

She tutted. I smiled and nudged Hester and Otis awake; they'd been snoozing in a makeshift nest in my discarded hoodie. 'Up for a run, you two?'

Hester's face screwed up. '*Run*? Fuck off.'

'I'll run. You can sit on my shoulder.'

Otis flapped his iridescent wings, flew upwards and immediately made himself comfortable. Hester continued to scowl but, unwilling to be left behind, climbed onto my other shoulder. 'Just don't jiggle around too much,' she yawned. 'I need another forty winks.' She nestled against my collar bone and started to snore.

I grinned and wished I didn't feel envious, then I nodded at Miriam and headed off.

I HADN'T EXACTLY LIED to Miriam: I *did* want to clear my head, and enjoying some time away from the rigours of training, even if I was running, was the best way to achieve clarity.

There was another reason, too, and I had a specific destination in mind. I'd caught glimpses of it a few times on other runs during the last few weeks, albeit from a distance. This time I would head directly there and finally give in to my natural nosiness. It wasn't far away; if I cut across the woods at the edge of Hugo's many acres, I'd be there within the hour.

When I veered off the path, Otis started to pay attention. When the ground became more uneven as I entered the woods, Hester woke up and began to look around. 'Where are we going?' she asked.

Otis answered for me. 'It's obvious, isn't it?'

I wove in and out of the trees, taking care to avoid the low-hanging branches.

'Lady Rose's house?' Hester asked, her voice hushed with awe.

'I believe so,' her brother replied.

She thumped the side of my neck. 'Is that where we're going? Daisy? Are we going to where Lady Rose lived?'

'Yep.' I jumped over a small bush and my feet squelched in the mud as I landed.

'You're going to help Gordon!'

I shook my head. 'I've not made my mind up about that yet. I won't do until I've spoken to Hugo.'

'She will help Gordon,' Hester whispered loudly to Otis. 'She'll look for Lady Rose.'

'That's not what Daisy said,' he replied.

'I know what she said. But I also know what she *meant*,' she added smugly.

'All we're doing is having a look at where Lady Rose lived, Hester,' I said. 'Nothing more, nothing less.'

'Uh-huh. If you say so.'

I gave up trying to persuade her otherwise and concentrated on staying upright. There was a lot of bracken to avoid and numerous gnarly roots that I could easily trip over if I didn't pay attention. It didn't help that I was assailed by bouts of light-headedness when I turned my head too swiftly. I gritted my teeth, willing the sensation to go away.

Eventually I reached a dry-stone wall that marked the boundary to Hugo's land. It was about two metres high, its solid and imposing presence adding to the suggestion that there had been bad blood between the Pembervilles and the Assigney family.

I gave a low whistle and looked around for a convenient place to scramble over before deciding the wall was too precarious to risk climbing. I steeled myself and leapt upwards, combining physical effort with a spurt of carefully directed air magic to boost me up and over. I even nailed the landing on the other side. Go me.

Hester and Otis had abandoned their spots on my shoulders in favour of flying over the wall. I'd expected at least a flicker of wonder at the way I'd conquered the wall, but they were both looking downhill at the Assigney mansion rather than at my inimitable fabulousness.

I couldn't blame them. As I followed their gaze, I gasped. The last of the swirling morning mist was curling around the large building, and swathes of ivy and overgrown weeds had sprung up the mansion's walls and along its paths and driveway. From where I was standing, it looked like an ethereal faery palace.

'Wow,' Hester breathed.

Wow, indeed.

I stayed where I was for a moment, marvelling at the view. I didn't know much about Lady Rose or her family because I'd only recently become part of the elven community, and I'd only heard of her a few months ago. I was aware that the Assigney mansion and grounds had been maintained for a few years after her disappearance, but it was clearly a long time since anyone had been here. Strangely, the place didn't look desolate or depressing; somehow its abandoned air only made it more magical.

I twitched, discomfited by the realisation. That shouldn't be the case; there should be a shroud of heavy tragedy, not an atmosphere of sparkling mystery.

I told myself firmly not to let my emotions get the better of me. This was a brief reconnaissance mission born out of curiosity: nothing more, nothing less. I pulled back my shoulders and jogged towards the mansion.

I didn't have a plan, I simply wanted to get a feel for the place and any lingering ghosts left by Lady Rose. Once I reached the house I circled it, pausing to peer through the windows in the vain hope that I'd spot something interesting. Every single one had been tightly shuttered; there was nothing to see apart from a few cobwebs clinging to the glass panes.

'We should leave now.' Otis shivered despite the gentle warmth from the morning sun. 'There's nothing to see.'

'We *could* leave.' Hester flapped her wings and arched a grin in my direction. 'Or we could break in and have a proper look around.'

Otis gasped with shock. 'We are not criminals, Hester!'

'We won't steal anything. We'll only be having a wee peek.'

'Tell her, Daisy,' Otis said. 'Tell her we won't be doing anything other than returning to Pemberville Castle.'

I looked at him then I looked at her. 'Come on,' I said eventually. 'Let's check out the back door.'

Hester pumped the air with her fists; Otis looked dejected.

'Nobody lives here, Otis,' Hester said. 'Breaking in is a victimless crime.'

'There's no such thing as a victimless crime,' he muttered. Perhaps he was right.

I moved to the door and knelt down to examine the lock. 'You could kick the door in,' Hester suggested helpfully.

That was a step too far; also, I doubted I'd achieve anything more than making a dirty scuff mark on the heavy wood. However, the lock appeared to be a simple affair so there could be a way of releasing the mechanism and opening it without causing any damage.

'This is such a bad idea,' Otis moaned, as I conjured up yet more air magic.

'Shh!' Hester said. 'Let Daisy concentrate.'

It was a testament to Hugo's magic lessons that I was in a

position to attempt this feat. Until recently, my magic had been more akin to a raging bull stampeding through the proverbial china shop, but Hugo had taught me the benefits of a delicate touch – and that was exactly the sort of power I needed now.

Holding my breath, I carefully combined the air molecules around me into a slender, invisible tool, then sent it forward and pushed the burst of air into the keyhole. I closed my eyes and concentrated hard, pushing the air into the locking mechanism and twisting it. The door rattled several times and the lock juddered. I tensed my muscles and fiddled further – and within less than a minute there was a satisfying click.

I beamed in triumph while Otis sighed heavily. I didn't look at him; I felt guilty enough without seeing my own culpability reflected in his expression. I straightened up, twisted the handle, and the door opened with a long, painful creak.

'You can stay out here, Otis,' Hester said importantly.

He huffed. 'I will do no such thing. I'm coming in with you to make sure you two don't do anything stupid.'

I couldn't imagine what he thought we might get up to inside the Assigney home. Maybe it was better not to ask.

I sucked in a deep breath and stepped across the threshold.

THREE

We found ourselves in a large kitchen. Every surface, from the floor to the countertops to the massive fireplace set into one wall, was thick with dust. Large sheets covered several bulky items; I lifted the corner of one of them to reveal a wooden cabinet filled with old crockery and glasses. Swirling motes of dust rose into the air and all three of us sneezed in quick succession.

'It's like stepping back in time,' Hester whispered as she wiped her nose.

I nodded in agreement. I understood why she was whispering: nobody could hear us, nobody was inside this house, but there was a distinct sensation that speaking normally would disturb the sleeping ghosts in this quiet place.

I dropped the sheet back over the cabinet. My eyes were drawn to a strange mark over the door which led outside; there was a large hole in the plaster and a spider's web of cracks around it. Puzzled, I squinted at it before eventually shrugging. It was an old building that hadn't been lived in for decades so it was bound to be in a state of disrepair.

I stepped over to a closed door that led deeper into the house. More dust flew up with every footstep. It must have been years since anyone had been inside here.

The door opened into a long hallway with covered picture frames hanging on the walls. Judging from the marks on the old oak floor, there had once been a rug running along it. It had probably been put into storage when all the furniture had been covered with sheets to await the return of Lady Rose. Except she hadn't returned – and there was nothing to suggest she ever would.

I considered risking a tiny fireball to bob along in front of me and light my way, but if I lost control of it for even a second, the house and all its contents might catch fire before I could stop it. Given my recent habit of losing control, I erred on the side of caution, slid out my phone instead and turned on the torch function. It didn't cast much light but it was better than nothing.

Holding it up in front of me, I walked forward gingerly, trying not to notice the way each floorboard creaked ominously. Five minutes, I decided; I'd wander around for five minutes and no more.

Hester and Otis flew close beside me; not even Hester appeared willing to overtake me. I didn't think it was because they were afraid; the sense of awe we'd felt outside persisted, despite the mansion's somewhat lugubrious and stale interior. Our unwillingness to rush was more out of respect for the building and its history than fear or wariness.

The hallway led to another door that opened into a grand vestibule. Once upon a time it had probably looked similar to the magnificent entrance at Pemberville Castle, albeit on a smaller scale. There were five closed doors, a sweeping staircase and several more pieces of furniture swathed in dust sheets.

I turned to the brownies with a questioning look. Otis shrugged unhappily but Hester pointed at the nearest door. I pursed my lips, then headed over to open it.

'A drawing room of some kind,' I said quietly. The air was fusty and the light dim, thanks to the shuttered windows. Despite that, Otis spotted something interesting.

'Look,' he said quietly, and pointed at a large painting on the far wall. The sheet covering it had fallen slightly, revealing part of a face. Unable to stop myself, I strode up to it and yanked it down then shone the phone light upwards to illuminate the picture.

'That's her,' Hester said. 'That has to be Lady Rose, right?'

I swallowed hard as I gazed at the portrait: it certainly could be her. The woman was dressed formally in a pretty cocktail dress with her red hair tied up in an elaborate style that belied her youthful features. The shade of her hair matched mine, but there was no way I could ever tame my unruly curls into a similar style.

The painter had captured a mischievous glint in Lady Rose's eyes, as if she were planning something exceptionally daring yet highly unbecoming for someone of her status. She looked like a girl I'd have enjoyed getting to know; she also looked painfully young, barely more than a teenager.

'She has a corsage of pink roses,' Otis said. 'And look – there are more flowers in the garden in the background and they're roses, too. This has to be Lady Rose.'

Hester squinted. 'There are lots of roses,' she agreed. 'But that building she's standing in front of isn't this one. It doesn't look British.'

She was right: Lady Rose, if that's who it was, had been painted beside a quaint cottage. Something about the quality of the light and the architecture suggested a building in a warmer climate. It might not exist in real life – the artist could have conjured it up from their imagination, along with the blooming rose bushes.

I wasn't interested in the location – it was Lady Rose who occupied my attention.

I stared at her pointed ears and her relaxed stance. Until that moment, she hadn't seemed quite real; she'd been a character in a tragic story. I realised I'd been thinking of her like I might think of Anne Boleyn or Joan of Arc or Boudicca, but Lady Rose wasn't ancient history. If she'd been alive today, she'd have been younger than Sir Nigel, younger than both my adoptive parents. She might have been someone with whom I could have become friends.

The painting brought her to life, at least in my mind, and I couldn't help thinking of what Gordon had said. She deserved to be found and her story deserved to be told. The longer I looked at her portrait, the more unsettled I felt. I suppressed a faint shiver. Otis had been right: we shouldn't be here. Breaking into Lady Rose's house had been a terrible idea.

'Let's go,' I said. 'Let's get out of here.'

'But we've barely scratched the surface!' Hester protested. 'There are lots of rooms. We've hardly looked anywhere!'

'We won't find anything else we need. I've already found what I was looking for.'

Her brow furrowed. 'What?'

Otis understood and pointed at the painting. 'Her.'

I nodded. 'Her.' I turned away. 'Come on.'

Retracing my steps, I left the drawing room, closed the door then swivelled to the right to return to the long hallway so we could go out through the kitchen door. I'd barely moved in that direction when Hester let out a strangled cry.

I stiffened in alarm. 'What is it? What's wrong?'

She didn't speak, just raised a shaky arm and pointed. When I saw what she was looking at, my eyes widened. The darkness made them hard to see clearly but, from the small chinks of daylight seeping through the shutters, it appeared that there was a set of footprints trailing through the dust from the front door to the staircase and beyond. A matching set trailed back in the opposite direction.

I looked around and registered the tracks of my own footsteps. We weren't the only people who'd been here in the recent past. My heart started beating faster, fluttering like a butterfly trying to escape an impenetrable net.

'Lady Rose.' Her voice hushed with amazement, Hester flew down to the nearest footprint. 'Lady Rose has been here after all.'

Not unless she wore size twelve boots, she hadn't. 'These almost certainly belong to a man,' I said. All the same, I looked from side to side, as if the woman herself were about to make an appearance.

Otis was already twitching. 'Do you think he's still here? Do you think he'll attack us? Do you think—?'

I put up my hand to reassure him before he had a full-blown panic attack. 'No. Whoever made these was here some time ago.' I slid a fingertip along the length of the print. 'Enough dust has settled to prove that.' I pointed. 'And look. They came through the front door, walked across the hall and went up the stairs. Then they came back again and left. We're alone.'

Hester flew towards the front door and used her full weight to tug down on the handle. 'It's locked.' She dipped down and gazed at the heavy lock. 'Whoever came in had a key. Maybe there's a caretaker who pops in from time to time,' she added doubtfully.

'To do what? Dust?' Otis asked. He waved his arms around

and sent a cloud of tiny motes flying about around his little body. 'If that's the case, they're not doing a very good job.'

'Let's not jump to conclusions before we know what's really going on.' I sounded far calmer than I felt. 'It might have been Gordon – I'm sure he's been here lots of times. He'll have a key to this place.'

'Uh-huh.' Hester's expression was still doubtful.

'Or maybe it was someone who used a similar magic tool to fiddle with the locks, like I did at the back door,' I added. 'Let's follow the trail and see where it leads.' I unsheathed Gladys. 'Just in case,' I said unnecessarily loudly.

The brownies nodded gratefully; for her part, Gladys hummed in what I supposed was a sentient sword's expression of happiness.

We edged towards the grand staircase and started to ascend.

The further up we went, the less distinct the prints became, often appearing to be little more than smudged marks. When we reached the first-floor landing, however, they reappeared as distinct boot marks leading to the next flight of stairs. I glanced at the brownies; despite their taut expressions, they nodded in silent agreement at my unspoken question. We crossed to the stairs and climbed some more.

This was a mansion with a lot of rooms. Yet another flight of stairs stretched up to another floor, but the dusty footprints veered left. Whoever had made them hadn't gone any further up but had walked to the room at the opposite end of the landing. I was no tracker, but I didn't think the intruder had hesitated at any point. Whoever had been here knew where they were going.

I licked my lips; my nervousness and my excitement were growing. I pulled back my shoulders and marched alongside the trail of prints to the door, put out my hand and rested it on the handle.

'Do it,' Hester whispered. 'Open it.'

I waited another beat then, with my heart in my mouth, I did as she said. Unlike the squeaky doors we'd opened so far, this one swung open noiselessly, suggesting that its hinges had been oiled. I tried not to allow that to bother me and peered inside the room. Although it was as dark as everywhere else in the house, the shapes of the dust-sheet covered furniture suggested it was a bedroom.

'Daisy was right.' Hester sounded relieved. 'Nobody is here.' She flew past me to an old light switch and pushed on it with both hands. It clicked down but no lights came on; the electricity must have been shut off years ago.

I edged around the room trying not to disturb the footprints. Reaching the nearest set of shutters, I heaved them open until there was enough light to see properly without using my phone.

This was definitely a bedroom. I looked at the large four-poster bed, unmistakable beneath the large sheets that covered its frame, and shivered. Was this where Lady Rose had slept? Why had the mysterious stranger who'd entered this house before us come into this particular room?

Hester and Otis flew slowly over the trail of bootprints and followed them until they were out of my eyeline. There was a moment of silence before Otis called, 'Er, Daisy?' He sounded worried. 'You should come and see this.'

They were hovering above a dressing table. Unlike the rest of the furniture, this wasn't covered. I moved faster until I was staring down at it, probably with the same expression as the brownies.

Oh.

The surface was marked in several places where various

accoutrements would once have stood. There were circles that might have been made by perfume bottles and a discoloured rectangle that could mark the position of a jewellery box. Those items must have been cleared away a long time ago – but the top of the dressing table wasn't empty.

Lying in its centre was a sealed white envelope, and written on the front of it in a looping, old-fashioned script was one lonely word: *Daisy*.

CHAPTER

FOUR

I stared slack-jawed at the envelope. Yet another distracting wave of light-headedness assailed me; I shook my head with annoyance and tried to focus.

'What does it mean, Daisy?' Otis asked.

Hester stretched out a hand to touch the envelope then thought better of it and pulled back. 'Who is it from?'

'I don't know. I don't recognise the handwriting.' I continued to look at it as if I were watching a bomb. The only way to defuse this explosive would be to pick up the envelope, open it and read the contents. I slowly returned Gladys to her sheath.

'Do it,' Hester whispered. 'Open the envelope.'

For once Otis agreed. 'You have to.'

I gazed at it for another moment. This was ridiculous: there was no reason to be afraid of a letter – unless it was a gas bill catching up with me from my little flat in Edinburgh. I allowed myself a tiny smile at the thought, then yielded to the inevitable, scooped up the envelope and ripped it open.

I removed the single sheet of paper and marched towards the unshuttered window where I could read it properly. The brownies came with me, flying so close to my face that I felt the tips of their wings brushing against my cheeks.

'Read it aloud,' Otis urged.

I swallowed and unfolded the paper.

'*Dearest Daisy,*' I read. '*I am certain that you will be surprised to receive this missive. I sincerely hope that you will carefully consider its contents. From what I already know of you, I am sure that you will give it your appropriate attention, regardless of whatever inane comments those two irritating brownies by your side may be making.*'

Hester gasped. 'How insulting!'

Otis hushed her and I continued.

'*The tragedy of Lady Rose Assigney is immense. She was a wonderful person who displayed great maturity despite her youth. She possessed excellent mastery of the magical elements and had an aptitude for water magic that was uncommon even amongst her supposedly talented peers. More than that, she was a warm, trusting young woman. Her heart was too easily led astray and her head did not lend itself to logic, but her faults were outweighed by her virtues. She was a braver woman than I realised. Rose was only ever a high elf, but she had the potential to be much, much more.*'

It was Otis's turn to interrupt. 'That doesn't make sense,' he said. 'How could she be more than a high elf?'

'Shh! Let Daisy finish!' Hester snapped.

'*The mystery of her disappearance deserves your full attention. I know you will be disinclined to do what I say because that is always the way with children and their parents. However, I urge you to investigate what happened to Rosie because the rewards will far outweigh the risks. I can assure you, my dear Daisy, that you can trust me in this.*'

I paused. '*With great love, A.*'

'*A*?' Hester asked.

My shoulders sagged and nausea rose unbidden in the pit of

my belly. 'Athair.' My fiendish alleged birth father had written this and left it here for me to find. And now I had even more questions than before.

I DIDN'T RUN BACK to Pemberville Castle – I didn't even jog; I walked slowly, my arms hanging heavily by my sides as my mind turned over and over. For once both brownies were sensitive to my mood and lapsed into silence.

My limbs were aching, my fatigue persisted and my various minor wounds from my training sessions were pulsating with pain, but none of those were bothering me. I had far more important things to worry about.

It was noon by the time I emerged from the woods on Hugo's side of the boundary wall. The sun was high and any lingering morning mist had long since dissipated. I gazed towards the familiar turrets of Pemberville Castle and spotted Hugo's battered Jeep parked close to the old moat bridge, next to another car. He had returned, but I couldn't decide whether that was a good thing or not. I could have done with some more time alone before I spoke to him and revealed what I'd discovered.

Fuck it. I sighed, reached into my pocket and extracted two spider's silk pills. When the muted buzz they provided disappointed me, I swallowed a third one – and I didn't let myself feel guilty about it. Not even when my ears rang with the buzz of drug-induced tinnitus and my heart rate fluttered worryingly. I told myself that, given the circumstances, I was holding together admirably.

I pushed away the temptation to delay and trudged the rest of the way to the castle entrance. I didn't even manage to get close to the front gate, though; Duchess was already on full alert.

She bounded out from beneath the bridge, planted her massive bare feet on the cobblestones, placed her hands on her hips and fixed me with a narrow glare. 'Password,' she demanded.

I wasn't in the mood for her troll games. 'Is this necessary? You know who I am, Duchess. In fact, you're living here because of me. Just let me pass.'

She gave a wide-mouthed cackle. 'Well, somebody is in a bad mood this morning. What's wrong, girlie? Is the sexual frustration getting to you? You should let Lord Snoot Face shag you and be done with it.'

'Lord Snoot Face?'

Duchess raised her massive shoulders in a shrug. 'If the shoe fits...'

I sighed. Hester giggled. 'I like it! What's my nickname?' she asked.

'Grumpy Goth,' Duchess answered without missing a beat. She pointed at Otis. 'And Goody Two Shoes.'

I didn't bother to ask what my nickname was but started forward, planning to push past Duchess whether she covered me in troll snot or not.

'Oi! Password first!' she yelled.

I gritted my teeth. 'I don't know the cumbubbling password, Duchess.'

I moved to my left; she matched me. I moved to my right; she did the same.

'If you don't have the password, you'll have to cross my palm with silver.'

'I don't have any money on me.'

She pursed her thin lips. 'Give me the sword, then. That's a fair exchange.'

I most definitely was not going to do that.

The massive door on the other side of the bridge opened and Hugo appeared. He was wearing black trousers and a white shirt, with the top two buttons undone. There was barely a scrap of his chest on display, but it was still incredibly hard not to gawk at it lasciviously. 'Daisy,' he greeted me. 'Where have you been? I've been looking all over for you.'

There was no easy way to answer that. 'It's a long story.'

He frowned and looked at me more closely. Clearly, my expression betrayed me. 'What's happened?'

'Hey!' Duchess stamped her foot. 'Password first. Chit-chat later!'

Hugo ran a frustrated hand through his tawny hair and raised his eyes heavenward. 'Duchess is the best troll an elf could wish for,' he said. She didn't move. Hugo's mouth tightened. 'She is truly wonderful and she deserves the best.'

'The *very* best,' Duchess said. 'Say it.'

'The very best,' Hugo repeated dutifully.

'You could sound as if you meant it,' she muttered. She pointed at me. 'Now you.'

'Don't do it, Daisy,' Hester whispered.

I didn't have much choice. 'Duchess is the best troll an elf could wish for. She is truly wonderful and she deserves the *very* best.'

She beamed. 'See? You did know the password after all.' She stepped aside, sweeping out one of her long, heavy arms to indicate that I could cross. 'On you go, Fated Flea.'

Fated Flea?

Duchess giggled girlishly at my expression. 'Caught in the spider's web, aren't you, girlie? And doomed as a result.'

Hugo scowled and prepared to snap at her but I shook my head at him in warning. Duchess wanted a reaction, and this wasn't the time to indulge her. Besides, she wasn't wrong: Fated Flea was as good a nickname for me as any.

I scooted past her. 'We need to have a conversation,' I said to Hugo, doing my best not to sound too ominous.

He nodded, his mouth still in a tight, flat line. 'Yes, Daisy,' he said. 'We do.' He pointed towards the garden room. 'Sir Nigel is here to see you.'

I dropped my hand into my pocket where Athair's letter was burning the proverbial hole. I knew why *I* was feeling tense, but I didn't know why Hugo appeared to be on a cliff edge of his own.

'Okay,' I said, massaging the back of my neck and trying not to look nervous. Or nauseous. 'Lead the way.'

REGARDLESS OF HOW Hugo and I were feeling, Sir Nigel was having a whale of a time. He'd settled into a comfortable old wicker chair and was sipping a cup of strong tea while Becky foisted a plate of small cakes upon him. 'They're very good,' the youngest member of Hugo's Primes insisted. 'Especially the lemon ones.'

Hester zipped through the air towards him. 'Don't eat the chocolate brownies!' she yelled. 'They're awful!'

Sir Nigel lifted his head and blinked.

'Ignore her. They're delicious,' I told him. 'Hester wants to keep them all for herself.' It was true: she'd been stockpiling the damned things under my bed. I smiled at Sir Nigel. 'It's good to see you again. Thank you for coming.'

He placed his teacup on a small table, stood up and extended his hand. 'It's the least I could do after missing the party last night, Daisy. I was waiting for the last of my contacts to get in touch. I wanted to have as much information as possible before I spoke to you.'

I shook his hand then sat opposite him when he resumed his seat. 'That sounds as if you actually have information for me.'

His expression grew more serious. 'I do.'

I reminded myself that lunging forward to grab him by the lapels and shake the information out of him was not the behaviour of civilised elves. I took the cup of tea that Becky was pushing in my direction and waited with as much patience as I could muster.

'We can leave you in private to hear this,' Hugo said. 'If you want.'

'No. I'd like you to stay,' I replied.

I didn't miss the answering flash of happiness in his blue eyes as he nodded and pulled up another chair. Becky shot me a questioning look, then did the same.

'As you know,' Sir Nigel said, 'I've been in touch with numerous fiend experts both in this country and abroad. There are three known cases where fiends have sired children.'

Behind me, Otis sucked in a breath. I remained very, very still as I said, 'So it is physically possible that Athair is my birth father.'

Sir Nigel didn't mince his words. 'Yes.'

'And those children?' I asked. 'What happened to them? What did they ... become?'

'Their circumstances were different to yours.'

I met his eyes. 'That's not what I asked.'

He sighed. 'I know.' His waxed moustache quivered. 'None of them are alive today, not in this realm anyway. The first one, a girl called Zitinillia, died when she was thirteen years old. It appears that the onset of puberty, combined with the unexpected force of her magic, caused her death.'

Bile rose in my mouth. 'I burned my house down at a similar age,' I whispered. 'I could have easily killed myself and my adoptive parents.'

Unbidden, Hugo's hand reached out and he entwined his fingers with mine. The unsettling cold that had been leeching into my bones at Sir Nigel's words started to dissipate. I smiled briefly at him to show that his touch was very welcome. His gaze was soft. He had my back; despite everything, he would stand beside me. Knowing that I wasn't alone meant more than I could put into words.

'Thank heavens for spider's silk,' he murmured in a lighter tone than he probably meant.

'I bet you never thought you'd say that six months ago,' I replied.

A ghost of a smile crossed his face. 'You can say that again.'

'I bet you never thought you'd—'

Hugo squeezed my fingers tighter and I stopped, but the flicker of levity had eased the tense atmosphere. Sir Nigel's moustache stopped trembling and Becky's shoulders relaxed as she leaned back in her chair. 'And the other two children?' she asked.

'One was called Fravock,' Sir Nigel said. 'He was born in the early twentieth century and died just before the Second World War.'

'He also died quite young, then,' I surmised.

'Yes.'

I nodded distractedly and plucked at an invisible thread. 'Did he...? Was he...? I mean did Fravock...?'

Fortunately, Sir Nigel understood what I was trying to ask. 'We don't believe he was a fiend. As an adult, he passed for a normal human. He was married, worked as a solicitor before he was killed, and had no children.'

'But he didn't die naturally?'

Sir Nigel's eyes slid away. 'Reports at the time suggest he was murdered by Athair.'

My ears started ringing with an ominous whine. 'My father was taking out potential future competition.'

Hugo's voice was dark. '*Alleged* father.'

'We can't know what Athair's motives were,' Sir Nigel said.

Yeah, yeah. 'And the third one?'

'His name was Meranz.'

I grunted. 'Weird name.'

Becky agreed. 'They're all weird names.'

Hester landed on my shoulder. 'Daisy isn't a weird name.'

Sir Nigel nodded. 'I did say that their circumstances were different to yours, Daisy. All three of those children were raised by the fiends who brought them into this world.'

'Nature versus nurture,' Hugo said.

I chose not to pass comment on that for now. 'What happened to Meranz?'

Sir Nigel's voice was very quiet. 'He was born in 1763. Meranz became what we would classify as a fiend.'

I half-closed my eyes. Okay, then. Okay. 'He's definitely not around any longer?' For the most part, fiends were immortal; I supposed that was part of the allure of becoming one in the first place.

'Meranz was magically banished by a trio of witches in 1875.'

My shoulders sagged. 'Because a fiend can only be banished to another demesne by skilled witches or be killed by another fiend.'

'Or be killed by *the child* of a fiend,' Otis burst out. 'Like the way you killed that fiend Baltar in the dragon's cave. *You're* not a fiend, Daisy. And you never will be.'

'But if you do end up becoming a fiend,' Hester added,

'you'll be the bestest, baddest fiend that the world has ever seen.'

Becky looked horrified, though Hugo nodded and appeared to be mildly amused. 'She's not wrong.'

I rolled my eyes but I did find myself sitting a little straighter. 'The fiends who sired all three,' I said. 'What about them?'

'Zitinillia's parents were fiends – it's the only time in history that there's a record of a married couple who were both fiends. They have since been banished. As for Meranz and Fravock, it was their fathers who were fiends. We believe that Meranz's mother was a human who was killed shortly after his birth. Fravock's mother was reportedly a human sorcerer. There's no information about what happened to her.'

Sir Nigel paused. 'I haven't found any information about who your birth mother might have been, Daisy. I am sorry.'

Hmm. 'So in effect,' I said, aware that the whole group was watching me with worried eyes, 'we still don't know anything. Athair might be my dad but he might not be. My birth mother could have been anyone. I might end up turning into a fiend or I might not. Nothing we've learned has changed anything.'

Sir Nigel cleared his throat. 'I must say, you're taking this better than I expected.'

What else could I do? I'd had six weeks to get used to the idea that I might have fiendish blood, and I wasn't the wallowing type. 'We still don't have any actual answers.'

Next to me, Hugo drew in a breath. 'I might.' He released my hand and reached into his pocket.

'If you have an envelope in that pocket with my name on it,' I said, 'I will sprint out of here and never return.'

He gave me a quizzical look. 'Eh?'

'Never mind. Go on, then. What do you have?'

He pulled out a small glass vial and held it up. 'This is the reason why I was out this morning. I was retrieving this.'

Inside the vial was a withered brown thing; if I squinted, it looked oddly familiar. 'Is that ... is that ... is that a severed finger?'

Hugo grinned. 'Yes, it is. Specifically, the severed finger of a bastard fiend called Athair.'

Otis squeaked, 'But when we saw him, he had all his fingers!'

'Fiends can re-grow their limbs,' I said, still staring at what was inside the vial. It was genuinely disgusting. 'Are you certain it was Athair's?'

'As certain as I can be. He lost his finger in a fight with a group of witches about sixty years ago. They tried to banish him, but obviously they failed. All but one of them died in the process, but they did manage to slice off this while they were defending themselves. The surviving witch stated categorically that this digit belonged to Athair. It's been kept in safe storage ever since. I had to pull in a lot of favours to get hold of it but,' Hugo gave me a long look, 'I reckon it'll be worth it.'

I knew exactly why. I reached up and plucked a single strand of my hair, making sure to pull it out at the root. 'Will that be enough for a DNA comparison?'

'It should be. It'll take a few weeks to get the results, but then we'll know the truth.' He hesitated. 'If you want to know, that is.'

'We're already too far down the rabbit hole to pull out now,' I said. 'I can't forget about all this. Athair is still out there – and he won't forget about me, either.'

It was my turn to reach into my pocket. 'I've got something to show you, too.' I slid out the envelope and took a deep breath, hoping that my hands weren't shaking too obviously. 'You're not going to like this.'

CHAPTER
FIVE

hree hours after Sir Nigel had departed, Hugo was still stalking around the castle with a face like thunder. I'd left him to it; I had drilling and practising to do, and he would come to me in his own time.

I continued to force my exhausted limbs beyond what I'd ever thought they were capable of. Hugo finally appeared when Slim was taking me through the finer points of using water magic from a distance.

'It's all very well conjuring up bursts of water right in front of you, Daisy,' he told me, 'but can you do it from the other side of a field? How far can you direct a stream of water?'

I concentrated hard on the opposite side of the disused ball-room where a small tin bucket was forlornly waiting for some magic. There were several puddles of water dotted around it but, alas, there was very little water in the bucket itself. Slim could conjure up precisely directed water magic from a distance of up to three miles; I couldn't manage it from three hundred feet.

Hugo leaned against the door frame as he watched my final attempt. I narrowed my gaze and focused on a spot directly above the bucket. Sensibly, Hester and Otis had removed themselves some distance away after I'd doused them several times by accident.

'Listen to your heartbeat,' Slim advised.

'I'm listening.'

'Slow your breathing.'

Yep. I was doing that.

'Visualise the molecules.'

A bead of sweat ran down my forehead. 'Gotcha.'

'And release.'

I flung the magic out of me, giving it all the energy I had, and a cupful of water splashed into the bucket. Another three litres missed it altogether and created a miniature river that ran across the ballroom floor to Hugo's feet. His mouth tightened.

I sighed and wished the palpitations in my chest would subside.

'You're making progress,' Slim said encouragingly.

Not much progress, but I thanked him anyway. He was a patient teacher and I was lucky to have him. I was lucky to have all of them. I smiled, curtsied – and finally faced Hugo.

'Can you give us five minutes, Slim?' he asked.

The older elf was already heading for the door. Otis rose up in the air and prepared to follow him, but Hester yanked him back. Neither brownie was going anywhere; they wanted to hear what Hugo had to say.

He closed the ballroom door and gestured to a few chairs grouped against one wall. I nodded and sat down. When Hugo joined me, I could see the strain etched into his features and the dark tension in his eyes.

I gave him all the time he needed; he'd speak when he was ready. This was a raw, vulnerable Hugo, a side to him that I'd rarely witnessed. He deserved my patience.

After several moments, he inhaled deeply and folded his

arms. 'Daisy, I need you to believe that I'm not a complete bastard,' he said.

I blinked. 'I don't think that, Hugo.'

'You used to.'

Yes, when we'd first met, but so much had changed since then. 'That was a long time ago. Everything is different now.' My feelings for Hugo were now running in a totally different direction.

He continued to avoid my gaze. 'It's not that I don't care about what happened to Lady Rose – whatever happened to her is an enormous tragedy – but it's been thirty years. Gordon Mackenzie isn't the first person to search for her and he won't be the last, but there's never been a trace of her anywhere. She's dead, and I don't believe her remains will ever be found.'

He finally raised his eyes and looked at me. 'My parents still receive hate mail on an almost daily basis, even though they're abroad. That sort of thing grinds you down.'

I wanted to reach out and hug him but it wasn't the right time; Hugo needed to say his piece first. I wasn't in his position and I could never truly understand it, but I was there for him, if only to listen. Most of our conversations lately had involved banter, training details or treasure hunting; this, was definitely not one of those.

I registered the flicker of anguish in his face. 'There's something about Lady Rose that my parents won't tell me,' he whispered.

Oh no.

'I don't know what it is. Whenever I've tried to bring it up, they've changed the topic or simply refused to speak to me about it. But they're my mum and dad and I know them as well as I know anyone. I'm certain there's something important that they won't tell me.'

I selected my next words very, very carefully. 'Do you think they had something to do with Lady Rose's disappearance?'

He shook his head, then he nodded. A moment later, he growled with frustration. 'I don't believe they'd hurt her, I truly don't. But...' He sighed. 'There's something there, something they know. What if...?' He couldn't finish the sentence. I didn't blame him.

'I shouldn't be complaining,' he continued. 'You've had far more to deal with – you're still dealing with far more.'

'It's not a misery competition, Hugo. You're entitled to your feelings.'

'It's a wonder to me that I ever thought you were anything less than amazing,' he said quietly.

From the other side of the room, Hester shouted, 'Yes, Hugo!' I pulled a face at her. This wasn't the time for her commentary, regardless of how well-meaning it was.

'I tried to find Lady Rose, you know,' he said. 'I searched for her for a long time when I was a teenager. I thought that if I could find her then all the nastiness directed at my parents would stop. I broke into her house like you did. It's one of the few hunts I've undertaken where I completely failed. The truth is that there's nothing to find. She's gone.'

'Gordon told me that if this magical skull he's looking for doesn't offer up any answers, he'll put the investigation to bed once and for all.'

'Others will pick up where Gordon leaves off,' Hugo said darkly. 'There are always others – and one of them appears to be your alleged father. His interest alone should be enough to dissuade you from helping Gordon. Athair's involvement can't be a good thing.'

We were in agreement about that. 'Did you notice how Athair talks about her in his letter?' I asked. 'The first time he mentions her, he calls her Lady Rose, then she's just Rose. The last time, he calls her Rosie. What if he knew her? What if he was responsible for whatever happened to her?'

'And what if he's pulling your strings because he wants to control you and everything you do? Athair is the most powerful remaining fiend in this country for a reason. He's cold and vicious and very intelligent. He's playing a game that you can't win, Daisy.'

'But this isn't only about Athair, or me. It's about Lady Rose and about Gordon. And it's about you.'

Hugo grimaced with obvious frustration. 'Athair wants you to get involved and whatever the reason, it won't be good. It's bad enough that he knew you'd sneak into the Assigney house.'

'I can't pretend he doesn't exist,' I pointed out. 'Athair is part of my life now, whether that DNA test confirms he's my father or not. He won't go away.'

'And dead or not, Lady Rose won't go away either.' That was true. 'You want to help Gordon find this skull, whatever it is?' he asked.

I nodded. 'I do. He wouldn't tell me what the skull does, although he seemed confident that it would provide answers. I understand what you're worried about, Hugo. It doesn't make you a bad person, it makes you normal.' I paused. 'If you tell me you don't want me to do this, I'll respect your wishes.'

'Why? Why would you do that for me?'

'Because I care about you,' I said simply.

His voice was rough. 'Care? Is that it?'

I didn't look away. 'You don't believe me?'

Hugo hissed through his teeth, stood up and marched several paces away. When he stopped, he didn't turn around to face me. 'I care about you too.' He sounded strained. 'I know I've put you through hell these last weeks.'

'You've been trying to help me.'

'But it hasn't worked, has it? You're no closer to fully

controlling your magic, and you're no closer to weaning yourself off spider's silk. I'm not stupid, Daisy. I know what's going on. I've seen the way you break into a cold sweat when you're doing nothing to warrant it. I've noticed how you suddenly start shaking. But you've done everything I've asked and more and you've never hesitated. You, Daisy Carter, are the bravest, strongest, and most wonderful person I've ever met.' He paused. 'I'm not like you. I'm not as strong as you. But you make me want to try.'

My eyes widened. I swallowed hard, stood up and went to him. When I reached his ramrod-straight body, he turned and faced me. 'We'll look for Gordon's little magical skull together,' he said. 'We'll be more successful as a team. Anyway, you desperately need a break in your training. Miriam keeps telling me that the regime is as likely to kill you as save you. Even Otis has pulled me aside to scold me for giving you too much to do.'

I glanced over at the little brownie. A guilty flush stained his cheeks as he shoved his hands in his pockets and looked away. Hester nudged him. 'Otis! You did that?'

He mumbled an answer. She flung herself at him and wrapped her arms around him.

'You should take the rest of the day off, Daisy,' Hugo said, drawing my attention back to him. 'Get some proper rest. I'll convene the Primes first thing tomorrow morning. We can take a good look at all the information Gordon has about the skull and come up with a plan.'

'Are you sure about this?' I whispered.

His hand reached up and cupped my cheek. 'I am.'

I couldn't help myself: I stiffened. 'That's the first time you've touched me since London,' I said. Six weeks ago.

Hugo's hand stayed where it was. 'I know.' His head dipped closer to mine. 'Believe me, Daisy, I know.'

As his warm breath brushed my skin, something deep and

nameless inside me quivered. I gazed into his eyes, then I muttered two words: 'Fuck it.'

My mouth rose to meet his. For one heart-stopping moment, he didn't react but then he groaned and curved an arm around me, pulling me closer and kissing me harder. He tasted of cinnamon and cloves, and the heat of his hard body as it pressed against mine almost made me gasp aloud. When his mouth left mine and he trailed a series of kisses down my neck towards my collarbone, I *did* gasp. And I moaned. Then again, so did Hugo.

'Um, Daisy?'

I barely heard Otis, and I certainly didn't pay him any attention. My hands curved down until I was cupping Hugo's gorgeous arse and then—

Hester screeched in my ear. 'Daisy!'

I stepped back, my heart hammering against my ribcage with more force than a dozen confrontations with Athair could invoke. 'What?'

She pointed downwards.

Oh.

I swallowed hard. Hugo glanced down and his skin paled beneath his flush of lust. Not only had I finally managed to fill the bucket with water, but it also appeared that I'd filled the entire ballroom. We were standing in three inches of tepid liquid that was covering every inch of the floor.

'If the two of you are going to keep at it and drown yourselves in the process,' Hester retorted, 'at least let us leave the room first.'

I thought of the three spider's silk pills I'd taken a few hours earlier; the drug's effects on my magic were diminishing day by day. Cumbubbling bollocks.

I drew in a ragged breath. 'I'm sorry, Hugo. That was a mistake.'

He gazed at me with hot, blue eyes. 'No, it wasn't. It was worth every damned inch of water.' He looked as if he meant it.

I licked my lips. When I realised I could still taste him on my tongue, something surged through me – and the water level rose another inch. Oops. 'Just so we're clear,' I said. 'I didn't kiss you because I'm happy that you'll help me look for Gordon's skull.'

The corner of Hugo's mouth crooked up and his dimple appeared. 'I know that, Daisy. You kissed me because I'm irresistible and you couldn't help yourself. I can't blame you.' He gestured to himself. 'It's hard to say no to this.' His eyes dropped to my mouth, then they travelled lower.

'Stop that!' I protested.

'Stop what?'

'Ogling!'

'Why? Is it making you melt?' He grinned; he was back to his usual self. 'You want me *so* badly right now.'

He wasn't wrong. I felt myself leaning towards him once more.

'No!' Hester yelled. 'No more! No flooding! No tsunamis!' She was right. I closed my eyes and stepped away.

When I opened them, Hugo had also moved. 'Go and get some rest, Daisy,' he said from the other side of the room. 'I'll clean this up.'

I considered arguing then thought better of it. With Otis pressing his hands to his cheeks and Hester pretending to fan herself, I took advantage of the moment and fled the room.

SIX

I f you'd opened a dictionary to look up the word 'astonished', you might well have found a photograph of Hugo's team of Primes when he told them he would help Gordon Mackenzie. Even Becky, who'd been in the room when I'd pulled out Athair's letter, was shocked. 'You're going to help that sorcerer search for Lady Rose?' she asked, blinking rapidly.

'No.' Hugo linked his hands behind his head and leaned back, putting on a very good display of a man who was utterly relaxed and at peace with his decision. 'I will help him search for a small magical item that may or may not help his investigation into Lady Rose's disappearance. There's a distinct difference.'

'You could have fooled me,' Rizwan muttered. His eyes flicked to me and away again. It was obvious they all realised who was at the bottom of Hugo's decision, though I couldn't tell yet whether anyone was dismayed by it.

Miriam smacked her lips together in approval. 'This is good, Hugs. Very good. It's about time all those old ghosts were laid to rest.'

Hester, who'd been examining the tray of biscuits laid out to fuel the morning's activities, jerked up. 'Ghosts?'

'Metaphorical ones,' Otis said.

Hester narrowed her eyes. 'They'd better be.' She stared around the room as if checking for any spectres who had suddenly decided to appear.

'Nobody is under any pressure to get involved,' Hugo said. 'If you want to sit this hunt out, I won't think any the worse of you.'

'Are you kidding?' Slim said. 'I've been itching to do some proper work for ages.' His gaze flashed to me and I spotted a trace of guilt in his expression. 'Uh, I mean— No offence, Daisy. I'm enjoying helping with your training, but treasure hunting is what we're all here for.'

I grinned. 'It's okay, Slim. I'm excited too.' I meant it. It wasn't simply that we'd be part of the investigation into Lady Rose, or that Athair was somehow involved, it was that treasure hunting was the most thrilling thing I could think of to do with my time.

Mark, a tall elf who was part of the research team, cleared his throat. 'Then let's get to it.' He could barely contain his smile. 'What do we know about this golden skull?'

I pushed a folder towards him. 'Gordon sent through all the information he has about its whereabouts. It's a magical object, although he's unwilling to reveal exactly what magic it contains.'

Becky stiffened. 'What if it's dangerous? We all know there's plenty of hidden treasure out there that *shouldn't* be found.'

'I don't think it'll be too long before we work out what the skull can do,' Hugo said. 'And let's not forget that Gordon is a cautious man. Despite his fervour, he wouldn't take any unnecessary risks.'

I raised an eyebrow; for someone who professed to hate

Gordon Mackenzie's actions, Hugo certainly had the measure of the man.

'That doesn't mean that we won't proceed with caution,' he continued. 'It won't be the first time we've searched for something with unknown properties.'

Rizwan nodded. 'Remember the Fabergé egg we found a few years ago?'

I spotted several amused expressions around the table.

'How could we forget?' Mark asked.

Miriam turned to me. 'Legend had it that Rasputin had bound magical healing powers into the egg. We were hired by a company based in Moscow to find it.'

'And?' I asked, fascinated.

'It had magical powers, alright.' Slim snorted. 'But not healing powers. Rasputin had more of a sense of humour than history gives him credit for.'

Miriam grinned. 'The egg attracted chickens. Lots and lots and lots of chickens.'

'We were inundated,' Becky said. 'There were thousands of them, flocking in from every direction.'

'Sometimes I still have nightmares about the smell,' Rizwan told me.

'Bird poo is pungent.' Hugo smiled slightly. 'But I think we can rest assured that this skull will not be a magical chicken magnet.'

'I have a great photo of Hugs with two fat hens perched on his head,' Becky said.

He looked exasperated but Rizwan was more amused than ever. 'It certainly made an interesting fashion statement.'

I sat up straighter. 'I'd like to see that photo.'

'Perhaps,' Hugo said drily, 'we should focus on the hunt?'

Miriam nodded. 'You're right, dear. A bird in the hand is better than two on your head.'

There was a ripple of laughter and I felt myself relax. The mood was good humoured, none of the Primes were upset that we were helping Gordon, and even Hugo seemed at ease with the idea. That was progress indeed.

Mark flipped open the folder and scanned the contents. I'd already read through them and I knew they didn't hold much information. Most of it made little sense to me, but I was confident that the Primes' combined knowledge and experience would shed light on where we should start to hunt for the skull.

'Hmm.' His fingers raked across the stubble on his chin, then he stood up, walked to the whiteboard and wrote down the key points. 'According to this, the skull is made of gold, is about three-inches high, and was last seen sometime in the seventeenth century when it was uncovered together with a hoard of Roman coins in Lincolnshire.'

'Who uncovered it?' Miriam asked.

'A local farmer. There's no reference to what happened to the skull after that, but the coins and the chest that contained them are on display in Doncaster Museum.'

'Do we have any contacts there?' Slim asked.

Hugo shook his head. 'No.' There was a familiar gleam in his eyes; regardless of the motives behind this treasure hunt, the thrill of the chase was affecting him. 'But we have a place to start.' He looked at me and smiled. 'Let's saddle up.'

Given the scanty information that Gordon had provided, half the team remained behind to see what else they could discover while the rest of us packed overnight bags and set off in convoy for the museum in Doncaster.

Hugo, Hester, Otis and I took the first car; Miriam, Slim and Becky took the second. We drove fast, keen to reach our destination before it closed for the day. Fortunately the roads were clear, so we pulled into the car park with twenty minutes to spare.

We'd informed Agatha Smiggleswith, the museum director, of our impending arrival and she was there to meet us at the entrance. To my surprise, she was a bogle. I had to bite my tongue to resist the urge to ask her if she knew my drug dealer, Arbuthnot. The bogle community was a small one, and not many of them chose to abandon a rural life for one amongst humans, elves and other such beings, so it was possible that she'd heard of him – though I doubted that mentioning him would be wise. Her job title suggested that she wasn't like other bogles; in this instance, silence would be golden.

'Hugo Pemberville.' She smiled in a business-like fashion and extended her hand. 'It truly is an honour to have you visit our small establishment.'

'Thank you for being here to greet us,' he responded in kind. 'I hope that our visit won't cause too much disturbance.'

'Not at all! We're thrilled to have you.' From her expression, she meant every word. Hugo was something of a cause célèbre both within and outside the archaeology and treasure-hunting world. The fact that so many people admired him would probably boost the museum's visitor numbers; if the wonderful Hugo Pemberville thought Doncaster Museum was worth a visit, many others would follow suit.

No doubt, Ms Smiggleswith would make time to take several photos of Hugo to display around the museum. That's what I'd have done if I'd been in her shoes.

'We have many Roman artefacts,' she said. 'There are several Roman forts in the area. We're particularly proud of the Danum shield, which was recovered in 1971 and has been dated to the late first century AD. But I believe it's the small cache of coins found near Caistor that has piqued your interest?'

'You believe correctly.'

'I'm afraid they're not particularly unusual or valuable. It's quite common to find hoards such as this one.' She eyed him. 'But you'll know that already.'

'To be honest,' Hugo said, 'every discovery and every hoard is amazing to me.'

Her eyes twinkled. 'In that case, I'll take you right to it. Follow me.'

We trailed after her. I let the others take the lead so I had a moment to fumble in my pocket for a surreptitious dose of spider's silk. My mouth was as dry as sandpaper and I could already feel the familiar heart palpitations; I had to keep my body under control and feed the beast inside.

I swallowed the pill dry and shuddered before wiping the sweat from my brow and blinking rapidly to try and clear my blurred vision. Bright colours flared across my eyes. I gulped until my body righted itself and I could look around the museum like a normal visitor.

I spotted a large display board with pictures of Roman artefacts drawn by local children, a plea for people who could tell interesting stories to join the museum team, and an advertisement for a presentation by a local historian. There was an impressive number of intriguing exhibits but I resisted the temptation to browse and caught up with the others before they reached the glass cabinet we wanted.

Ms Smigglesswith's attention remained wholly on Hugo, which suited me because it meant I could examine the coins and their original chest without interruption. Smooth-talking suited Hugo but it wasn't my forte. Miriam, Becky, Slim and Hester also paid little attention to what the museum director was saying. Otis, however, hovered by Hugo's shoulder and appeared to be listening intently to every word.

I leaned over the glass cabinet and peered at the coins. I could see why Ms Smigglesmith wasn't particularly excited by them; there were thirteen in total, and they'd all been damaged by the elements, so it was difficult to decipher their marks or their original values. In comparison to other hoards this was small and unremarkable; even so, I felt a delicious thrill when I looked at it. Historical artefacts had that effect on me. There again, so did Hugo.

I switched my attention from the coins to the small wooden chest they'd been found in. It was also in a bad condition, although I could see the ancient, rusted hinges and several marks etched into it.

Becky crouched next to me. 'That looks like a rune,' she whispered. She pointed. 'See?' I followed her finger and squinted. She was right, it did look like a rune.

Ms Smigglesmith was in the middle of a long explanation about Roman roads. As soon as she paused for breath, I jumped in. 'This rune on the side of the chest. Do you know what it means?'

'Oh, yes.' She nodded enthusiastically. 'We had it translated by a local sorcerer. It's a plea for forgiveness.'

We were all interested now and turned to her eagerly. Slim started bouncing up and down on his toes. If the museum director was taken aback by our sudden attentiveness, she didn't show it.

Agatha Smigglesmith struck me as someone who took life and its foibles in her stride. She hadn't commented on the brownies, which was unusual given their rarity, and despite her exuberant welcome she didn't appear overawed by Hugo. Her interest in him seemed to be purely because of her desire to publicise the museum. I liked a person who had priorities that couldn't be swayed; it made them easier to understand – and easier to deal with.

Hugo looked puzzled. 'Romans didn't use sorcerers,' he said. 'There's no evidence that they ever made use of runes.'

Smiggleswith was already nodding. 'For a long time it was believed that they eschewed magic in all its forms but we've discovered that's not true. Although the Roman authorities tried to forbid magical practices, there were witches in abundance. Roman witches weren't like the ones we are used to today, but many of their practices were similar. Their use of herbs was more limited so instead they bound spells into gemstones, creating amulets for protection and tablets for curses. Most magical Roman artefacts that we find nowadays are of precious metals and stones.'

She gestured at the necklace I was wearing, a Christmas gift from my parents – my *real* parents, the ones who had adopted me and put in the hard graft to bring me up. 'Rather like that pendant you're wearing.'

My curiosity increased, even though my necklace was modern and possessed no magical properties. Perhaps the little golden skull we were searching for was Roman in origin? Not for the first time, I wondered what on earth it could do and why Gordon Mackenzie thought it would be so useful.

Smiggleswith continued. 'Both the wooden chest and the rune are more modern than the coins. They date from the sixteenth century.'

'Very modern, then,' Hester muttered.

The museum director smiled. 'There are many interpretations of the word "history". Yesterday is history, two thousand years ago is history. It's all relative.'

Before we got involved in a lengthy philosophical discussion, Miriam brought the conversation back to what we needed. 'So the chest was created at a later date to hold the coins?'

'Yes. It's an interesting story. The coins were discovered near Caistor, about forty miles from here, which has strong

Roman connections. We don't know who buried them originally, but they were found on a small hill in the seventeenth
century by the farmer who owned the land. He dug them up
from beneath a large rock known as the Fonaby Sack Stone.

'Legend has it that the stone was once a sack of corn that
was transformed in the seventh century by a missionary who
asked a local farmer to spare some grain. When the farmer
refused, the missionary took umbrage and turned the sack into
rock.'

She beamed beatifically. 'Of course, we don't know if the
story is true – and we certainly no longer possess the sort of
alchemical magic that can transform materials in that way.'

Slim was still examining the coins. 'A Roman buried them
two thousand years ago, and fourteen hundred years ago a
stone appeared in the same spot? Then four hundred years ago,
somebody dug the coins up. Where does the forgiveness rune
come in?'

'The missionary didn't only turn the sack of corn into
stone.' Smiggleswith lowered her voice dramatically. 'He cursed
it as well.' Her bright smile was totally at odds with her story.
'Or so the legend goes. When the seventeenth-century farmer
dug up the coins, the curse attached itself to him. Eventually he
was so beset by misfortune that he placed the coins in the
chest, added the rune and re-buried them, together with some
other items that had been dug up at the time.'

I did my best to keep my expression bland. One of those
'other items' could have been our little golden skull, but it
would be wise not to let Agatha Smiggleswith know what we
were searching for. We didn't want any interference – or
competition.

'We don't know whether his actions rid the farmer of the
curse or not, but there are other instances of it affecting local
folk. A local mason hammered a chunk off the stone, intending

to turn it into a gift for his fiancée, then died violently soon afterwards. Another farmer in the late nineteenth century moved the stone to plough the land underneath it. In the process, he discovered the chest and the coins and promptly sold them to the highest bidder. The money didn't do him much good – his horses all died, his crops failed and his eldest son was taken ill.'

Hester gasped loudly.

'That farmer couldn't retrieve the coins from the buyer, but he did return the stone to its original position – and then his son miraculously recovered.'

Hugo was already nodding. 'The curse is on the stone, not on the coins.'

Smiggleswith looked at him approvingly. 'Which is why the coins are here rather than buried beneath the stone. They were donated to the museum many decades ago because the family who owned them were wary of any misfortune they might bring.' Her cheery expression didn't alter. 'I can assure you that we've never endured any hardship because of their presence.'

Slim scratched his chin. 'And the Fonaby Sack Stone?' he asked.

'Is on the same land and in the same place. It has been many years since anyone has dared to disturb it.' She arched her eyebrows. 'If you're planning to do so, Lord Pemberville, I'd be very wary of the consequences. Such things are best left alone.'

We exchanged glances. Otis shivered, and so did I. For once my reaction had nothing to do with spider's silk.

'Thank you for the warning,' Hugo said. 'And for your time. You've been very helpful.'

Smiggleswith inclined her head then raised a hand. A young man bearing a camera appeared from behind a pillar. 'You're very welcome. Shall we take a few photos to mark the moment?'

The rest of us dutifully stepped aside to allow her to pose with Hugo.

I looked again at the thirteen old coins, protected by the glass display case.

'Interesting, isn't it, that there are thirteen coins?' Miriam said. 'It's an unlucky number.'

'You believe in the curse, then?' I asked.

'You've not read through our risk assessments, have you?'

I shook my head.

'We should remedy that.' Slim gave me a meaningful look. 'Top of our health-and-safety list is dealing with curses.'

Becky tilted her head towards me. 'Welcome to yet another of the grim realities of treasure hunting.'

CHAPTER

SEVEN

'Daisy,' Otis said as we clambered into the Jeep after saying farewell to Agatha Smiggleswith, 'perhaps you could consider an alternative career. Treasure hunting is a far too risky a business.'

Hester was already nodding agreement. 'Bomb disposal. That would be safer.'

'Firefighting,' Otis suggested.

'Front-line operations with the military,' she said.

'Very funny.' I pulled a face at them. 'You don't have to worry. Now we know about the curse, we can take precautions to avoid invoking it.'

'Indeed,' Hugo said. 'There's almost nothing to be concerned about.'

Hester snorted. 'So says the man who walked around with chickens on his head.' She flew up, landed on top of his skull and started to squawk. Loudly.

'Hester,' I scolded. 'Stop that.'

Hugo raised his hand and brushed her away. 'You know, Hester,' he said, 'there's no guarantee that the skull is buried beneath the stone. It might not have been returned when the coins were, or it might have been dug up since then. It could be somewhere else.'

'Let's go *there*, then!' she exclaimed. 'Let's go somewhere else and avoid the cursed sack stone altogether!'

'Right now, the stone is our best lead,' I said. 'We'll check there first.'

Otis joined in her protest. 'It'll be dark soon.'

'You can stay here if you like,' I offered.

They both folded their arms and glared at me. 'We're not letting you have all the fun!' Hester objected.

'And we're the ones with experience in curses,' Otis added. 'We're the ones who were trapped inside a necklace for decades because of a sorcerer's curse.'

Good point. 'Any tips for avoiding a fate worse than death?' I asked.

'Yeah,' Hester said. 'Don't get caught.'

Hugo shrugged. 'Works for me.'

We exchanged smiles. There was a loud beep as Miriam, driving like a demon and pulling past us with her wheels screeching, wound down the window of her Jeep. Slim ducked his head out. 'Last one to the cursed stone buys dinner!'

'Hugo!' I ordered. 'Switch on that engine and get going! They cannot beat us!'

The Jeep roared into life. 'Don't fret.' Hugo put his foot down and smirked. 'We'll be the first ones to get cursed around here, not them.'

Hester and Otis buried their heads in their hands. 'We're doomed,' Hester muttered.

'All doomed,' Otis agreed.

They were probably right. I punched Hugo's arm lightly. 'Drive faster.'

∾

IN THE END both vehicles got stuck behind a tractor and we pulled into a layby not far from the Fonaby Sack Stone at the same time. I jumped out of the Jeep, checked the location on my phone and glanced around. There was a narrow path leading up a low hill towards a copse of pine trees. 'I think it's that way,' I said.

'It doesn't look spooky or cursed,' Hester said. 'It just looks like farmland.'

'Maybe we'll get lucky and discover the tales of the curse have been exaggerated,' I told her. She stared at me without blinking. 'Yeah,' I said. 'Alright. I know. Given the way our lives have been going, I'll knock the stone over by accident and we'll be cursed for a thousand generations.'

'Sounds about right,' Otis muttered and I grinned.

We headed for the path. Although it hadn't rained for several days, the ground was thick with dark mud and our footsteps squelched noisily; at one point, Slim's wellington boot got stuck and we had to pull him free. If this had been merely a casual stroll, I might have been tempted to use a skein of magic to suck away the moisture and make the ground easier to cross, but we were heading for a spot steeped in its own unpleasant magic. Until we knew exactly what we were dealing with, even an innocuous spell seemed like a bad idea.

Our slow progress meant that the sun was already dipping by the time we reached the place where the Sack Stone was supposed to be. 'This is the spot.' Hugo frowned. 'I don't see any stones.'

'Maybe Smiggleswith was playing us,' Slim offered.

Miriam clicked her tongue. 'You're not looking hard enough.' She pointed at several fallen branches several metres away from the path. 'See?'

We turned and looked. She was right: there was a large, moss-covered stone, but it was almost entirely hidden from view by the branches and only one corner of it was visible from the path. Had someone shielded it on purpose to deter curious hikers from invoking the curse? A shudder ran down my spine.

The shape of the stone did remind me of a sack of corn. This was what we'd come to find so we couldn't simply stand and gawk, although strangely nobody seemed willing to abandon the path and move closer. The playful, competitive atmosphere had vanished.

'I know it's getting dark,' Becky whispered, 'but shouldn't there be more noise?' She was right. This was the countryside in late spring: there should have been a cacophony of nesting birds, buzzing insects and rustling from the undergrowth. I couldn't hear a single thing – and now that I was aware of the deathly silence, I felt unsettled.

Otis flew towards me and buried himself in the folds of my jacket. 'I don't like it here.' Hester watched his head disappear beneath my collar. A second later, she followed him, burrowing even deeper.

My gaze lifted to Hugo. For a few seconds, we shared a mutual – albeit silent – look of deep foreboding. 'I think that we can all agree the curse is real,' he said quietly.

I steeled myself and stepped off the path. Night was on its way and the sky wouldn't get any lighter until the morning; we had to act now before we lost what little visibility there was. Although I didn't say anything, I was relieved when the rest of the group followed me. Soon we were all standing around the strange stone and staring down at it.

'We can't risk moving it,' Miriam said. 'Not even by an inch.'

'Agreed.' Hugo scratched his chin. 'Thankfully we have a special technique, created by Daisy herself, that will help us search for any items buried beneath it.'

'Using earth magic to sense for what's buried there is a good idea,' Slim said. 'But we can't remove anything without disturbing the stone.'

I toed the ground. 'The skull is small. We could dig a small tunnel and send the brownies in to retrieve it.'

Hester's head immediately popped up from inside my jacket. 'Oh, fine,' she snapped. 'Give us the hard jobs, why don't you? Give us the opportunity to be cursed for the rest of time.' She glared at me. 'Save yourselves, sacrifice the brownies.'

'You don't have to do it if you don't want to. In fact, if you have a better idea, Hes, I'm more than willing to hear it,' I said.

She wrinkled her nose.

'I'll do it.' Otis's voice was muffled and shaky but still audible. 'I'll burrow underneath and find the skull.'

'It could be close to the surface – we might be able to retrieve it without you.' Becky sounded doubtful but she was right: until we knew exactly where the skull was, we couldn't tell what digging would be required.

I nodded. 'Step back. I'll do a quick magical search and see what I find.'

Otis and Hester reluctantly extricated themselves from their hiding spot while I delved into my pocket and drew out another two pills of spider's silk. Hugo's jaw tightened but he knew as well as I did that I couldn't let my magic get the better of me and mess this up.

I swallowed the pills then unclipped Gladys from my side and handed her to Hugo. Pretending that my heart wasn't thumping loudly enough to rattle my rib cage, and that my stomach was not churning with greasy nausea, I forced a smile. Then, before my trepidation got the better of me, I pushed out a brief nudge of questing earth magic.

The flash of pain that reverberated through my bones came instantly. I winced and beamed at the same time; annoying as the pain was, it indicated that there was definitely something underneath the Sack Stone that didn't belong there – and it wasn't far beneath the surface. Retrieving it might be easier than we'd expected.

Suddenly buoyed up, I ignored the grim aura and damp moss clinging to the Fonaby Stone and lowered myself to the ground. The gloopy mud would wash off. 'Keep out of the way,' I said to the others. 'If anything goes wrong and I end up triggering the curse, it'll be better if it only affects me rather than all of us.'

Before anyone could dissuade me, I started to scrabble downwards, taking great care to avoid touching the stone itself. If I dug at an angle, I reckoned I could retrieve the hidden item without disturbing the lump of rock. Patience was key: given how much my hands were shaking, I had to take my time and do everything I could to control my movements.

I pulled out several handfuls of dark mud and flung them aside. 'You're in luck, Otis,' I said. 'If the ground was harder we could create a tiny tunnel for you to burrow through, but it's too soft and squelchy. It's pretty disgusting but it's not difficult. You can stay where you are.' I pushed my hand deeper. 'There are only a few more inches to go. I'm almost there.'

I drew out a few pebbles, then scooped away several more handfuls of thick, wet earth. 'Almost there,' I muttered again, and planted the side of my face in the mud as I tried to get closer to my target.

My heart skipped a beat, then another, and I paused and waited for my traitorous body to sort itself out. When it returned to a regular rhythm, I stretched my fingertips forward, squeezing them through yet more dirt. Finally, I felt something.

It wasn't another pebble, and it certainly wasn't more mud. 'Guys,' I whispered. 'I think I have it.'

I hooked the object with my index finger and clawed it out inch by laborious inch. After what felt like an age, I could wrap my hand around it. I angled my body to the left to make sure I didn't brush against the cursed stone, then yanked hard.

There was a loud sucking noise as my arm, hand and the tiny object pulled free. I tumbled backwards and held my prize aloft with a crow of delight. Without waiting for the others, I wiped away as much of the mud as I could. It was wrapped in some sort of sack cloth, and it was the right size to be Gordon's skull.

'Cross your fingers, everyone,' I said. 'This might actually be it.'

I peeled away the fabric. The mud had seeped through the cloth, so I had to rub it against my thigh to clean off the worst of it, but as soon as I did a slow smile spread across my face.

I was holding a small, three-inch-high golden skull. Its tiny eye sockets were filled with even more mud and there was something chilling about its empty grin, but I could feel the thrum of its magical power beneath my trembling fingers.

'We've found it,' I breathed. 'That was easier than I thought it would be.' Gordon would be delighted – hell, *I* was delighted. There was nothing like the sensation of pure success.

And then my feeling of elation and my bright smile began to dim. *Hang on a minute.* I glanced to my left then to my right. Heart pounding, I scrambled up and spun around, staring at the path.

Yes, it was dark, but it wasn't so dark that I couldn't see what was in front of me. Or rather, what *wasn't* in front of me.

Hugo, Miriam, Slim and Becky – together with Hester and Otis – had all disappeared.

EIGHT

'This isn't funny,' I said. Nobody answered. 'Come on, you lot. You can come out now.' Still nothing. My voice sharpened. 'I appreciate a prank as much as the next person, but this isn't the time.'

Nothing rustled, nobody giggled, and nobody jumped out from behind a bush to say boo. Cumbubbling bollocks, what the hell had happened?

I slowly turned and double-checked the area. I rubbed my eyes, then I gazed hard at the Fonaby Stone. I hadn't touched it, not once. 'I'm sorry,' I said. 'But I didn't do anything so the curse shouldn't have been invoked. And nothing in those old stories mentioned sudden disappearances!'

Unsurprisingly, the stone didn't reply.

'I didn't touch you! I didn't even *breathe* on you!' I ground my teeth. My fingers tightened around the little skull as I turned, searching through the encroaching darkness for signs of life.

It was on my fourth spin that I thought I saw something. My eyes narrowed. It was difficult to tell what it was and going towards it would take me away from the path and the layby where the Jeeps were parked. From this distance it was a mere faint glimmer, but I had no other clues.

I pushed away my rising panic, shoved the skull into my inside pocket and set off determinedly in its direction.

The closer I got, the more certain I was that the dim light had nothing to do with my missing companions. It was too small, it wasn't moving, and it definitely wasn't making any sort of noise. Nevertheless, I plunged ahead.

I was only ten metres away when I realised that the glow was attached to a spindly pine tree. I marched towards it and hunkered down. A strange blue splodge of goo covered several inches of the bark. I'd never seen anything like it before.

I reached out as if to touch it, then thought better of it and pulled back. The hairs on the back of my neck were raised and my stomach was churning. Every thought in my head was scattered and fearful.

'Think, Daisy. Just think.' I reached into my jacket pocket and took out another two spider's silk pills. Seven pills in one day; that would be a record, and not a good one.

I stared at them as they lay in the palm of my hand, then I grimaced and tossed them into my mouth, allowing their familiar, bitter fizz to calm my panicked thoughts. As I expected, my tinnitus flared up and the heart palpitations made me inhale sharply, but it was okay. My head was clearing.

I realised that I wasn't alone, not entirely.

Pulling out my phone, I sagged with relief when I saw there was a weak signal. I could call for help; I didn't have to deal with this on my own. In fact, there was a whole team of competent people at Pemberville Castle who could provide answers. Or so I hoped.

Rizwan picked up on the second ring. 'Hi,' I said quickly. 'It's Daisy. I've got a problem.'

To his credit he didn't panic, but neither did he sound

particularly surprised. Perhaps sudden emergency situations were par for the course when you were part of Hugo's Primes. 'Tell me.'

'Everyone's disappeared.'

There was a beat of silence. 'Pardon?'

I licked my lips and started from the beginning. 'I located the golden skull buried beneath an old stone near Caistor. Everyone was behind me while I dug it up. Once I'd retrieved it, I turned around and nobody was there. Hugo, Miriam, Becky, Slim and the brownies have vanished. The stone is cursed – I'm certain I didn't touch it but maybe it shifted slightly without me noticing when I pulled out the skull. Maybe somehow that invoked the curse.'

'Shit,' Rizwan muttered. 'Okay.'

'There's more.' I stared at the glowing blue splodge. 'There's some ... goop nearby.'

'Goop?'

'Maybe thirty metres away from the stone, just off the path, I found some blue goop. It's stuck to a tree and it's – er – glowing slightly.'

'Glowing blue goop?' Rizwan delivered each word very slowly as if he didn't believe me.

'Yep.'

'Okay, hang on. Let me get Mark.'

As I waited impatiently, I scanned the darkness. When I spotted another blue blob, I exhaled sharply, then crouched down, phone in hand, and checked the ground.

'Daisy?' Mark's voice sounded tinny.

I straightened up. Words tumbled out of my mouth at top speed. 'There's more – there's more goop. I think it's some kind of trail. And I can see footprints heading in the same direction. The others must have followed it.'

'Okay, okay. That's good.' He was trying to reassure me but I could hear the tension in his voice. 'Whatever you do, Daisy, don't follow the trail until we know exactly what we're dealing with.'

I was already moving. 'Sure, yep. No following.'

Several dry twigs snapped under my feet. If somebody or something had taken hold of my team and done anything to hurt them, they'd live to regret the day they were born. I had no idea what creatures might live out here in rural Lincolnshire among the cows and cursed stones, but I would find them.

I stopped abruptly. 'Ask Duchess. Ask if she knows what it might be.'

Mark sounded confused. 'Duchess?'

'She's a troll. She's used to rural areas. If anyone knows what the blue goop is or what's happened to the others, she will.'

'Okay, okay. But make sure Gladys is unsheathed and you're prepared while I find her.'

'I—' My voice faltered. Double cumbubbling bollocks: I'd handed Gladys to Hugo because of my untrustworthy magic. But Mark was already worried; I didn't need to make things worse by telling him. I swallowed. 'Alright,' I said.

Picking my way through the trees, I followed both the illuminated glow in front of me and the footsteps on the ground beside me. A large field with some unidentifiable crops lay to my left, and a mess of ancient bracken, old trees and deep mud was to my right.

A pleasant buzz from the spider's silk was coursing through my system and my heart was thumping anxiously against my ribcage: my adrenaline levels were high. That was good, I told myself. They would keep me alert and ready for anything.

With that thought in mind, I slapped both my ears hard, as if the action could somehow knock away my tinnitus. It didn't stop the whiney ringing, but the self-inflicted pain made me feel slightly better. I focused on moving as quickly and quietly as I could and tried not to think about what danger my friends might be in.

I'd passed the second splodge of blue goop and seen the third one by the time Duchess's voice crackled down the phone. 'Glowing blue goop?' she cackled. 'How many drugs have you taken today, Fated Flea?'

I held my temper. Just. 'Duchess, if you don't know what it is, pass the phone to Mark.'

She snorted. 'I know what it is. Of course I know! You're in trouble, girlie.'

I clambered over a fallen tree trunk and snagged my jeans on something sharp. I scowled as I extricated myself. 'Clearly you don't know anything. Go back to your bridge.'

Offended, Duchess gave her answer without thinking. 'I do! I do know! I ain't stupid. You're in wisp territory!'

Wisp? I blinked rapidly. Will-o'-the-wisp? Suddenly everything made perfect – albeit terrifying – sense.

'Thanks, Duchess,' I heard Mark mutter, and there was a brief scuffling sound as he wrestled the phone from her. 'A will-o'-the-wisp,' he breathed. 'I should have thought of them sooner, but there are so few of them left these days.'

He was right. From what little I'd read when I'd been trying to teach myself about the world of magic, there was more chance you'd be struck by lightning than that you'd fall into a will-o'-the-wisp's trap. The lightning would be preferable, though.

'Rizwan is looking them up. Hang on, Daisy.' Mark clicked his tongue. 'Hugo should have known better than to allow this to happen. He's been far too distracted lately.'

I stiffened. I was the one who'd been distracting him, and I felt the sting of guilt.

Within moments, Rizwan was speaking. 'Duchess is right.

The blue goop is excreted by the wisp in the same way that you or I might sweat.'

Ick.

'If you follow the trail, it should lead you directly to the wisp's lair. Be extra careful because a wisp can hypnotise unwary people into a trance – that's probably what happened to Hugo and the others. You weren't affected because you weren't looking at it.'

'Saved by the golden skull,' I muttered. 'What does the wisp want with them? What is it after?' In other words, would it try and kill anyone? And worse, was there a chance they were already dead?

'That depends,' Rizwan replied. 'Some will-o'-the-wisps are nothing more than mischief makers. They lead travellers astray for their own amusement.'

'And others?' I asked, suspecting something far more sinister.

'Others are evil bastards that will viciously attack their prey without a second thought.'

Of course they were. I sighed. 'Gotcha.'

'The thing is, Daisy,' Mark cautioned, 'you stumbled into its territory. You know what the law says. You can't harm it.'

I nodded and swore at the same time. Magical creatures living in the wild had legal protection, whether they were giant snakes, talking dragons or nasty will-o'-the-wisps. In some cases, you could fight back if the situation called for it – but not if you had wandered into their habitat and disturbed them.

If I hurt the will-o'-the-wisp, I'd be facing a jail sentence regardless of what it had done to me or the others because it had the right to defend itself in its own home. Until we'd shown up the wisp hadn't been bothering anyone, so it was a law that I agreed with. That didn't help me right now, of course.

'There should have been some warning signs,' I protested.

'You can put in a written complaint to the authorities later,' Mark said.

Yeah, yeah. I pushed back my hair and quashed the desperate urge to swallow yet more spider's silk. 'Any tips for dealing with it without harming it?'

'Don't look directly into its eyes. If you do, you'll fall into the same trance as the others.'

'Anything else?' I crossed my fingers hopefully; even a scrap of an idea about what to do would be helpful.

There were several seconds of silence. 'We'll keep searching for anything in the books and let you know.' Translation: he had nothing more to tell me and I was on my own.

I sniffed. No problem.

I HAD to walk further than I'd expected, at least a mile, and the longer I kept going the boggier the ground became. At least that meant the footprints were easily visible so I didn't have to worry that I was heading in the wrong direction. Given that the splodges of blue goop were few and far between, I could easily have gotten lost.

A little of my tension eased when I started to hear the usual rustling of nocturnal wildlife and the occasional hoot from an owl on the hunt; the curse leaking from the Fonaby stone obviously had a limited range and probably had little to do with the will-o'-the-wisp. That didn't make the situation any less dire, but it did mean there was less to worry about. I was only equipped to deal with one disaster at a time.

The first indication that I was drawing close to the will-o'-the-wisp's lair was the singing. The notes drifted across the landscape, curling around the leaves and trees and saturating the air like a mist. The wisp was female – and a damned good soprano, to boot.

I slowed my steps, placing each foot carefully on the ground so I didn't alert her. As I inched closer, the will-o'-the-wisp's song faded and I felt oddly bereft at the loss of the enchanting music.

I didn't have long to mourn its disappearance because seconds later she spoke. 'Which one will we eat first?' I stiffened. She continued. 'The small ones will be bony and unsatisfying, but they might be tasty.' There was a smacking sound. 'Yes, they will make an excellent snack. Chuchi will enjoy eating them.'

A carnivorous will-o'-the-wisp? Why couldn't I stumble across one that was vegan? And who was Chuchi? Would I have to deal with two of these fuckers?

The wisp continued chattering to herself. 'This woman is old and her flesh will be tough, but it will make fine jerky to keep for winter.' I doubted Miriam would be thrilled at that thought.

'This younger woman has more meat on her bones. Perhaps I will leave her for last, and we can eat her with the brown-haired man. He looks stringy. But this other man – wow! He will be a delectable feast. Elves are good. Chuchi says their meat has a spicy bite. Yum-yum.'

There was a pause. 'There are so many of them. Perhaps I can keep one, just for a while. Chuchi won't mind if I only keep one.' She hesitated again. 'Will he?'

I reached an oak tree that was broader and taller than the pine trees and provided more cover. I pressed my spine against it then risked a peek around its trunk. The will-o'-the-wisp's lair was in a small clearing. Judging from the moisture in the air, the rotting smell and the way the ground was glinting in the soft moonlight, it was some sort of marsh. I couldn't sprint across it to perform a surprise rescue – I'd be more likely to take three steps and sink to my knees. From the way Hugo, Becky, Miriam and Slim were standing, that was exactly what had happened to them.

They were shoulder to shoulder in a row, arms hanging loosely by their sides. Becky and Hugo were calf deep in mud; Slim, who was taller, was only submerged to his ankles, but Miriam was encased up to her knees. Their jaws were slack and their eyes were vacant: they looked like zombies.

Slumped on Hugo's shoulders, neither Otis nor Hester was in any better shape. I couldn't make out their expressions but there was little doubt that they were in the same condition. I couldn't see Gladys.

'Yes. I can keep one. One won't matter. And Chuchi will want to visit now,' the will-o'-the-wisp said. 'Now I have meat to give him, he'll definitely come. He'll stay for many days.' She trilled happily and bustled around, picking up bits of litter that had blown in with the wind.

I watched her flit to and fro. I'd seen photographs of will-o'-the-wisps before, and I had a dim recollection of an old Attenborough documentary that had featured one of them, but it was weird to be this close to one.

She was round and squat like a little beach ball and she was hovering several inches above the ground, with only the tip of what I supposed was her tail trailing in the mud. Will-o'-the-wisps didn't have legs – they didn't need them. Although they weren't birds and they couldn't fly, they possessed a natural buoyancy that pushed against the effects of gravity. As far as I knew, they never touched the ground, not even when they slept.

This will-o'-the-wisp was glowing a brighter blue than the secretions I'd followed and doing a better job of lighting the dark marsh than the moon. She was pretty, with wide green eyes that gave her a cartoon-princess air and an upturned nose speckled with what I assumed counted as freckles in wisp physiology.

She turned her back and busied herself with something on the far side of the marsh. My phone, which was on silent in my pocket, vibrated. I slid it out, hoping that Rizwan and Mark had finally found something useful that would help me rescue everyone.

It was a text message. I scanned the contents, carefully shielding the screen so its glow didn't alert the will-o'-the-wisp.

Her name is Baudi. Proceed with extreme caution. She's dangerous. The last known report of her is from 2003 when she attacked two lost hikers. They said she almost killed them. This WOTW is one of the nasty ones.

I grimaced; yeah, I'd already worked that last part out. It was interesting that she hadn't been heard of for more than twenty years. Given the lack of warning signs in the area, I suspected the curse that was bound into the Fonaby Stone kept most people away. Even if some intrepid wanderers reached it, the grim atmosphere would likely make them turn back.

I hastily typed a reply. *Another wisp called Chuchi?*

Three little dots appeared: either Mark or Rizwan was typing. I waited – and waited. A moment later, the dots vanished. I scowled and checked the phone signal, and my heart sank when I saw it had disappeared. So much for help from the outside.

I tucked away the phone and considered my options. I could wait until daylight or go back to the Jeep and call for help, but there was no guarantee that Baudi would wait before starting dinner. I might not have that much time.

I risked another peek. Her back was still turned as she focused on her task and I squinted to see what was holding her attention. Unfortunately, in my bid to get a better look I shifted my feet. My stomach lurched with nausea strong enough to make me gasp aloud – and I slipped. My heel landed on a twig, snapping it in two.

Baudi swung around then zipped several metres through the air in my direction. Her bright-green eyes narrowed as she scanned the area. Heart pounding, I pressed against the tree trunk and prayed she'd dismiss the noise as nothing more than a badger snuffling nearby.

Long seconds ticked by as I strained my ears for any sign that she was approaching. There was nothing. After a couple of minutes had passed, I started to relax. She wasn't coming for me; I'd fucked up, but my luck was holding. I exhaled softly.

And that was when there was a rush of air and Baudi's glowing blue body whisked around the tree to face me. 'Excellent,' she said, smacking her lips. 'Another elf for my cooking pot.'

CHAPTER
NINE

I squeaked and ducked, just in time to avoid her hand smacking me in the face, then I skidded around the tree and sprinted around the edge of her marshy lair. But Baudi had the advantage: her feet didn't sink repeatedly into the thick mud so she could move much faster than me. She also knew the territory like the back of her blue hand.

I barely managed six metres before she was on me again, her hand swiping towards my neck. I managed to pull forward and prevent her fingers wrapping around my throat, but she still caught hold of my jacket collar. I frantically tried to yank free; when that didn't work, I fumbled for the zip of my coat. It was one of my favourites and I'd miss it, but I'd rather lose it than end up as a will-o'-the-wisp's dinner.

My fingers were caked in mud and they felt fat and clumsy. When the zip caught halfway down, I knew I wouldn't be able to shrug it off quickly enough. With one hand snarled in my collar, Baudi used her other hand to spin around my helpless body, then her face loomed towards mine.

I dropped my gaze instantly: one glance into her eyes and

I'd end up zombified like the others. This was not good; this was not good at all.

I twisted and wrenched, desperate to get free, but I couldn't attack her and I didn't want to hurt her. That didn't mean I was out of options for defending myself, though. Scenarios tumbled one after another through my head, while Baudi's cold breath chilled my skin and she half-snarled and half-smiled.

'It's so wonderful to have another visitor to my humble home.' She grabbed my chin and hauled it upwards to force me to meet her eyes.

I jerked my head in the same direction and looked over her shoulder into the shadowy trees on the far side of the clearing. Then I jolted out several bursts of air magic to make the leaves and twigs in several different locations rustle and twist.

Baudi stiffened and immediately released her hold on me as she turned to look.

'Get ready!' I yelled towards the trees, addressing an invisible – and non-existent – cavalry. 'Get ready to attack!'

'There are more of you?' She grinned, revealing pointed, yellowing teeth. 'Marvellous!' She lurched towards the trees, determined to catch more prey. It wouldn't take her long to realise that she'd fallen for the oldest trick in the book.

If I tried to run away, I wouldn't get far before she came after me. I had to reach the others and try to free them from their trance. If even one of them was fully conscious, we might get out of this situation unharmed.

I headed for Hugo first. Baudi was crashing around in the trees only metres away, so I knew I didn't have long. I shook him hard and, when he didn't react, I slapped his cheek. He still didn't react. I conjured up a burst of water and threw it in his face but it didn't do a damned thing: I couldn't wake him.

There wasn't time to haul his body out of the clearing – and anyway, I was already up to my ankles in gloopy mud. I hissed and grabbed Otis and Hester from his shoulders. That was the moment when Baudi careened out of the tree line and came for me again.

'You thought you could fool me!' She aimed a fist towards my head that I couldn't dodge. It caught my cheekbone and sent a jolt of pain reverberating through my skull. As I reeled backwards, I dropped Otis and Hester who landed in the mud with a wet splat. The mud was like quicksand; they would be swallowed up within seconds.

Desperate to retrieve them, I scrabbled forward, pinched Otis's legs and pulled him up. I hastily dropped him into the dubious safety of my pocket.

'Look at me!' Baudi screeched. 'Look! At! Me!' She aimed another blow and another, both of which connected with vicious, agonising pain. Yep, she was thoroughly kicking my arse.

I managed to scoop Hester up in the palm of my hand and felt her limbs stir beneath my fingers; perhaps the seconds she'd been trapped in the mud had knocked her out of her trance. I didn't have time to check because Baudi smacked me hard on the back of my head and I collapsed once more into the quagmire.

I sensed rather than saw her body circling around mine. 'What's your name?' she asked.

I didn't answer, mostly because my mouth was full of mud. She hit me again. 'I said what's your name?'

I spat out the dirt. 'Daisy.'

'Where are you from?'

'I live in Edinburgh but I'm originally from the north of England.'

'Do you dye your hair that colour or is it natural?'

Eh? 'It's natural.'

'If you could choose between fighting one hundred duck-sized elephants or one elephant-sized duck, which would you pick?' *What?* 'Answer me!'

'One elephant-sized duck,' I said quickly.

'You're stupid,' she muttered. 'Why did you come here?' She wasn't pausing for breath but firing out questions like a skilled interrogator. And some of those questions were very strange indeed.

Before I could answer, Hester's tiny body spasmed and she started to cough. Delight coursed through me. As I raised my head to look at her, my gaze snagged on Gladys propped up against a pile of wood only a few metres away. Ah-ha.

A half-baked plan started to form. Baudi was a will-o'-the-wisp who lived in the middle of nowhere. The last reports about her activities were from years ago, and she was clearly a creature who attacked first and asked questions later, so she probably didn't know about the law that protected her in her habitat. She certainly didn't know that I always tried to stick to that law, so all I needed to do was threaten her enough for her to release us. I simply needed to convince her that I was bigger, badder and scarier than she was – and Gladys could help me do that. So could my innate magic.

I spat out more mud, then reached inside myself and tugged on my power. I conjured up a vast, powerful spurt of air magic and angled it behind Gladys before releasing it and using the techniques I'd been working on with Slim.

It worked. Despite her hefty weight, Gladys was thrown forward until the tip of her blade scraped against my cheek. I grabbed her hilt with my free hand and hauled myself up, tossing out several more bursts of magic at the same time. None of them were aimed at Baudi because I didn't want her to feel their effect, but I did want her to witness what I was capable of.

A heaving flash of earth magic rocked the ground and sent splatters of mud flying up into the night air. Water magic crashed down on both sides of the wisp's body and pooled by her feet. A ring of fire magic appeared in mid-air and surrounded the whole clearing with flickering flames.

'I came here to kill you,' I said, hoping she wouldn't catch the lie. I kept my eyes fixed on a point over her shoulder so I couldn't judge her expression.

When she started to laugh hysterically, it was clear what she was thinking. 'Kill me? Kill *me*?' she spluttered. 'You won't be the first elf to come here and try that, and I hope you won't be the last. I will keep you till last. You'll be here for months and you can watch me kill your companions. You and I will be spending a lot of time together.' She sounded pleased at the prospect; the one thing she didn't sound was scared.

Hester coughed again and I gave her tiny body a reassuring squeeze before I swung Gladys menacingly in the air. The sword, helpful as ever, vibrated and hummed in response.

'Your sword doesn't scare me,' Baudi said. She lunged forward in a blur of motion.

I steeled myself for the blow but the will-o'-the-wisp was cannier than I'd given her credit for. She feinted left so that I thought she was aiming for Hester. With a flash of fear, I altered my stance – and loosened my grip on Gladys. At the very last second, Baudi switched her attack: instead of trying to grab Hester, she knocked Gladys clean out of my hand.

Hester muttered something and fluttered against my fingers. I opened my hand and she flew upwards, shaking herself off and retreating to a safe distance. 'Hester?' I called. 'Are you alright?'

'What the fuck do you think?'

I exhaled. 'Don't look at her. Don't look at the will-o'-the-wisp's face.'

Baudi laughed again. 'You're only delaying the inevitable.'

I scowled and bent down to get hold of Gladys again, but

Baudi was wise to my plan and ready for it. As soon as I moved, she slammed into me and forced me backwards, further away from Gladys. 'Look at me,' she commanded.

I forced my head down.

'Look at me.'

I clenched my jaw. I wasn't giving up yet.

'Look at me!' she roared.

I made a show of shaking my head and my gaze snagged on a neat pile of leaves, mushrooms and berries that had been arranged into sections. I frowned – then Baudi smacked me again. At this rate, I'd soon be seeing pretty lights dancing in front of my eyes.

My heart was rattling against my ribcage, while the blood that was coursing through my veins seemed to be heating up. My mouth felt painfully dry. I didn't want to break the law, and I didn't want to hurt Baudi, but if there was no other option then I would. It wasn't only my life on the line, it was everyone else's too.

'Look at me.' Baudi's voice dropped to a silky whisper. 'Look into my eyes or I will start killing your companions. I'll do it right in front of you. I won't wait.'

Something snapped and the heat in my blood became scalding fury as it overtook the spider's silk in my system. Coherent thought fled.

I raised my hands high into the air and stretched.

'Uh, Daisy?' Hester sounded scared but I barely heard her. My hands were twitching now. I'd take Baudi down. I'd do what needed to be done. I'd—

'That's not elf magic,' Baudi said. The confusion in her voice drew me back to myself. As I glanced up at my hands, I saw tiny flickers of lightning jumping from fingertip to fingertip. In an instant, the heat in my body subsided to a distinct chill.

The only people I'd seen use magic like that were fiends.

Now the will-o'-the-wisp was backing away, putting distance between us. I still didn't look at her; my focus remained on the sparks at my fingertips. I licked my lips and concentrated. A beat later, a single lightning bolt shot upwards, flashing from my right hand into the sky. Cumbubbling bollocks.

I concentrated harder on dousing the sparks, and one by one they flickered out. I stepped forward and picked up Gladys. A preternatural calm had overtaken my fury.

By now, Baudi was at the edge of the clearing. 'Do it,' Hester hissed. 'You have to do it! Kill her and everyone will be freed. You can make it quick so she doesn't suffer.'

As I tightened my grip on Gladys's hilt, I thought about Agatha Smiggleswith at the museum. I'd liked her because I'd understood her motivation.

I glanced at the collection of leaves, berries and fungi and then looked around the quiet little marsh. I thought about everything that Baudi had said and done. Then I lowered Gladys and dropped my shoulders. 'You talk to yourself,' I said to the wisp.

Baudi's answer was swift and defiant. 'So? I'm not mad.'

'I wouldn't suggest anything of the sort. I often talk to myself, too, though I don't do it so much now that I spend less time on my own.'

'I'm not always on my own!'

Uh-huh. 'When did Chuchi last visit?' She didn't respond, which gave me all the answer I needed.

'Baudi,' I said softly, 'it's been twenty years since anyone came here, hasn't it? You live alone and your usual diet is vegetarian. You asked me several daft questions because you wanted to talk. You were happy about capturing all my friends because you thought it meant that Chuchi would visit, not because you cared about having a few spicy elven meals.'

'He will visit,' she muttered. 'Chuchi *will* visit.'

'You were happy at the prospect of having me here for months before you killed me. You're lonely.' I paused. 'Aren't you?'

'No!'

'You don't want to kill anyone, and you don't want to eat anyone either. You've not really hurt any of us.' I shrugged. 'Sure, you smacked me around a bit and made a lot of threats, but I've got nothing more than a few bruises. If you'd wanted to, you could have hurt me a whole lot more. You were fast enough and strong enough to break my skull if you chose to, but you chose *not* to. I know what you really want.'

'I want to eat you all!' Baudi bellowed, still keeping her distance from me.

'Nah.' I shook my head. I thought about the information Mark had given me and I felt more sure of myself. Baudi had attacked two hikers in 2003 and they'd reported that she'd nearly killed them, but she obviously *didn't* kill them or they wouldn't have lived to tell the tale. They'd obviously escaped and not ended up in a cauldron of will-o'-the-wisp soup.

'All you want is a bit of company,' I continued. 'It can't be easy out here on your own all the time. The curse on the Fonaby Stone means you don't get many visitors.' I corrected myself. 'In fact, it means you don't get *any* visitors. There are no unwitting travellers to lead astray, nobody to chat to. That's rough.'

Baudi didn't say anything.

'Being alone can be really hard,' I said softly. I lifted my head and, for the first time, looked directly into her eyes. 'I think I can help with that.'

TEN

The negotiations went surprisingly smoothly. I'd had to leave the clearing to get a phone signal and Baudi had trailed me all the way, muttering, but Agatha Smiggleswith had answered her phone almost immediately and was more enthusiastic than I'd expected.

'I have a few conditions,' she said on speaker once I'd put my suggestion to her. 'We'll need to engage the services of a sorcerer to bind the wisp for the duration of each visit. It wouldn't go down well if she decided to attack any of the museum visitors.'

I raised my eyebrows questioningly towards Baudi. Rather than looking offended, she seemed pleased by the idea that she was a dangerous creature who had to be magicked into submission. 'That's not a problem,' she said.

'We'll also have to put her on probation to begin with. A trial period of, say, two months?'

Baudi's mouth twisted. 'One month.' We eventually settled on six weeks, thus appeasing both parties.

'I have a few conditions of my own,' Baudi said loudly, keen to wrestle some control over the situation. 'I want to be paid.

I'm not giving my time up for free. In return for every hour I spend at the museum, I demand one bushel of apples. No stinting – I want a full bushel.'

I didn't have the faintest idea how large a bushel was but apparently Smiggleswith did. She agreed without question.

'Somebody will need to pick her up,' I said. 'I don't think Baudi can travel into Doncaster on her own.'

'That can be arranged, as long as she agrees to meet us by the road,' Smiggleswith said. 'I won't risk any of my people tramping past the Fonaby Stone every two weeks.'

'The curse doesn't frighten me!' Baudi said loudly.

I ignored her. 'That's settled then. Every two weeks Baudi will give a presentation to the public at Doncaster Museum. I am sure there are any number of topics on which she can wax lyrical.'

The will-o'-the-wisp nodded emphatically. 'Damned right there are.'

'She'll be a very popular addition,' Smiggleswith agreed. 'No other museum in the country can boast of a will-o'-the-wisp on its staff. That was a fabulous idea of Lord Pemberville's. The man is a genius.'

She wouldn't have said that if she could have seen him at that moment, standing slack-jawed and stock-still in a smelly marsh. There was even a dribble of drool hanging from the corner of his mouth.

I refrained from commenting and ended the call. Hester flew up to my ear. 'It's not too late to kill her, you know. You can still do it.'

I waved her away and looked at Baudi. 'Your turn,' I said. 'Let the others go.'

'Perhaps I could keep them until the end of the week?' she said.

I folded my arms and stared at her. She sighed. 'Alright,

then. Come on.' She turned around and hovered back towards her lair. I followed, texting Mark and Rizwan as I walked: *Disaster averted. All good now.*

The three little dots appeared again. A moment later, a reply appeared: *Very glad to hear it.* More dots. *We could only find one mention of a Chuchi. He was a nasty ogre who was known for manipulating weaker magical creatures to do his dirty work.*

Hmm; like persuading will-o'-the-wisps to entrap travellers and imprison them until he arrived to crunch on their bones. I gazed at Baudi's retreating blue back and typed another message. *Was?*

The response came quickly: *He was killed in a fight in the nineties.*

A wave of sympathy for Baudi washed through me. If she'd been holding out for a scammy ogre for thirty years, it was a wonder she'd done as well as she had. She deserved better; any living creature did.

I looked down at my traitorous hands and noticed a single spark flickering at the tip of my left index finger. Apart from fiends, I thought; fiends didn't deserve a damned thing.

HUGO WAS STARING AT ME. 'You saved us,' he said.

I wasn't convinced they'd needed saving – Baudi would probably have released them before too long – but I agreed anyway. There was no harm in receiving Hugo's eternal gratitude. 'Not only did I save you, but I also found the treasure all on my own.' I pulled out the little golden skull. 'Go me.'

'Go you indeed.'

I suppressed a grin. 'I'm a treasure hunter *extraordinaire*, Hugo, and it's not the first time your arse has needed rescuing.

It won't be the last, either. Honestly, you're lucky you've got me around.'

He snorted. 'I've saved your arse too.'

'I'm in the lead. I've saved you more times than you've saved me.'

He stepped towards me. 'So we're keeping track now?' He scanned my face then continued lightly, 'Because none of us would have been in this situation if you weren't so determined to help Gordon.'

Yeah, alright. I could admit it. 'Fine. It was my fault. No good deed goes unpunished.'

'We're even, then.'

I rolled my eyes.

'Say it, Daisy.'

'Can't you just admit that I'm better?'

He folded his arms, his eyes dancing, and I shook my head in mock irritation. 'We're even,' I muttered.

He smiled with satisfaction and headed in the direction – and relative safety – of the path. My amusement ebbed away. 'I'll always come and save you, Hugo,' I whispered. He didn't look around and I wasn't sure that he'd heard me.

'Can we leave now?' Hester demanded. 'I want to get as far away from this place as we can.'

'Lead the way.' I turned and waved at Baudi, who was eyeing us from the centre of the clearing. 'Stay in touch,' I told her. 'Let me know if you have any problems.'

Otis gave me an approving nod. Miriam, Slim and Becky managed tight smiles in Baudi's direction, and then we left.

WE DROVE through the night and arrived outside Gordon Mackenzie's little house on the fringes of Edinburgh at the same time as the postman. I yawned and watched as he slipped a collection of letters through the door, then I glanced at Hugo.

'You should come in with me,' I said. 'This was your treasure hunt as much as mine.' I gestured to the Jeep behind us. 'I'm sure that Gordon would be happy to see Miriam, Becky and Slim, too. We all had a hand to play in retrieving the skull for him.'

Hugo turned off the engine, took the keys out of the ignition and fiddled with them. It was the only hint that he was concerned about what would happen next. 'You're the one who did the heavy lifting,' he said. 'And I don't think Gordon will want me inside his home – he's nervous enough as it is. It's best if you hand over the skull on your own.' The keys jangled in his hands.

'It's your call,' I said. I was disappointed but I understood. 'I'll make sure he tells me what the skull does and what will happen next. This is your story, Hugo, not mine.'

He shook his head. 'It's not my story, and it's not yours either. Neither is it Gordon's. This tale belongs to Lady Rose. Maybe this will finally shed light on what happened to her.' He sounded doubtful.

'Your parents—' I began.

He interrupted me. 'Let's not go there. Let's wait and see what happens with the skull first.'

I gave a tiny nod then, without thinking, I leaned across and brushed my lips against his stubbled cheek. 'I won't be long,' I promised.

He gazed into my eyes. 'You smell of stinky marsh. He won't *want* you to stay for long.'

I laughed. 'You smell worse.'

'I can't argue with that.'

I stepped out. Otis and Hester came with me. 'Hugo's not

coming but we can, right?' Otis asked. 'I want to see why this skull is so special.'

Hester's eyes were wide with anticipation. 'I want fireworks!'

'I hope there will be nothing of the sort,' I said primly. I crooked my finger at them and they settled in their usual positions on my shoulders. I cast another look at Hugo's tense expression; the faster this was done, the better.

Gordon opened the front door before I reached it, smiled awkwardly at me in greeting, and looked at Hugo and the second Jeep. 'They'll wait out here,' I said.

He blinked, suggesting that he understood Hugo's reasons for staying outside. Maybe he did. He held open the door. 'Welcome to my home,' he said. 'You have no idea how happy I am that you're here, Daisy. I'm so glad you found the skull. This will change everything.' He sounded certain, and I hoped he was right.

I headed down a narrow corridor with polished wooden flooring into a small kitchen. I hadn't given much thought to Gordon's house, but I suppose I'd expected an empty bachelor pad with the inevitable collection of nerdy memorabilia neatly displayed and meticulously dusted. That image couldn't have been farther from the truth.

Gordon's home was certainly clean, but it was cluttered and homely. Family photographs decorated the walls alongside little watercolours of local beauty spots. There were some items I'd expect to see in a sorcerer's house, such as old books relating to runes, but mostly what was on display was pretty crockery, simple wooden carvings and well-tended plants.

He was obviously a competent cook as well: the kitchen was bursting to the seams with equipment. There was an old mixer that looked as if it had come from the 1950s, a heavy marble rolling pin, and several tubs of carefully labelled baking ingredients. The heavenly scent of baking bread wafted from the old oven. I was impressed.

Hester gave a low whistle. 'Nice! Are you a baker?'

Gordon's cheeks flushed. 'I try.'

'Wonderful!' Otis beamed.

'Thank you.' He clasped his hands. 'Would you like something to drink? I can brew a pot of coffee, or I have a collection of nice teas.'

Given that Hugo and the others were waiting outside, I thought it wise not to linger. 'That's very kind of you, Gordon,' I said. 'But we won't stay for long.' Hester pouted.

I delved into my pocket and tried my hardest not to add a dramatic flourish as I pulled out the skull. I'd cleaned it, and when I placed it on the kitchen table the sunlight streaming in through the window made it glint.

Gordon breathed out. 'Oh.' He paused. 'Oh. I wasn't expecting it to be so pretty. Was it difficult to find?'

I considered telling him the whole story then decided against it. 'All in a day's work,' I said. Which was kind of true. 'Now, can you tell me what it does? I can feel its magic every time I touch it. It's obviously powerful.'

'It certainly is.' He was still gazing reverently at the skull. 'This will do it. This will reveal the truth about Lady Rose's disappearance once for and all.'

'How?'

Gordon picked it up and turned it over. 'Well,' he said, 'you might not believe this but—'

He didn't get the chance to finish his sentence because the doorbell rang. He jerked and his brow creased, and he handed the skull to me. 'Wait a minute. I'll go and see who that is.'

I wondered idly if it was Hugo; perhaps he'd decided to join us after all. Warmed by the thought, I followed Gordon. I paused by the kitchen door and squinted towards the end of the hallway; the brown-haired man standing at the front porch was wearing a postman's uniform.

As soon as I saw him, my skin started to itch. I opened my mouth and gave a strangled yell. 'Gordon!' He hesitated. 'Gordon! Get back here!'

He turned. 'What is it?'

'That's no postman – your postman has already been and gone.' I stared fearfully at the man. He looked human and he didn't appear threatening, but I already knew that powerful fiends could take on other forms. And from the way my body was prickling, I knew exactly which fiend was on Gordon's doorstep.

The 'postman' leaned forward. 'Hello, daughter.'

My body screamed at me. I lunged for Gordon to pull him safely behind me, but my limbs wouldn't obey me; terror had taken over. The floor of the sweet little house juddered as uncontrolled earth magic flowed out of me. Heat surrounded me and, when I looked down, flames were licking outwards from my body.

'That's it. Keep going,' Athair said encouragingly.

'Daisy,' Gordon hissed. 'What's happening?'

I opened my mouth but no words would come.

Otis shrieked and threw himself into my pocket as Hester yelled in my ear, 'Your hands! Daisy!'

I gazed at the tiny flickers of lightning sparking between each fingertip. I was still clutching the skull and, horrifyingly, I felt it change temperature. Within three beats of my adrenaline-fuelled heart, it was icy cold. I gasped, dropped it and it thudded at my feet.

That was when its eye sockets started to glow.

I dimly heard Athair say something before he stepped off the doorstep and vanished.

Gordon's eyes widened. 'No,' he whispered, staring at the

skull. 'No, not yet. We're not ready.' He raised his hands and started to etch a rune in the air, his fingers dancing at high speed. The skull started to spin on the spot, moving faster and faster.

'Daisy!' Hester shrieked in panic. 'Daisy!'

Gordon completed the rune and lurched forward in a bid to reach me, but he couldn't get close. The sparks from my fingertips scorched the air and forced him back.

The house was still shaking and cracks were appearing in the plaster around us. The noise was tremendous, roaring through my ears.

I bent down to grab the skull, but before I could touch it Gordon gave a sharp cry. I looked up as a large chunk of plaster fell from the ceiling and landed on his head. He crumpled in an instant.

Then I saw a blinding flash of white light and heard a high-pitched ringing in my ears. Losing control not only of my magic but my body too, I tumbled forward. Cumbubbling bollocks.

CHAPTER
ELEVEN

The tinnitus was worse than ever, coupled this time with a prickling pain behind my eyelids. I groaned, aware of little except the shaking sensation in my limbs and the cold, clammy sweat that was drenching my body. I slowly gathered my thoughts – and that was when fear thudded through me again. Athair: he was here.

I opened my eyes and leapt up, ignoring the agonising pain that ripped through my body. But the front door was closed and there was no sign of Athair; neither was there any sign of Gordon or the collapsed ceiling. I rubbed my eyes and looked again. What on earth was going on?

There was a flutter of movement by my feet. Hester stirred then flew straight up, her tiny fists raised. 'Where is he?' she snarled. 'Where's that fiend? I'm going to—' She faltered. 'What?' Her head whipped around. '*What?*'

I glanced down to check on Otis. He was also awake and sitting cross-legged on the patterned carpet, gazing around the narrow hallway. I stared at him, then I stared at the carpet. Wait: moments ago hadn't that been wooden laminate flooring? I took in the floral wallpaper and the picture of a buxom country girl tending her sheep, neither of which had been present five minutes ago.

'This isn't Gordon's house,' Otis whispered. 'It smells different.'

I wanted to tell him that didn't make sense – we couldn't be anywhere other than in Gordon's house – but before I could speak there was a squawk behind me. I spun around and was confronted by a middle-aged woman brandishing a frying pan. She was gripping its handle so hard that her knuckles were white, and her eyes were wide with terror.

'Get out!' she screeched. 'Get out of my house!' She waved the pan in much the same way that I wielded Gladys. At that thought, my hand strayed to my side. To my relief, my trusty sword was still in her sheath.

Unfortunately, feeling for Gladys might have reassured me but it really worried the woman. She threw the frying pan at my head, where it bounced painfully off my skull, then she grabbed a large, old-fashioned telephone from a side table and jabbed in three numbers.

'Wait,' I said, 'I'm not—'

I heard a tinny voice on the other end of the line before the woman started babbling. 'Police! I need the police! There's an intruder in my house. She's got a sword. And there are two fairies with her. She's going to attack! I don't know what she wants! Help me!'

'I'm not a fucking fairy!' Hester yelled, squaring up to the poor woman in a very unhelpful manner.

I grabbed Hester in one hand and Otis in the other, wrenched open the front door and ran outside. It was dark, but it looked like I was in Gordon's street. I glanced back; it was the same front door, the same address. However, that woman was definitely not Gordon – and there was no sign of Hugo or the others outside.

Something crashed onto the path beside me: the woman was throwing plates. She aimed one at my head with a look of fixed concentration. I gave up trying to work out what was going on and sprinted down the barely lit street. I didn't know what had happened to the dawn I'd witnessed only minutes ago; I didn't know what was happening at all.

All I could do was run and run and run.

I WAS breathless by the time I had to stop because my legs would no longer obey my orders and I was on the verge of collapse. As I dropped onto the edge of the pavement and gasped for air, Otis and Hester watched me with worried eyes. 'Her face is very red,' Hester commented. 'Do you think she's unwell?'

I glared at her and continued to suck gulps of air into my lungs.

Otis wrinkled his nose. 'Shh!'

Hester nodded. 'Yeah, Daisy, shh. You sound like a steam train with all that wheezing.'

'I'm shushing you, Hes, not Daisy!'

'Why would you shush me?' she asked her brother. 'I'm not the one who sounds like a dying walrus.'

'I'm going,' I gasped, 'to barbecue you ... the ... next ... chance ... I ... get.'

Hester smiled. 'She's fine.'

I finally brought my breathing under control and pulled out my phone. There was no signal. Great.

Otis wrung his hands. 'You shouldn't have run away, Daisy.

You should have waited for the police. As soon as you explained what happened, they'd have looked for Gordon to make sure he's okay.'

Gordon. My body shook. If Athair did anything to hurt him, anything at all... 'I panicked,' I said. Even to my own ears it sounded like a lame excuse.

I stood up and pushed away the sweat-soaked curls that were plastered to my forehead. There was a large egg-shaped bruise on my temple where the frying pan had hit me. 'That woman was terrified, and she wasn't going to listen to anything we said. She needed us to leave as quickly as possible.'

'Why is it night time again?' Hester asked. 'Why did we suddenly appear in a random stranger's house? Why did that stupid skull do all that weird spinning stuff? Why did Athair show up? Why—?'

I held up my hands to stop the tirade of questions. 'I don't know. I don't have any answers.'

'What happened to Hugo?' Otis asked.

'I don't know that either.' I looked at the tenement buildings around us; we were definitely still in Edinburgh. 'But I think I know where we are. I've made deliveries to this street before. Let's go to the Royal Elvish Institute. With any luck, Hugo will be waiting for us there, and Gordon will be receiving medical attention.'

'And Athair?' Hester raised a sceptical eyebrow.

I didn't answer but Otis did. 'Hopefully he'll have fucked off back to his cumbubbling hole.' Hester and I both stared at him. 'What? Do you disagree?'

Not for a second. I grinned faintly and pointed down the street. 'Come on,' I said. 'It's this way.'

A car drove past, a belch of smoke burping from its exhaust and 'Baby I Love Your Way' by Big Mountain blaring out of the speakers. I frowned then looked at the other cars parked in the street. 'What is it, Daisy?' Hester asked.

Despite my burning cheeks, there was a sudden chill in my bones. 'Nothing.'

She jabbed me. 'You're lying.'

Yes. Yes, I was.

I spotted a dim glow coming from a newsagent's shop a few yards away. 'Let's go there first.'

'Why?'

I wouldn't say what I was thinking until I was sure. I looked at my phone again: still no signal. I swallowed hard. The tinnitus had faded, but my fingers were trembling enough to make my phone shake. 'Humour me,' I said.

Hester brightened. 'What do you call a man with a spade in his head?'

'Idiot! That's not what Daisy meant.' Otis glared at her, then added, 'Well?'

She sniffed sullenly. 'Well, what?'

'What *do* you call a man with a spade in his head?'

Hester folded her arms. 'Not telling you now.'

'Tell me!'

She sighed. 'Doug.'

Otis stared at her. 'I don't get it. How is that funny?'

I'd already stopped listening. I put my phone away, checked Gladys again and started to jog towards the small shop.

A wire mesh covered the glass door. When I peered through it, I saw a man leaning over the counter with a pen in his hand. Excellent. As I went in, he jerked upright and reached for something beneath the counter. Then he checked my face and relaxed.

'Sorry,' he said. 'I'm a bit jumpy. You shouldn't be out at this hour, you know. You're welcome to shelter here. I'm only open for deliveries, but early customers are always welcome to come in and wait for dawn.'

Huh. I chewed the inside of my cheek. 'Uh, thanks. I guess I lost track of time.' I gestured to his watch with a questioning look.

'Just gone five-thirty. It won't start getting light for another twenty minutes.' His eyes dropped to Gladys and his mouth tightened. 'I guess you know what you're doing, though.'

When in doubt, brazen it out. I smiled confidently. 'Absolutely.'

He scratched his chin. 'Hmm.' He stared at Hester and Otis. 'Are they brownies?'

'Yep.'

'We can talk for ourselves,' Hester said.

'At least he didn't call us fairies, Hes,' Otis muttered.

I didn't allow my smile to dim; instead, I slowly inspected the contents of the shop. There was an array of sweets and chocolate bars to my right: Snickers, Mars bars, Milky Ways. I paused. Opal Fruits.

The man was watching me warily. Beside him was a stack of newspapers and behind him were rows of brightly packaged cigarettes.

I was starting to feel nauseous. I licked my lips. 'Can I get one of those papers?' I asked.

'Sure.' He lifted the top one from the pile.

I picked it up and stared at the large photo emblazoned on the front page of Liz Hurley wearing a slashed black dress held together by over-sized golden safety pins.

Otis blinked rapidly. 'What *is* that woman wearing?'

'Shocking, right?' the man said. 'I don't know what the world is coming to when someone goes out wearing something like that. There should be laws against it.'

'It's fabulous!' Hester cooed. 'I want a dress just like that!' The man scowled.

'This is today's paper?' I asked.

He grunted. 'Yes.'

I jabbed at the date. 'The fourteenth of May?'

'Yeah.'

Gordon. What have you done? 'The fourteenth of May,' I repeated. '1994?'

He gave me a long look; it appeared that his initial guess that I was deranged was being confirmed. 'Yes. And that will be twenty pence.'

I felt my heart hammering faster.

Otis and Hester were staring at the paper, no longer interested in the daring dress. 'Daisy,' Otis whispered.

I shook my head in warning; whatever he was about to say would be best said in private. I dug into my pocket, pushed past the small bag containing my remaining spider's silk pills and located a pound coin. As I handed it to the shopkeeper, I hoped he wouldn't notice my trembling fingers.

He squinted at the coin. 'What's this?' He turned it over. 'Some kind of foreign money? I'm not accepting that.'

Shit. There was nothing wrong with it; it was a normal pound coin. My shoulders sank. Normal in 2024. 'Uh ... you're right.' I dropped the paper on the countertop. 'Never mind. I'll come back after I've been to the bank.'

The suspicion in his eyes increased tenfold as I backed away. 'Hester! Otis!' I said sharply. 'We're leaving now!'

'But—'

'Now!'

We left the shop at high speed. I could feel the man's eyes burning into my back as I marched away and rounded the corner. Only when we were out of sight did I come to a stuttering halt.

Otis and Hester immediately began shouting into my face.

'1994?'

'It can't be 1994!'

'What happened?'

'Daisy!'

'This is a joke, right?'

I gazed at them both dully. 'The cars on the street are old. The décor in Gordon's house – which isn't Gordon's house – is old-fashioned. That shop sells cigarettes openly. They had Opal Fruits on the shelf! I'm sure that's what Starburst used to be called before the name was changed.'

There was an odd roaring in my ears. 'It all makes sense. This is why Gordon wanted the skull, why he was so sure it could give him answers about Lady Rose. He wanted to travel into the past to witness what happened to her. Perhaps he thought he could stop it. Perhaps he thought he could save her.'

Hester's cheeks were bright red. 'Then why the hell are *we* here instead of Gordon?'

'Athair.' My voice was barely audible. 'He showed up, I went into a panic and lost control of my magic, and I triggered the skull by accident. Now we're here and Gordon's not.'

Otis shook his head violently. 'No. No way. I've only just got used to 2024 – I don't want to have to adjust again. We shouldn't be here. Use the skull and send us back to where we belong.'

Hester was wide-eyed. 'He's right. Set off your freaky magic again and let's go home.'

I shook my head. 'I can't.'

Her voice rose. 'Why the fuck not?'

Magic was starting to leak out of me. The ground beneath my feet shook and cracks appeared in the pavement. A strong wind was circling around us, whipping up my hair and making it almost impossible for the brownies to remain airborne. Otis squeaked and threw himself at me for safety; Hester did the same and burrowed beneath my coat.

'I don't have it,' I muttered. Flames licked upwards from my fingertips. 'The skull didn't come with us – the skull is in 2024.' A second later, the flames transformed into fireballs that blazed up into the still dark sky.

And I felt worse than ever.

CHAPTER

TWELVE

We didn't hang around. Between the shopkeeper's suspicions and my accidental surge of magic, it didn't seem wise to stay in the area.

An hour or so later, the three of us had found our way to Holyrood Park, the large city park in the centre of Edinburgh, which included Arthur's Seat, the remains of an extinct volcano. The open space and the lightening sky had calmed me considerably, but there was still a knot of deep anxiety in the pit of my belly.

'Things aren't that bad,' I said aloud.

'Are you trying to reassure us or yourself?' Hester asked.

I managed a tight smile. 'Both. We need to look at the positives.'

They both looked dubious so I elaborated. 'We're alive.'

Otis conceded that point. 'True.'

'We've only gone thirty years into the past – if we'd travelled three hundred years, we'd have real problems.'

Hester said grudgingly, 'I suppose Otis and I didn't get to experience the 1990s the first time around. It might be fun.'

I nodded. 'Nobody else that I've heard of has ever time travelled. We're pioneers. That's exciting. Plus,' I was warming to the topic, 'we're not necessarily stuck here. At this moment, the golden skull is buried beneath the Fonaby Sack Stone. All we have to do is travel to Doncaster and retrieve it for a second time.'

Hester brightened further. 'Great!' Then her shoulders dropped and she scowled. 'No, not great. You said we should be glad we'd only travelled thirty years and not three hundred, but we're probably here because Gordon did that rune thing when you set off the skull. He controlled what happened. We need a sorcerer as good as Gordon Mackenzie – and one who understands what he's doing – to get us back to where we belong. That won't be easy.' She pointed at me. 'You might end up losing control again and we'll end up three *thousand* years in the past.'

Otis blanched. 'Also,' he said, 'if we dig up the skull now, it won't be there for us to dig up a second time in 2024.'

Hester snapped her fingers. 'If it's not there in 2024 and we can't dig it up then, surely we can't travel into the past so we won't be here now.' She hesitated. 'Right?'

'But we *are* here now,' Otis said. He looked at me, bafflement in his eyes.

I grimaced. 'I've got to be honest, I don't understand how any of it works. I don't know if we can affect the future that's already happened. We should avoid doing anything that might cause ripples in the – er,' I scratched my head, 'space-time continuum.'

'The space-time what?'

I drew in a breath to explain, but my understanding of physics came from watching *Star Trek* as a kid; I didn't really understand the science at all. 'We'll try to keep everything the same as it should be,' I said lamely. Somehow.

The brownies exchanged looks, then nodded. Apparently

they'd decided by mutual agreement that any discussion of the mechanics and implications of time travel was pretty pointless.

'We focus on what we *can* control,' I said firmly.

'That's not much,' Hester told me.

Otis was more positive. 'Do you have a plan, Daisy?'

'Not really,' I said. 'But I'm sure something will come to mind soon. What we need to do is to deal with our problems one by one. Let's take care of the small stuff and perhaps solutions for the big stuff will present themselves.'

Before Hester could tell me that I was burying my head in the sand and being hopelessly optimistic, I leaned towards her and her brother. 'Right now, we don't have any money. The cash I've got won't be accepted because it's not been minted yet. My bank card won't work because my bank account doesn't exist. We're penniless – literally. The first thing we have to do is solve our cash-flow problem.'

'That part's easy,' Hester said. 'We steal five pounds from one person and use it as a bet. A horse race would be easiest. We're from the future so we know the outcome already. We keep betting until we become millionaires. It'll only take a few days.'

Otis gasped. 'I've always wanted to be a millionaire.'

'Why stop at a million?' Hester said. 'How about a billion?' She grinned suddenly. 'Forget returning to 2024. Let's stay here and become rich beyond our wildest dreams!'

I frowned at them. 'That won't work.'

Otis and Hester glanced at each other again. 'Hugo,' they chorused.

'No,' I said, 'I—'

Hester interrupted me. 'Don't worry, Daisy. You can meet up with him again in 2024 when you're sixty years old. He'll still be thirty-two, but you'll be rich enough to definitely rock a toyboy.'

I gritted my teeth. 'I'm not talking about Hugo.' I gazed at them both in frustration. 'Yes, we're from the future, but do any of us know which horses won which races in 1994?'

They stared at me blankly.

'Football matches?' Otis asked hopefully.

I had a sneaking suspicion the World Cup was about to take place. Maybe Brazil won? Or was it Argentina? I didn't know. 'Nope.'

Hester squinted. 'Tennis?' I shrugged. 'Do you know *anything* useful about 1994?' she asked.

'Nothing specific is coming to mind.'

She groaned. 'We're going to be the worst time travellers the world has ever seen.'

'We're the *only* time travellers the world has ever seen,' I said cheerfully. 'We'll work something out.'

'We're doomed,' she muttered.

'There's something else we need to think about,' Otis said. 'Gordon was coming here to solve the mystery of Lady Rose. Should we go looking for her, warn her something is going to happen to her? She doesn't go missing for another few weeks, right?'

'Less. She disappeared on May 30th – it's only six days away.' Right now she was alive and well, and we had time to prevent something bad happening to her. 'Let's get some money together then see if we can talk to her.'

Otis protested, 'But you already said we shouldn't change things. If we prevent her disappearance, won't that affect the future?'

I didn't reply. There was something else I needed to consider, too. Athair – and a few of the other fiends I'd come across a couple of months ago – had known me but I hadn't known them. There was every possibility that they'd met me in the past before I met them in the future – and that meant I'd been destined to be here in 1994 from the very beginning.

WE ENDED up on Princes Street, Edinburgh's main shopping area which ran for almost a full mile and provided stunning views of the castle, with not a single useful penny in our pockets. I considered returning to my original plan of heading for the Royal Elvish Institute and asking for help, but if they weren't keen to let unknown low elves through their hallowed doors in 2024, they certainly wouldn't have done so in 1994.

The thought of trying to explain to a group of wealthy high elves that I was from the future gave me imaginary hives. If Hugo had been with us, we might have had a chance; he had a smooth tongue and he understood how they operated. On my own, and without his trusty presence by my side, it would be next to impossible to get their help. Besides, there were other avenues I could try first.

Princes Street in 1994 was both very similar and very different to the 2024 version. The buildings were the same, but many of the occupants were different. The fancy Jenners Department Store was not only still open for business but teeming with customers – it wouldn't close permanently until 2020. And there were other stores that I hadn't seen for years, such as Littlewoods, Woolworths and Virgin.

A few busking bagpipers remained in situ, and there were lots of buses, but the clothing and hairstyles of the passers-by, while not starkly different, made me feel out of place. The atmosphere wasn't what I expected, either; the mood of the city seemed lighter than in 2024. The Cold War was over and it wasn't yet the millennium. The internet existed – but only in primordial form compared to the all-encompassing behemoth it was now.

I thought of all the disasters and problems the world was due to face in the next thirty years. Thirty years wasn't a lifetime by any stretch of imagination, but it still felt like a huge gulf.

Thinking that we'd be more successful if my elven identity was hidden, I found a spot in front of Waverley train station. I'd suspected that Hester would be too proud to beg, but she and Otis approached the task with gusto. She gazed mournfully at every person who wandered past us, pleading in a pitiful voice, 'We don't have any money for food. Please spare some change.'

'I'm very hungry,' Otis added time and time again. 'So very hungry.'

'Any spare change will make a huge difference,' I added to their sterling efforts.

None of it was a lie but, after an hour or two, I wasn't convinced that it being true made any difference. Thousands of people passed us and most pretended we didn't exist. Many looked disgusted and swerved away, as if poverty were contagious. However, some were kind, and by lunchtime we'd earned a sausage roll, a packet of crisps and the grand total of £4.23 in small coins. It wasn't great but it was better than nothing.

I was subduing the worst of the growls of hunger in my stomach with the sausage roll when a young family emerged from the station. A mother, father and a young boy of around eight years old who were well dressed and walking hand in hand.

The boy noticed us first. No doubt unused to busy city centres, he was staring wide-eyed at the throng of people. When his eyes landed on me, he stopped. I smiled automatically and, a second later, he tugged at his mother. 'We need to give her some money,' he said, in a high-pitched Scottish accent. 'Mummy, give the homeless lady some money.'

His mother looked at me, went very pale and looked away again. She tightened her grip on her son's hand and started to move faster. Her partner shot me a narrow glance and did the same. 'No, Angus. We're not going to do that. She'll only use it for drugs.'

I stiffened and my smile disappeared. A moment later the three of them had gone, replaced by more disinterested passers-by.

I reached into my pocket and fingered my small bag of spider's silk pills. The encounter had been humiliating, made worse by knowing that the woman was right. Yes, we needed money for food and shelter, but I also needed money so I could find a dealer and get some more spider's silk. My stash would only last a few more days, and after that I'd drop into sudden, life-threatening withdrawal. Given the way my magic had been acting up over the last day or so, it wouldn't only be my own life that would be threatened. I bit my lip, trying to keep my anxiety at bay.

'Don't worry about the likes of her,' a young female voice said from close by. 'She'll never know what it's like to be one of us.'

The speaker was in her early twenties. Her well-worn clothes were clean and her eyes were warm, but her cheeks had the slightly gaunt shape of someone who was struggling to make ends meet. I felt a tremendous surge of guilt. I'd been broke and homeless for half a day; this was someone for whom it was a daily experience.

I tried to smile. 'Yeah,' I muttered. 'Thanks.'

'I'm Tracey,' she said. 'I've not seen you here before.'

'I just arrived in the city today.' In a sense it was the truth. 'I'm Daisy.'

Tracey grinned and nodded at the brownies. 'Lots of us have dogs but I've never seen someone with fairies by their side.'

I winced, expecting Hester to begin her usual anger-laden speech about mislabelling, but she simply said, 'We're brownies, not fairies, but it's an easy mistake to make.'

Otis's jaw dropped.

'I'm sorry!' Tracey sounded as if she meant it. 'I've never seen a brownie before.'

'That's okay.' Hester looked her up and down. 'You're a witch, right?'

Tracey blinked. 'You can tell by looking?'

Hester pointed. 'Your fingers are green.'

The young woman glanced down then gave an embarrassed laugh. 'Yeah, they are. I've been collecting plants from the gardens over there.' She placed a finger to her mouth. 'Don't tell anyone. The authorities don't like it when unauthorised witches harvest around here. We're supposed to have a permit, but that costs three hundred quid and there's no way I can find that kind of money.'

'Your secret is safe with us,' I assured her.

'Thanks.' She eyed me. 'You got somewhere to stay tonight?'

It was barely afternoon; what happened tonight was far from my immediate concern. 'Not yet.'

Her expression grew serious. 'You can't sleep out at night, it's not safe. There's a shelter not far from here. As long as you get there by eight, they'll find space for you. You don't want to become another statistic.'

Otis flapped upwards. 'What do you mean it's not safe?' he asked in a quavering voice.

'You know,' Tracey said. The three of us gazed back blankly. She frowned and tapped her teeth with a grubby, green-tinged fingernail. 'Vampires, of course. There are swarms of them all over the city.'

My mind flashed back to the way the newsagent had reacted when I'd walked into his shop. 'Yes,' I breathed. A huge grin spread across my face. '*Yes!*' I looked at Otis and Hester in sudden triumph. I should have thought of it before. 'I know exactly how we can make all the money we need. You, Tracey,' I told her, 'are a genius.'

Her face clouded with confusion but I was already getting to my feet and scooping up the small collection of coins. This would be brilliant.

THIRTEEN

Hester and Otis were considerably less thrilled. 'You want to do *what?*' Hester's screech was high-pitched enough to make a passing Labrador stop and jerk towards us. Its owner tugged its lead and they started moving again, but the chubby dog continued to swing his glossy head around and stare at her.

'Stealing is a better idea than this,' Otis said. Genuinely surprised at his words, I raised my eyebrows. His cheeks coloured. 'Alright,' he muttered. 'I didn't mean that. But there must be a better way.'

'We've dealt with vampires before,' I reassured him.

'*You*'ve dealt with vampires before,' Hester said. 'My ethos – and it's one that I'm proud of because it's kept me alive up until now – is to avoid them at all costs.'

I wouldn't let her dampen my enthusiasm. 'I've studied this. In the late-twentieth century, most cities – Edinburgh included – suffered extensive vampire infestations. The authorities tried to bring their numbers under control but they didn't make any real headway in reducing the fanged population until

HELEN HARPER

vamp spray became popular a few years before the millennium. Before that, they relied on vampire hunters.'

'Vampire hunters?' Otis looked dubious.

'Yep. There was a reward for anyone who brought down a vampire.' I crossed the street and nodded at the small police station on the corner. 'I'm pretty certain it was a good reward, too. You simply presented yourself at a police station with evidence of a dispatched vamp and you received a reward.'

'That sounds like a recipe for getting killed,' Hester said.

I nodded enthusiastically. 'Oh yes, it was a terrible idea. From what I remember, more hunters were killed by vampires than the other way around.'

'And that doesn't tell you something?' Otis asked. 'That you should run away now and forget you ever had such a foolish idea?'

I tapped my temple with my index finger. 'I'm smarter than the average vampire hunter.'

'I doubt that's true,' Hester said.

'Well, I've got more experience.'

'Probably not true either.'

'I've got lots of magic.'

She sighed. 'That you can barely control at the best of times.'

'And there's Gladys.' I touched the sword at my side.

'You won't change your mind, will you?'

'Nope,' I said cheerfully.

'We're going to die,' Otis said mournfully.

I grinned. 'Not today, I promise.'

I marched into the police station, shoulders back and head high. I meant business. A young, uniformed police officer was standing behind the desk. She smiled at me. 'Good afternoon. I'm WPC Hurst. How can I help you?'

I blurted out before I could stop myself, 'WPC?'

Her smiled dimmed slightly. 'Woman Police Constable.'

I raised an eyebrow. Surely the 'woman' bit was clear? I tried to rearrange my features into a blank expression. Alright: 1994 wasn't all good.

'Uh, my name is Daisy,' I said. 'Daisy Carter. I'm here because I want to enquire about the vampire hunting programme.'

Constable Hurst stared at me. 'Seriously? You don't mean—?'

'I want to know what the reward is for bagging a vampire, what proof you need, and how long it takes to receive the reward.'

'I'm not sure that's a very good idea.'

'It's a *fabulous* idea,' I told her. Better than fabulous.

She swallowed and picked up a black phone. 'Wait a few minutes,' she said. 'I'll get someone to come down and explain the process.'

I'd barely settled onto the blue plastic chair in the waiting area before an older and far more grizzled police officer appeared. Unlike the WPC, he made no attempt to be pleasant; he didn't even introduce himself.

'So,' he said, without bothering to sit down, 'I hear that you want to bag a vamp and make a quick buck.' He pointed at the door. 'You should turn around and get out of here. You need to get those sorts of foolish thoughts out of your pretty little head.'

The brownies immediately flew to the door. 'Okay, then!' Otis trilled.

'No problem!' Hester added.

I ignored them, stood up and faced the officer. 'What is the reward for killing a vampire?'

He gave me a long look that left no doubt as to his opinion of me. He tapped his foot and raised his eyebrows; only when it was clear that I was going to stand my ground did he answer. 'Five hundred pounds.'

Bloody hell. That was a lot more than I'd been expecting.

The police officer gave a sharp laugh at my expression. 'Yeah. But there's a good reason why the reward is so high. Hunting vampires is dangerous – you're far more likely to get killed and give someone like me a pile of extra paperwork to complete than you are to bring me their fangs to prove their death.'

I didn't miss a beat. 'That's what you need? Their fangs?' I frowned. Extracting a vamp's teeth would be messy but it was do-able.

'Listen, girlie.' He sighed heavily. 'You might think you can kill a vampire but you can't.'

This was getting tiresome. 'I'm an elf. I've got magic.'

'So? Two high elves were killed by vampires last month. Being an elf won't make a bit of difference,' he sneered. 'Neither will magic.'

For the first time I hesitated. 'Two high elves? Really?' That was unusual.

'A normal vamp would be too much for someone like you – and the vampires out there are worse than normal. They're brutal. They'll show you no mercy. And they're intelligent,' he added dourly.

Nah: 2024 vampires were stupid and I didn't doubt that 1994 vampires were equally dumb. 'When do I get the money?'

He rolled his eyes. 'You don't. You'll only get dead.'

Hester somersaulted and returned to my shoulder. 'No, she won't,' she sniffed. 'This is Daisy Carter and she's amazing. No vampire can kill her.'

She'd changed her tune. Hester didn't like being told no, and she didn't like anyone who disparaged me. I suppressed a grin and nodded. 'Exactly. Once I come back here with the vampire fangs in my hand, how long before I get paid?'

He clicked his tongue. 'Payment is immediate.'

I knew not to bother asking if I could use PayPal. 'Uh, by cheque?'

'If you want.'

'Can I have cash instead?'

'*You* will not kill any damned vampires.'

I folded my arms.

He sighed again. 'Yes. If you bring vampire fangs to prove a kill, a cash payment can be arranged.'

Brilliant. I smiled and curtsied. 'Thank you so much for your time.'

'Don't do it.'

My smile grew as I headed for the door. 'Bye!' I threw the word over my shoulder. 'I'll see you first thing tomorrow morning! Make sure that money is ready and waiting.'

If the police officer replied, I didn't hear him; I was already on the pavement, rubbing my palms together in glee.

'You need to show that policeman what's what,' Hester said in my left ear. 'Show him that Daisy Carter is strong and powerful, and far more capable than he is.'

'You need to abandon this foolish idea immediately,' Otis said in my right ear. 'There are other ways to make money.'

Not fast enough to serve our needs there weren't. I waved them both off and scanned the crowds in front of Waverley station. When I spotted Tracey sitting in the spot I'd vacated, I sighed with relief and made a beeline for her.

'Spare any change, love?' she asked. She looked up, saw it was me and pulled a face. 'Oh, sorry.'

I glanced at the coins in front of her; she'd done better at begging than I had, but not much better. 'I need your help again, Tracey,' I said. 'I'll make it worth your while.' Her eyes narrowed suspiciously. 'It's all legal,' I assured her. 'All above board.' I hunkered down beside her. 'I only need your witchy skills, nothing too complex, I promise.'

She still looked wary but she didn't tell me to piss off. 'Go on,' she said.

'Can you get hold of some wild garlic?'

'It's getting a bit late in the season for this part of the world, but yes – I know where to get some.'

'If I get some holy water, could you combine the two ingredients with a spell to ward off vampires?'

Tracey did a double-take. 'What?'

My understanding of witchery didn't go beyond the basics. 'Uh, some kind of defensive thing that could be put into a spray bottle and used against a vampire. Could you manage something like that?'

'You're not seriously planning to try and kill a vampire, are you? I know people who used to think they could do that.'

'Where are those people now?' Otis asked.

Tracey's response was flat. 'Dead.'

Otis shot me a pointed look. 'I think this vamp spray thing might work,' I said, avoiding his gaze.

She shook her head. 'Lots of people have tried holy water and garlic.'

'Sixty percent holy water, forty percent wild garlic – and it has to be wild. If those ingredients are bound together by the right witch, I reckon they might just do the trick.' I paused. 'Add a touch of thyme too.' I didn't know what effect the thyme had, but I knew it made a difference.

Tracey still didn't look convinced. 'If you try to go up against a vampire, you will die.'

I grinned. 'I've been hearing that a lot today. Trust me, this will work. I'll go hunting for vampires tonight then collect the reward in the morning from the police. I'll give you fifty percent of whatever I make.'

She raised a sceptical eyebrow. 'That *sounds* like a lot, but we both know that fifty percent of nothing is nothing.'

'You've got nothing to lose.'

'No, but *you've* got everything to lose.' She glanced at my expression and sighed. 'Fine. I'll give it my best shot.' She was easier to persuade than the police.

'Thank you. I'll go and find some holy water. Meet you here in two hours? Will that give you enough time to harvest the garlic?'

'Should do.' She gnawed at her bottom lip. 'But listen. There's more to life than money. Cash is not worth risking your life for.'

I waved a hand to suggest airy confidence. 'With your special vamp spray, there won't be any risk.'

Otis snorted sarcastically. 'Yeah,' he said, under his breath. 'Right.'

I turned to him. 'The only risk will be to the undead.'

'This isn't you, Daisy,' he said mournfully. 'You don't take unnecessary risks and you're not usually over-confident.'

'It's not over-confidence, Otis. And it's not risky. They're only vampires, they're not that big a deal.' I smiled and repeated, 'They're only vampires.'

His bottom lip jutted out. 'I wish Hugo was here.'

So did I, desperately. But I didn't need him for this. Even without his help, bagging a few vampires would be easy: *undead* easy.

CHAPTER

FOURTEEN

'I think the best plan is for you to sally forth, Daisy, while Otis and I wait here,' Hester said.

'I thought you'd changed your mind and you were behind my plan?'

She nodded. 'I'm all the way behind it. At least half a mile behind it, in fact.'

It would be for the best: if I didn't have to worry about Hester and Otis getting hurt, I could concentrate on any vampires who appeared. 'Alright,' I said. 'But you stay right here. You do not leave this spot.'

'Don't die,' Otis whispered.

Hester agreed. 'We need you to get us back to where we belong.'

'You're all heart.'

She bobbed her head solemnly. 'You know it.'

I raised my hand in farewell and slipped out of the dark alleyway. The bottle of vamp spray that Tracey had concocted lay nestled in my pocket, and I'd swallowed as much spider's silk as I dared. I was as ready as I could be – but now that I was out here in the cold, quiet night, my earlier confidence was deserting me.

'Only vampires,' I muttered to myself. 'Only vampires. Nothing to worry about.'

Unsurprisingly, the Edinburgh streets were empty. Local people clearly heeded the dangers presented by the burgeoning population of fanged fuckers and hurried home as soon it was dark.

There were plenty of lamp posts, and their orange glow provided more than enough light to see what was up ahead, but somehow their eerie reflections in the small puddles of water and on the slick cobblestones discomfited me. The whistling breeze that was echoing up and down the empty street and ruffling my hair didn't help matters.

I turned up my collar against the chill and moved quickly. With any luck, a passing vampire would notice me and come running over for a quick meal. I only needed one; I didn't need to be greedy.

I turned right at the bottom of the hill and passed a dilapidated building that I knew would soon be torn down and replaced by student flats. There was a flicker of movement and I half turned, pausing for a moment until I spotted a small mouse scurrying in the gutter. I tipped an imaginary hat in its direction then continued on my way.

I didn't have a particular destination in mind, and I'd hoped that a direction-less amble would quickly yield results, but when several minutes passed and the tiny mouse was the only creature I'd seen, I decided to alter my approach. There was an old graveyard past the next row of tenements; maybe I'd hit paydirt there.

As soon as I stepped off the pavement to cross the road, I heard snuffling. Yahtzee.

The vampire was a sorry-looking creature. His clothes were hanging off him in tattered, rotting strips, and his flesh was sunken and grey. He was shuffling along the middle of the cobbled road, dragging his left foot behind him; from the angle, it was badly broken. Vampires rarely felt pain; they possessed less awareness of their physical situation than the mouse I'd passed. Even so, as I watched his slow approach I reasoned that I was doing him a favour by putting him out of his misery so he could be laid to rest for good.

My right hand reached for Gladys and I slid her two inches out of her sheath. My left hand reached for Tracey's vamp spray; thankfully, it only shook slightly when I gripped it. I straightened my spine, raised my head and gave a long, low whistle.

It took the vampire a few seconds to register the sound. When he did, he froze for half a beat before twisting his head towards me. I heard the bones in his neck cracking as he fixed his gaze – and then he came for me.

I took three side steps to position myself in the middle of the road so I had plenty of room to manoeuvre and wouldn't end up boxed in. The vampire opened his mouth in a silent scream and showed me his fangs to prove that he meant business.

I waited until he was close enough before I acted. When he was less than a metre away and my nostrils started tickling at the stench of his rotting, undead body, I directed the small plastic spray bottle at his face and sent a cloud of fine droplets towards him.

The vamp's reaction was instantaneous: as soon as the magicked combination of holy water and wild garlic hit him, he screeched and started clawing at his face. I smacked my lips in satisfaction as the concoction ate at his flesh and blinded him. Then I swung Gladys at his exposed neck and, with one swift strike, lopped off his head. Gladys hummed with glee as he crumpled to the cobbles.

The process had taken less than five seconds. 'Only a vampire,' I whispered and smiled.

I returned Gladys to her sheath and retrieved the penknife Tracey had lent me, then knelt down to start the unpleasant task of extracting the vampire's fangs before I set the body alight to stop it ever rising again.

I'd barely made an incision when Gladys buzzed in warning. I stopped moving and listened hard. I could hear the hiss of laboured breath. Cumbubbling bollocks: something was behind me.

I slowly straightened up and glanced around. *Oh no*.

There were six vampires surrounding me, two behind, two in front and one on either side, and they were all in much better condition than the corpse at my feet. I was trapped.

The vampires were drawing closer and closer, matching their strides and maintaining the same distance from each other. They were working together, none of them allowing their bloodlust to take over and none of them going for an immediate attack. I'd never seen such a thing before.

As I shook my head in amazement, I wondered if they'd sent the first vamp out as bait to lull me into a false sense of security. But no, that didn't make any sense because vampires were mindless automatons whose festering brain cells allowed no intelligent or rational thought. This was most definitely not supposed to happen.

Then an annoying, prickling sensation started at the nape of my neck and descended through my body. I knew instantly what it meant. There was a fiend nearby.

I quashed my terror as soon as it began, flattened my mouth into a grim line and hoped the fiend was Baltar. I had killed him in 2024 – no-one had been more surprised than me when I'd defeated him in the depths of an old dragon lair. When I'd first seen him, he'd spoken as if we'd met before. If this was Baltar, history dictated that I could beat him and stay alive. I doubted I'd have much of a chance if Athair was lurking in the shadows.

In any case, I needed to prioritise and deal with the posse of vampires first. I swallowed hard, unsheathed Gladys again and tried to remember Miriam's training as the six of them closed in.

I turned slowly. They were clearly preparing to attack simultaneously, and I doubted I could take on all the bastards in close combat, but I was far from beaten. I had much more than Gladys at my disposal.

It wasn't clear how the hidden fiend was communicating with the vampires; for all I knew, the bloodsuckers were under its control and instructions were being relayed with telepathic immediacy. I had to assume the worst and act accordingly.

I gripped Gladys with both hands and aimed her blade high as I completed another slow 360-degree turn, sweeping my sword through the air with glittering intent – and glorious misdirection. Then I inhaled deeply and flung out an arc of earth magic.

The effect was immediate. The ground shook and the cobblestones loosened, some flying several feet upwards before clattering down again. The road ruptured, first in a perfect circle that mimicked my sword sweep, then in radial cracks.

Four of the vampires fell backwards, and one lurched forward and snagged her leg in the hole my magic had created. She grunted and jerked as she tried to free herself. I focused on the sixth vampire, the only one who was still advancing.

Rather than blast him with more magic, I gave Gladys the honour of killing him. She sang as I swiped her tip forward, and she pierced the vamp's eye before entering his skull. He didn't make a sound, just gazed at me in confusion before falling to his knees and toppling forward.

There wasn't time to congratulate myself. Three of the other vampires were already back on their feet. 'Alright then,' I said. 'Come at me.'

Whatever control the concealed fiend had been exerting was fading away; the vampires' faces were contorting and the wild hunger I was used to seeing in their eyes was taking over. I felt genuinely relieved that the natural order of things was reappearing, though I didn't have long to feel pleased. All three of them meant business.

My skin was itching even more – the fiend must be getting closer. I shook away the sensation and blasted the nearest vampire with a jet of scorching fire magic. He roared as his body was engulfed in flames, though it didn't stop his advance. His focus was so single-minded that he continued running at me, flaming arms akimbo. As I gulped and jumped out of the way, I almost fell into the hole I'd made.

The other two vampires followed, bloodlust speeding up their movements. I threw out a burst of water magic to douse the burning vampire and the force of the water knocked him down. The resulting steam blocked the view of his two companions for a few seconds, but that was all I needed.

Instead of running away, I ran at them. I pumped Tracey's spray bottle vigorously, dispersing the anti-vamp potion into the steam – then I shrugged, yanked off the top and chucked in the rest of the contents. The answering shrieks were enough to tell me I'd hit paydirt.

I dropped the bottle and backed away several metres before blowing out a gentle gust of air magic to clear away the steam and see the damage for myself. The vampire who'd been on fire was down and out; his left arm was twitching but his body was charred beyond recognition. The two vampires who'd joined his attack were on their knees, their hands raised to their faces. Tracey's vamp spray really was potent stuff: I could see exposed bone down the side of one of the vampire's skulls. Her potion had eaten his flesh. Now all I had to do was use Gladys to finish them off for good.

Unfortunately, I didn't get the chance. The two remaining vampires were back on their feet. The one who'd snagged herself in the hole created by my earth magic had freed herself while the other one, who'd been knocked over by the same blast, had also recovered. The female sprinted at me from my right as the male hurtled forward on all fours like an animal from my left.

Time seemed to slow down. I didn't know whether it was because of all the training I'd received from Hugo and his Primes or whether my own instincts kicked in, but I held my ground for one beat, then two. In the split second before both vamps were on me, I jumped backwards. Instead of throwing themselves onto my body, they collided with each other. Not realising that I'd moved out of the way, they went for each other and started tearing off chunks of flesh, screeching at the top of their rotting lungs.

Something altered in the cool night air and for a moment I was confused. I felt a strange stillness overtake the atmosphere; it was as if the world itself were taking a breath. Then a wave of powerful magic rippled from behind me, gathering in the air and rushing past my body. It engulfed first me and then the group of vampires.

A whimper escaped my lips as I stumbled onto my hands and knees and my chest constricted. Some sort of invisible force was pushing me down. I gulped in air, trying to recover and fight whatever nasty magic was surrounding me. With a great effort, I raised my head in time to see all the surviving vampires collapse in a synchronised thud onto the slick cobblestones.

A voice rang out across the street. 'Well, I suppose if you want a job done properly you have to do it yourself.'

I turned my head. Less than twenty metres away, illuminated by both moonlight and the orange-tinted light from the nearby lampposts, stood the glittering golden body of a fiend. No doubt this was who had been controlling the vampires.

And no doubt this was when the real battle would begin.

FIFTEEN

The strange rippling magic ebbed away. I gave a shuddering breath and forced myself to my feet, ignoring my fluttering heartbeat and the sudden surge of drug-induced dizziness. I needed to face the fiend properly.

It was a male that I didn't recognise. This wasn't Baltar, and it wasn't Athair. That didn't mean I could relax, not by a long shot, but I was incredibly relieved that I wasn't having to confront my supposed father.

I eyed him carefully. Despite the cool air, he was wearing a pair of bright purple, pink and orange Bermuda shorts, as if he were about to hit the surf on a sunny Californian beach instead of launching a full-scale attack upon a solitary elf on a chilly Scottish street. Unlike the younger fiends I'd encountered, this one had perfectly smooth, golden skin, which meant he was both old and experienced. In fact, I thought grimly, he was probably several hundred years old. Unlike an elf's, his ears were rounded rather than pointed.

I scanned his body in all its brazen golden glory; it was lean and sinewy in a way that wasn't wholly unfamiliar. 'Sorcerer,' I said aloud, without meaning to.

The fiend gave me a salacious grin. 'Once upon a time,' he said. 'But I'm so much more now.'

I responded flatly, 'I know what you are. I know *exactly* what you are.'

'Not many elves do, so I find it gratifying when I meet one who is aware of my kind.' His lip curled. 'If there were justice in this world, I would be worshipped as a god.'

I almost laughed. 'You're no god.'

The fiend swept an arm to indicate the devastation that surrounded us both. 'Who but a god can control creatures such as those?' His voice rose. 'One day – one day I will be recognised for what I am. There will be statues of me in every city in this land. I will be granted the respect and the love that I am owed.' His eyes met mine. 'But you will not be around to see it because you will not see tomorrow's dawn.'

'I wouldn't be so sure about that,' I said, sounding considerably calmer than I felt.

'You are strong, but you are not a witch. You cannot banish me from this realm. And if you truly know what I am, you know that the likes of you cannot kill me.'

I smiled. 'Ah, but that's where you're wrong. Because you don't know what *I* am.'

No sooner had the words left my mouth than I threw out the strongest blast of air magic I could muster. I'd hoped that it would knock him off his feet but unfortunately, although it made the nearby windows rattle violently and sent several large bins careening towards him, it didn't affect the fiend himself. As he was bald, I didn't even have the satisfaction of seeing it flatten his hair.

'Bravo,' he said. 'You're powerful, even for a high elf. But as you can see, you're not remotely strong enough to beat me.' His accent was odd, strangely clipped. It was possible that at some time he'd lived in some distant country, or perhaps he was simply unused to talking.

Although my recent experience suggested otherwise, fiends were typically solitary creatures. If this one was used to little more than the company of vampires, he probably never enjoyed the pleasures of a real conversation.

I shrugged. It didn't matter to me whether he was a social butterfly or a hermit; he was a fiend. And he was in my way.

I gave an insouciant shrug, 'I guess we'll have to see about that.' I sent out another blast of strong air magic. This time, however, I didn't aim for the fiend but at one of the parked cars on the side of the road. I used the heavy explosion of air to raise the chunk of metal a foot into the air before following with a second blast of air that threw the car in the fiend's direction.

From his expression, in the second before a tonne of Volkswagen metal smacked him in the face, that wasn't something he'd been expecting.

The noise was tremendous as it reverberated down the street, and the damage to the car was extraordinary, too. The windscreen shattered and the metal doors twisted; it was particularly gratifying to see the vehicle roll three times and pin the fiend to the cobblestones. Go me. And go German engineering.

Unfortunately, my delight was short lived. Before I could follow up to ensure that the fiend was taken care of, a voice drifted out of the darkness. 'Boss? You okay?'

My stomach tightened. Another one? I'd only had a slim chance of beating one fiend but I'd definitely lose against two of the bastards. I supposed I could still run for my life; I doubted I'd get very far but I'd give it my best shot.

I scanned the shadows for the source of the voice. There was a creak of metal as the trapped fiend used his own magic to push the fallen vehicle away from his body. 'No, Chuchi!' he spat. 'This is my fight!'

My mouth dropped open as, a second later, the hulking figure of an ogre stepped out from the dark opening of a nearby alley. 'Alright,' he rumbled. He folded his massive arms, which had to be the size of bloody tree trunks, and leaned against the wall. Then he grinned and winked at me. 'You'll pay for that, sweetheart.'

I had no doubt that this was the same Chuchi who had manipulated Baudi into entrapping passers-by. How many ogres could there be with that name? But an ogre was better than a fiend; at least I had a chance with an ogre.

The fiend stood up and dusted himself down with a mildly irritated scowl. 'Clever move,' he said. 'But not clever enough.' He crooked his little finger and etched out a quick rune in the air in front of him. It flared bright scarlet – and then I was thrown upwards.

My stomach rose into my mouth as I jerked into the air. This was no simple magic attack, and I wasn't rising a few metres only to come down to earth with a hard thump. Within three seconds, I was ten metres in the air. Then fifteen. Then twenty. My arms and legs flailed but I was powerless to stop my ascent.

I spotted a white face staring out from one of the tenement windows. All the residents must have been awake by now, but few of them would be brave enough to peer out for fear of being dragged into whatever battle was underway.

But not all of them were cowering. 'I'm calling the police!' a shaky voice shouted. 'I'm calling them now!'

I saw another face at a different window that was wide open: it was an older woman, dressed in a white nightgown. Cumbubbling bollocks. I waved at her frantically. 'Stay away!' I shouted. 'Don't get involved!'

It was too late. The fiend far below me was already drawing

another attack rune and I knew this one wasn't aimed at me. He was planning to hurt that woman; in fact, he meant to kill her.

I had to stop him. I was still moving higher and higher; in another moment, I'd be above the roofline. At some point the bastard below was going to release me and enjoy watching my body go splat in front of him when it hit the ground again.

My mouth flattened. If I was in the sky, then I might as well act like the sky. It was time to show the fiend that I was more than he thought.

I fixed on his position below me as he drew the last curls on the rune, then I sucked in a breath and shot out a bolt of lightning from my fingertips. It arced down and struck him on the top of his bald, golden skull. His body jerked and he started to collapse – but unfortunately so did I.

I was descending far faster than I'd ascended and, as air rushed past me, I lost my grip on Gladys's hilt. I yelped and writhed. In the nick of time, I pushed a surge of air magic into the space beneath my falling body. Half a second before I hit the ground, its counterforce pushed me upwards. Instead of spilling my organs onto the street, I landed on all fours only slightly winded. Gladys clattered to the ground a few metres away. Phew. That had been close.

The fiend was still in a heap – I couldn't tell whether I'd killed him or not – but suddenly he was the least of my worries. Chuchi burst from the alleyway, roaring at the top of his lungs.

Panicking, I sent out a jet of fire magic in his direction but he was incredibly nippy for such a large creature and dodged it easily. Before I could muster another magical attack, he raised his fists. I tensed as I waited for the inevitable blow, half-expecting him to knock my head clean off my shoulders. Instead, there was another blast of magic – and this one didn't come from me.

I didn't know exactly what the fiend had done, but whatever rune he'd etched had summoned up enough power to burn the ogre's eyeballs and burst open his vast ribcage to reveal his still-beating heart.

Chuchi let out a single long scream and fell forward. I scrambled away in the nick of time to avoid being squashed by his dead weight. He gave a final shuddering gasp and then he was still.

I turned my head and stared at the fiend.

'Minions aren't what they used to be,' he said. As he got to his feet, he rubbed the burn on the top of his head where my lightning had struck him. 'I told him to stay out of this. It's his own fucking fault.'

I could do little more than gape; I couldn't begin to compete against his sort of power. I was so very, very screwed.

The fiend adjusted his shorts, pulled the waistband higher, then ambled towards me. 'I believe introductions are in order.' His nose twitched. 'You know, you smell most peculiar – like … stinky marshland.' He shrugged amiably and held out his hand. 'I am Vargas.'

Uncontrolled earth magic flooded out from me and rocked the ground beneath our feet. Vargas tilted his head, dropped his hand, and looked at me curiously. 'Sorry,' I muttered, then I winced. Why the fuck was I apologising to a bloody fiend?

Rather than attacking me again, he raised a hairless eyebrow. 'Interesting,' he said. 'You do not have full control. And yet, you are … what? Thirty years old?'

I eyed him warily. 'Nearly.'

'How have you managed to live so long without burning yourself out?'

So he hadn't spotted the tell-tale ring of silver around my eyes. 'Dumb luck, I guess.'

He scratched his chin. 'You are not a fiend – not yet anyway – but your powers indicate that you were sired by a fiend.' His face loomed towards me. 'I will know your name,' he said in a commanding tone. 'And I will know your parents. Tell me who they are.'

He was within touching distance now. My mouth felt painfully dry and I shivered. *Stop it, Daisy,* I told myself sternly. *Don't let him see your fear.*

I raised my head and met his blood-red eyes. 'My name is Daisy Carter.'

'Who sired you, Daisy Carter? Where have you come from?'

This time I didn't answer; I was trying to work out how to play this new angle. Perhaps I wouldn't be dead soon after all.

'Magic like that doesn't manifest in fiend-born children unless their parents are very powerful, so that rules out most of the other fiend fuckers. You're either Zashtum's get – and I'd have heard about it if she'd gotten herself pregnant – or you're a product of Baltar or Athair.'

Vargas started to circle me. 'And Baltar gave up on his attempts to create a child of his own more than a hundred years ago.'

I glanced to my right. Gladys still lay too far away on the cobbles; I wouldn't get to her before Vargas got to me. I glanced away again, then lifted my chin mutinously.

'But if Athair had an adult child,' Vargas said silkily, 'I would have heard about it by now. He likes to boast, but he has never mentioned you. He would take great pleasure in telling me about you, especially after he went to such trouble to ensure my son, Fravock, did not live to meet his full potential.'

I sucked in a sharp breath, then I took a huge gamble. 'He doesn't know,' I said in little more than a whisper. For all I knew, in 1994 that was the truth. 'He doesn't know I exist.'

Vargas circled me again. 'I see.' He clicked his tongue. 'That is somewhat annoying, if it is true. There will be little enjoyment in watching Athair's face when I tell him I have killed his long-awaited child if he doesn't know that child exists. But kill you I must. Athair on his own is bad enough – Athair with a dynasty would be far worse.'

I snorted. Loudly. Vargas stopped circling my body. 'What?'

'You think I want to be part of a dynasty with Athair?' I spat. 'I'll see him dead long before that happens.'

'You cannot kill a fiend,' Vargas said. 'And you certainly cannot kill Athair.'

'You're wrong. Enough of Athair's blood runs through my veins that I'm more than capable of killing a fiend. In fact,' I said airily, 'I've already done so.'

Vargas's head snapped towards mine. 'Who?'

'Does it matter?' I didn't take my eyes from him. 'You know I'm not lying.'

He narrowed his gaze. 'No,' he said softly. 'I don't believe you are.' He stared at me for another moment or two then stepped back. 'It would be so delicious for you to meet Athair in battle,' he breathed. 'He would kill you before he knew the truth. He has wanted a child of his for so many generations. This would indeed be poetic.'

I chose my words with care. 'You sound as if you don't like him.'

'Don't *like* him? I do not *like* Athair?' Vargas scoffed. 'I *despise* that fucker! He murdered my child. He lords it over the rest of us. He thinks he is better than us – but he is not. He plays with the undead, but he does not command an army of them like I do.'

He waved at the collection of fallen vampires and Chuchi, none of whom were looking like particularly effective soldiers given that they were all very dead. 'He does not respect what I do! He does not respect me!' He thumped his chest and his eyes sparked with scarlet fury.

'Uh-huh.' I licked my lips. 'Vargas, before you kill me,

promise me one thing.' He stared at me, and I continued quickly while I had his attention. 'Promise me that one day you will kill Athair. I can go to my grave easily knowing that you will be strong enough to overthrow him.'

A scornful laugh escaped Vargas's mouth but he covered it hastily. He didn't want me to know that he would never be strong enough or brave enough to risk taking on Athair; if he were, he'd have attempted it when Athair killed his son. It was obvious Vargas valued his own existence far too much.

'Perhaps,' he said slowly, 'there is another way. Perhaps I do not have to kill you.'

I waited. The idea had to come from him.

He nodded and his golden jowls jiggled. 'Perhaps I can help *you* to kill Athair.'

I lowered my eyes so he didn't see the glow of satisfaction in them. He didn't believe for a moment that I was strong enough to hurt Athair; he only wanted to inflict as much psychological damage on his fiendish rival as he could. 'You're toying with me,' I said aloud. 'I know I cannot trust you.'

'Oh really?' Vargas sounded cool and I felt a flash of concern that I'd been too obvious. 'You can trust me in this, Daisy Carter, daughter of Athair. I will prove it to you.' He dipped his head towards mine. 'If you want to control your magic, you have to lose it first.'

I stiffened. That was not what I'd been expecting. 'What?'

'Release all your magic in one go, empty yourself of every scrap of power. Once you have done that, and once your energy returns, you will be able to control yourself and the magic within you.'

I almost stopped breathing. Could that be right? Was that all it took to master my powers?

Vargas laughed at my expression. 'It is true – try it and you will see. Then maybe you will have a chance against Athair. Stranger things have happened.'

'You will fight him alongside me?' I asked.

'I will do what is necessary,' he replied. Clearly, he wasn't prepared to make any promises.

I nodded. Then I brushed myself down and straightened the cuffs of my jacket. I checked the empty sheath by my side and went over to Gladys. With a thoughtful expression, I picked her up and re-sheathed her. She vibrated once: she understood.

I turned to Vargas and held out my hand. Triumph gleamed in his expression. He strode forward and stretched out his own hand to shake mine.

I smiled. Then, with as much speed and strength as I could muster, I snapped my hand back, yanked Gladys free and plunged her into Vargas's chest.

His eyes widened and a gurgling sound emitted from his throat. I rammed Gladys deeper into his body and leaned in so I could whisper in his ear. 'As if I would ever make a deal with a fiend.'

Vargas choked and dropped to his knees. His red eyes stared at me in horror for moment before the light in them went out for good and he collapsed. I nudged his body with my toe. He wouldn't get up this time.

SIXTEEN

I snatched a few hours uncomfortable sleep in a cold doorway while Hester and Otis kept an eye out for any other vampires that might wander by. It wasn't enough to fully refresh me but it was better than nothing.

The adrenaline rush from my night's activities meant that I was grinning like a maniac despite my grubby appearance when I presented myself at the police station the following morning. The spider's silk I'd swallowed had helped, and I pretended not to feel the ensuing palpitations and ignored the tremble in my hands. I was under a lot of stress so naturally I would experience side effects. That's what I tried to tell myself anyway.

WPC Hurst was on duty at the front desk again. When she saw me, her eyes widened with delight. It gave me a warm, zippy feeling to know that the country's police officers were glad I wasn't dead – or at least one of them was.

'You made it! When I heard the reports this morning about a huge fight close to Cowgate, I wasn't sure that you were okay. It's great to see you.' She emerged from behind the desk and strode towards me to pump my hand.

'It's good to see you, too,' I said.

Hester, who was perched on my shoulder, nodded. 'Daisy wouldn't let a few vampires, a nasty ogre or a silly fiend hurt her.'

WPC Hurst blinked. 'Fiend? What's a fiend?'

I wondered if I ought to tell her. Most of the general public – and a good number of people in authority, too – didn't know that either blood magic or fiends existed. Before I could make my mind up, however, the grizzled policeman from the day before appeared through the doorway behind her. 'So,' he growled, 'you've decided to show up.'

My smile didn't falter. 'Naturally.' I splayed out my arms in a gesture of triumph. 'I assume you've got my reward money ready.'

A spark of amusement lit his eyes – and gave me pause. 'Oh, we're ready,' he said, sounding surprisingly pleased.

Hester and Otis sprang into action, each extracting a series of objects in a coordinated dance that they'd choreographed for maximum drama. It involved a considerable amount of flitting between my pockets and the desk in front of us, but it made them happy so I let them continue until all fourteen vampiric fangs were laid out.

'Not just one dead vampire,' I said with a flourish that almost matched the brownies' antics, 'but seven. I even wiped away the blood.' I grinned. 'You're welcome.'

'Uh-huh.' The policeman barely glanced at the gleaming fangs, but at least WPC Hurst leaned over them with a fascinated expression on her face.

'I'll take my money now,' I said. 'You promised cash. Seven dead vampires equal three-and-a-half grand.' That would be more than enough to serve my needs.

'Uh-huh,' he said again.

I was starting to get a sinking feeling. 'Is there a problem?' I asked.

'Well,' he drawled, in a tone that suggested he was enjoying himself immensely, 'your arithmetic is accurate. Seven dead vampires do indeed equate to £3,500.' He sucked air in through his teeth. 'However, you've left out a few sums.'

Cumbubbling bollocks: here we go. I should have known it wouldn't be that simple. While both Hester and Otis bristled by my side, I folded my arms and waited.

'Several officers have attended the scene where you dispatched the vampires. We know it's the right place because numerous calls were made to the emergency services at around two in the morning, and there were descriptions of a woman who looks just like you.' He raised a questioning eyebrow. 'Brighton Street, to be specific.'

I tapped my foot. 'Yes, that's where I killed the vampires. But I might add that I saw no sign of any police. It must have taken your lot a long time to show up.'

WPC Hurst flinched but the older policeman only shrugged. 'When vampires are involved, only specialist officers and equipment can attend the scene. That takes time to organise.'

I regarded him flatly.

'You are to be congratulated on your ability not only to kill so many bloodsuckers in one night, but also to appear relatively unscathed.' He paused. 'Alas, Brighton Street is somewhat less unscathed.'

He held up a sheet of paper. 'Obviously at the moment this is only an estimate. There was considerable damage to the road and pavement. A large area of cobblestones will have to repaired, and the gas and electric lines nearby will need to be checked for safety. The repair costs will total around £20,000.'

I gaped at him.

'At least one vehicle which was parked nearby will have to be written off, and several others will need extensive repairs before they are deemed to be roadworthy. It is possible that the insurance companies will come to you to recoup their losses. I don't know how much that will be but it will be ... a lot.'

WPC Hurst looked very pale; I probably did, too.

'There is fire damage to some of the historic buildings nearby. Initial estimates suggest costs of around £5,000 for those repairs. General clean-up costs, including removing the charred bone fragments and ash from the scene, will add another few thousand pounds.'

I'd thought I was being a good citizen by setting each body – Chuchi and Vargas included – on fire. I wondered what the clean-up costs would have been if I hadn't bothered.

'So,' he finished, 'we owe you £3,500. Unfortunately, you now owe the city of Edinburgh an estimated £29,000.' He waved the piece of paper. 'Once that amount is settled, I will release your reward.' He smirked. 'In cash, as you prefer.'

Hester was furious and even Otis vented his frustration aloud. 'You ... you ... you ... you can't do that!'

'Oh, but I can. It's the law.'

'Daisy killed seven vampires! She made your streets safer! She deserves a medal, not a bill!' Otis squeaked.

He pursed his lips. 'Them's the breaks.'

'But—'

I grabbed hold of Otis and gestured for him to be quiet, then I shook my head at Hester, who had rolled up her sleeves and formed tiny fists with her hands. The last thing we needed was to add assaulting a police officer to our woes. 'No wonder there's such a big vampire problem,' I said icily.

'Anyone who's smart knows to stay inside once the sun goes down,' the policeman replied.

Hurst dropped her head. 'Sorry,' she muttered. Her apology was heartfelt but it didn't do me any good. Sorry wouldn't buy me food or shelter.

I rolled my eyes and walked out of the little police station with far less of a spring in my step than when I'd entered.

'I HATE 1994!' Hester moaned as we plodded dejectedly down bustling Princes Street. I wasn't convinced that matters would be any different thirty years from now, apart from a lack of vampires to kill. There wouldn't be many of the fanged fuckers around in the future, although it was astonishing how often the remaining ones seemed to find me.

'Me too, Hes,' Otis said. 'Me too.'

I had less than five pounds in my pocket and a fast-dwindling supply of spider's silk. I shook my head. 'We'll have to throw ourselves on the mercy of the Royal Elvish Institute. I don't know who was in charge in 1994, and it's doubtful that anyone will believe we've time travelled, but we must try to get them to believe us. There has to be a way to convince them of the truth. We're out of other options.'

I looked at Hester and Otis, hoping they might have some ideas, but neither of them was looking back at me; they were both staring ahead. 'Isn't that Tracey?' Otis asked.

I squinted. There was a large crowd of people around the entrance to Waverley train station and I couldn't see what – or who – was holding their attention. My stomach tightened. I desperately hoped there wasn't a problem and that Tracey was alright.

Feeling very tense, I half-marched, half-ran the final twenty metres before pushing my way through the crowd. A sharp pain stabbed at my chest when I saw that Tracey was indeed at its centre – but then I realised that she was fine. More than fine.

She was sitting on the ground surrounded by an array of small spray bottles. The people around her were thrusting money in her direction.

'I'll give you ten pounds for one!' a man shouted.

'I'll make it twenty!' said the woman next to him.

When I tried to get closer, the man next to me jabbed me in the ribs with his elbow. 'Hey! There's a queue here. Wait your turn!'

I held up my palms, unwilling to get into a fight. My morning had started out badly and I didn't need another battle on my hands, so I stepped back and watched the proceedings instead.

There was no doubt that what Tracey was doing was illegal, and if PC Grizzly Plod at the police station found out she was selling bottles of an unknown liquid on the street, she'd end up with a hefty fine. But what he didn't know wouldn't hurt him.

I rocked back on my heels and, for the first time since I'd walked out of the police station, I smiled.

'How do I know it'll work?' somebody asked.

'Seven dead vampires on Brighton Street last night says it does,' came the answer.

A buzz of delight zipped through me. Otis whispered in my ear, 'Tracey is selling vamp spray.'

'Yep.'

'You told her what to put in it.'

'Yep.'

'But you only know what's in vamp spray because it's popular in the future.'

'Yep.'

'So who actually invented vamp spray?'

I shrugged. Hester cackled. 'Daisy invented it!'

In a manner of speaking, I guess I did. I giggled. This vamp-killing venture hadn't been a complete write-off after all.

Within minutes, Tracey had sold all her stock and a lot of people who hadn't been able to snag any vamp spray were looking very upset. 'Same time tomorrow folks!' she trilled. 'I'll replenish my supplies overnight.'

The grumbling crowd started to disperse. Tracey glanced up, caught my eye and let out a thrilled squeal before rushing forward to give me a tight hug. 'You're fine! I knew all along you would be! I hope you don't mind but I made up more of that potion.' She beamed. 'It's selling like hotcakes! Everyone wants some.' She pulled back and thrust a wad of notes into my hand. 'Here, this is your cut.'

My cheeks flushed and I shoved the notes back at her. 'I'm the one who owes you money,' I said with a flash of guilt. 'The police won't give me the reward. I'm so sorry, Tracey.'

'Don't be sorry! Didn't you see all those people? I'm onto a winner here! This could be exactly what I need to get myself off the streets.' She hugged me again. 'I can't thank you enough. You have to take your share.'

I opened my mouth to protest further, then caught Otis and Hester glaring at me. I dropped my head, took the money and mumbled, 'Thanks, Tracey.'

Her eyes were shining. 'I'm taking off – I need to make another batch. I should come up with a name for this stuff as well.'

'Vamp Spray,' Otis and Hester chorused.

Tracey looked at me. 'Sounds good to me,' I said. 'It's best to stick to an obvious name so people know what it is.'

'Then Vamp Spray it is. Do you want to help me sell it tomorrow? We can make a killing, especially now that we know it works.'

I looked at the crumpled notes in my hand. I finally had

what I needed. I was in a position to do what Gordon had intended all along. 'That's a kind offer, but there's somewhere I need to be. There's an elven woman who needs my help.'

'She'll be lucky to have it. You're amazing, Daisy.'

I bit my lip. I genuinely doubted I was amazing enough to alter history and save Lady Rose – but I would certainly give it my best shot.

CHAPTER

SEVENTEEN

T hanks to Tracey's success at raising money, I could not only afford a cheap B&B, where I could clean myself up and get a decent night's sleep, but also the services of a spider's silk dealer. The relief I felt at replenishing my supplies was almost as good as my eight hours' sleep; the gnawing fear that I'd end up in withdrawal had been nibbling away at me, and it had been getting exhausting.

There was enough money left over to pay for a set of clothes from a charity shop and for my travel the following morning. I was both renewed and refreshed; I no longer smelled like a marsh and I no longer felt like a grubby marsh monster. My mood was so buoyant that I felt I could take on the whole world, regardless of what year it was. I tried to ignore the fact that the shaking in my hands kept recurring, and the heart palpitations, tinnitus and cold sweats continued to flare up when I least wanted them.

The train route was unchanged from what I knew it would be in the future. Finally I hopped off at a vaguely familiar platform and glanced around. Pemberville Castle, Hugo's family seat, was less than four miles away; the Assigney mansion was roughly the same distance, albeit in the opposite direction.

Hester cracked her knuckles. 'I am ready for our next heroic encounter,' she declared. 'Let's save Lady Rose!'

I turned to the right and started walking. 'Um, Daisy? Lady Rose's house is the other way,' Otis murmured.

'We'll go to Hugo's place first,' I said firmly.

He was astonished. 'Why would we do that? If he's there, he'll only be a baby. He won't be much use.'

Actually, in 1994 Hugo would be two years old, still in nappies but no longer a babe in arms. 'We can't just rock up at Lady Rose's house, knock on the door and tell her she's in danger. We need to establish the lay of the land. Hugo's parents are Lady Rose's immediate neighbours, and we know that they tried to speak to Rose several times before she vanished. If we talk to them first, we might learn more about what's going on.'

Hester sniffed. 'We might also interrupt them in the middle of sawing Lady Rose's body into bits before burying them in their vegetable garden.'

I certainly hoped not, for Hugo's sake. 'Well,' I said lightly, 'at least that'll solve the mystery of what happened to her. And we've got days yet before Rose vanishes for good, so they won't be sawing her up yet.'

'Do you think that they killed her?' Otis asked worriedly.

'I'm keeping an open mind. But until any evidence presents itself to the contrary, they deserve the benefit of the doubt.'

Innocent until proven guilty. I'd never met Hugo's mum and dad but I found it hard to believe they'd have the motive or the desire to kill off their neighbour and hide her body. Call me naïve, but it seemed unlikely.

Neither Otis nor Hester said anything. I turned around and glanced at them. They were pulling faces at each other and gesturing pointedly. 'What?' I asked, faintly exasperated.

Hester arched a mocking grin in my direction. 'You can tell the truth, Daisy.'

'Yeah,' Otis said. 'We won't judge you.'

'No.' Hester shook her head. 'We *will* judge you. But you don't have to lie.'

I gazed at them. 'I'm not going to Pemberville Castle first because I want to see Hugo as a kid. I have a carefully laid plan. I've considered this a great deal, and it's the sensible thing to do.'

'Yup.' Otis grinned broadly.

'Sure thing, Daisy,' Hester added.

'It's true!' Mostly true.

'Uh-huh.'

'Yep.'

I turned away. 'Come on.'

They snickered loudly. Vargas had been right on one count: minions weren't what they used to be.

WHEN I TURNED onto the long driveway and Pemberville Castle and its grounds finally came into sight, a flicker of relief warmed my insides. It looked exactly the same now as it would in thirty years, and that familiarity was comforting. The hedges lining the road were pruned in the same manner, the apple trees in the orchard to the east displayed the same blossom, and the castle didn't look any different, even though I knew that Hugo had carried out a lot of necessary repairs.

Other than the row of unfamiliar – and very expensive – cars parked outside the castle, the main difference was that Duchess wouldn't be lurking beneath the bridge that crossed the old moat. I'd miss her presence; in fact, when I reached the bridge I paused for a moment to acknowledge her. Strangely, it seemed the right thing to do. I didn't linger for long, though.

With my shoulders pulled back and my chin high, I walked to the massive oak front door and rang the heavy bell. 'You've got this, Daisy,' I muttered under my breath.

I didn't have to wait for long. Within half a minute, the door creaked open and I was looking into the smiling face of a woman in her fifties. She was wearing a long apron that almost reached her ankles. I gazed into her twinkling eyes and, for one stupid moment, thought I was looking at Hugo's mother until I realised she was far too old and was probably a member of staff.

'Good morning,' I said briskly, hoping that my charity-shop suit and business-like tone would make her think I was some sort of professional. 'My name is Gertrude Van Winkle. I am from the Royal Elvish Institute and I have an appointment with Lord and Lady Pemberville. I'm slightly early. I do hope that's alright.'

The woman's eyes slid from me to Otis and Hester. Thankfully, both brownies decided to play along.

'Kimberley Kardashian,' Hester said, with a mid-air curtsey.

Otis bowed. 'Mark Zuckerberg. We are Ms Van Winkle's assistants.'

The woman blinked. 'I don't have any record of an appointment.'

I let a tiny frown cross my face. 'Kim,' I said, addressing Hester, 'you did call yesterday to confirm, didn't you?'

Hester looked momentarily panic-stricken. 'I ... uh ... I...'

I tutted loudly. 'We've come a long way for this.'

The woman took pity on us. 'Not to worry. The Pembervilles are in a meeting at the moment, but I expect they'll be finished soon. You're welcome to wait inside while I see if they've got time to talk to you.'

'That's very kind of you,' I told her, making sure to glare pointedly at Hester at the same time.

'It's not a problem.' The housekeeper stepped back. 'Follow me.'

As soon as she turned away, Hester punched me repeatedly with both her tiny fists. Otis giggled. I winked at them and motioned to them to behave.

We walked into the grand entrance of Pemberville Castle. The paintings on the walls were the same; the suits of armour were the same; the only difference was the faint but pleasant scent of beeswax and lemon.

The woman directed us to an ornate wooden bench opposite the sweeping staircase. I nodded my thanks and settled down, scratching the back of my neck and twitching slightly as I did so. 'Would you like something to drink while you're waiting?' she asked. 'A pot of tea, perhaps?'

Before I could answer, a strange rattling sound followed by a loud dinging bell echoed towards us. The woman raised her eyes heavenward. A moment later, a tiny figure on a toy trike careened around the corridor and skidded towards us. 'Master Hugo!' she said. 'You're not supposed to be in this part of the house!'

My mouth went dry and I couldn't stop myself from staring. I was not a fan of small children – they were unpredictable and made me feel nervous – but Hugo was quite possibly the cutest child I'd ever seen.

He turned his head towards the housekeeper and grinned impishly, revealing the same dimple that I would know so well in thirty years' time, then he scooted over to me. Completely fascinated, Hester, Otis and I stared at this tiny version of Hugo.

I leaned down and smiled at him. 'Hello, there.'

He burbled something incomprehensible before reaching up

with one chubby hand until his fingers latched onto my necklace, which was hanging forward between us.

'Master Hugo! Let the nice lady go!' the housekeeper said.

Hugo tightened his grip and suddenly I saw echoes of the man he would become. He giggled and tugged, determined to yank the pendant from my neck. 'Puh – ritty!' he chortled. 'Mine!'

I carefully extracted his fingers and pulled back, then tucked the necklace out of sight beneath my shirt. Almost immediately, his face crumpled and his cheeks turned bright red. Uh-oh.

'You've done it now,' Hester murmured in my ear.

Hugo's wide blue eyes flicked to her. Forgetting his impending tantrum, he thrust out his hand and tried to grab her in the same way he'd grabbed my necklace. Before he could, the housekeeper scooped him up in her arms. 'I'm sorry about that,' she said with fond exasperation. 'He's a handful.'

'He's very cute,' Otis told her.

'Yes.' She smiled. 'He'll be a real heartbreaker when he grows up.'

Hester drew in a breath as she prepared to speak. I glared at her before she said something I'd regret. 'I have no doubt,' I murmured non-commitally.

'I'll take him to the nursery,' the housekeeper said. 'If you wait here, Lord and Lady Pemberville should be free soon.'

I watched as she headed up the stairs with Hugo squirming all the way. 'Happy now?' Hester asked.

'I—' I began. Then I stopped.

'What's wrong, Daisy?' Otis frowned at me. 'You've gone all pale.'

I rubbed my neck and a moment later rolled up my sleeves and scratched my arms. Seeing my actions, Hester and Otis immediately stiffened then shot up into the air in alarm as they scanned the empty entrance hall with panicked eyes.

A door to the right opened; I knew it led to the sun-filled garden room with its south facing windows and glorious views. With my heart hammering against my ribcage, I sprang to my feet and waved wildly at both brownies, who immediately took refuge behind the nearest suit of armour. My right hand strayed towards Gladys's hilt.

'I do so appreciate your time,' said a smooth, cultured male voice.

'You're very welcome, doctor,' a woman replied. 'Although our families haven't always seen eye to eye, I'd hate to think that poor Rose is in any trouble. She's so very young.' She stepped out of the doorway and smiled, revealing her own little dimple.

I sucked in a sharp breath: this was Hugo's mum. Beside her was a tall, well-dressed man with tawny hair. As I watched, Lord and Lady Pemberville stepped forward out of the garden room. Only then did I get a good look at their companion.

He didn't look like a fiend, although I supposed he'd hardly be in his natural form. I glanced briefly at his grey suit and checked tie, then stared in stark horror at his face.

'I am certain,' he said to the couple, 'that if you can persuade her to leave her house and take in some fresh air, even if only for a turn around her gardens, she will start to feel like her old self again. The healing properties of nature are not to be underestimated.'

Lord Pemberville nodded gravely while Lady Pemberville twisted her hands together in obvious concern. I barely looked at them, however, because my attention was focused on the self-styled doctor, who was smiling gently at them.

The face he was wearing was one I'd seen before; in thirty years' time, that very same face would be at Gordon Mackenzie's front door in the guise of a postal worker. That could only mean it was Athair – in Hugo's home, chatting amiably to Hugo's parents and less than five metres away from me.

Cumbubbling bollocks.

EIGHTEEN

My first impulse was to draw Gladys from her sheath and attack him; he wouldn't be expecting it and I'd have as good a chance as any to bring him down for good. But it was obvious that neither Lord nor Lady Pemberville knew what he was; if I launched myself at Athair with the intention of killing him, they would likely get involved – and they would not be on my side. Two-year-old Hugo was upstairs and he was vulnerable, plus I didn't know who else was in the castle – I could end up battling dozens.

I would never win, but if Athair made a move towards me I would defend myself to the death.

Athair shook hands with Hugo's dad and then with his mum. As he turned towards the door, he finally spotted me and I held my breath. At first his eyes slid dismissively past me, but before I could relax, a frown marred his features and he looked at me again. I knew he didn't recognise me because he didn't yet know who I was, but he was definitely puzzled.

'Forgive me,' he said. 'Have we met? You look incredibly familiar.'

The lie slipped out easily. 'No, I don't believe so.'

Something flashed in his eyes: he knew I was lying. Vargas had seemed to possess an affinity for the truth and it appeared that Athair had the same trait.

'In fact, I've got a great memory for faces,' I said hastily. 'I'm sure we've never met before this day.' That was the absolute truth – technically. 'My name is Daisy.' I gave what I hoped looked like a genuine smile. 'Daisy Carter.'

Athair stared at me for another few seconds; it felt like an hour, and I prickled and itched the entire time. 'It's nice to meet you, Daisy Carter,' he said finally. He nodded at Lord and Lady Pemberville, then thankfully he left.

Hugo's parents were smiling at me with polite but confused expressions. I watched Athair's departing figure as the house-keeper reappeared at the top of the stairs.

'Lord and Lady Pemberville! You're finished with the doctor.' She hurried towards us. 'This is Gertrude Van Winkle from the Royal Elvish Institute. She thought she had an appointment with you, but I think there's been a mistake in the diary. Do you have time to speak to her now?'

Hugo's mother tilted her head in an action wholly reminiscent of her son whenever he felt suspicious. 'I thought you said your name was Daisy Carter?'

Five minutes inside Hugo's home and I'd already fucked things up. Well done, Daisy, I thought sarcastically.

'Gertrude is my real name,' I said. 'But, uh, the Royal Elvish Institute doesn't like it when I reveal who I am to anyone who's not an elf.' I nodded towards the door through which Athair had departed. 'I didn't know who he was, so I thought it wise to use a nom de plume.'

It felt like the stupidest excuse in the world, but I folded my hands in front of me and smiled as if inventing names for myself was the most natural thing in the world.

Thankfully Lord Pemberville believed me. 'The Royal Elvish

Institute strikes again.' He rolled his eyes. 'It is time they stopped treating everyone who is not a high elf as the enemy.'

I agreed wholeheartedly. 'We should all put in a stern complaint,' I said. 'In writing.'

There was a loud snort from behind the suit of armour. 'Okay, Karen,' Hester muttered.

The Pembervilles frowned at me. 'Your name is Karen now?' Hugo's mother asked.

I had to bite back the temptation to stuff Hester inside the shiny armour and leave her there. 'That's a nickname.'

Hug's parents stared at me as I tried to look innocent.

'Alright, then.' Lady Pemberville's brow remained creased. 'Although you should remember that there's nothing wrong with humans. And that particular human is Dr James Taggart.'

That isn't his name.

'We've known him for several months.'

You don't know him at all.

Her expression was earnest. 'He's eminently trustworthy.'

No. He really isn't.

'He's very dedicated to his work. Our neighbour, Rose Assigney, is one of his patients. He comes regularly to check on her.'

Oh God.

'You know what?' I said, dissembling quickly. 'I think the diary error was probably mine. Let's reschedule the appointment for another day.'

'We've got time now,' Lord Pemberville said. 'There's no need for that.'

I was already backing towards the door and waving at Otis and Hester to come out from behind the armour. 'I have other appointments today. Another time will be fine.'

The housekeeper coughed gently. 'You don't have any more

spare time until next week,' she said to the Pembervilles. 'Not until Tuesday.'

Before there could be any further discussion, I jumped in. 'Tuesday it is! Two o'clock?' Without waiting for an answer, I burbled, 'I'll see you then. Thank you so much!' I reached the door and ran outside, leaving it ajar.

Lord Pemberville's words drifted to my ears. 'What a very peculiar woman.' I grimaced.

A sleek black car, which had been parked outside with the other vehicles, was already on its way down the long driveway leading to the main road. I gritted my teeth in annoyance.

'Daisy,' Otis hissed. 'What's going on? What are you doing?'

'Yeah,' Hester said. 'I thought you wanted to talk to them. Why are we leaving?'

'You know that was Athair,' I said. I turned towards the other vehicles, marched to the nearest one and tried the door. It was locked. 'He's pretending to be Lady Rose's doctor. He was talking to the Pembervilles about her.'

'So *he's* the one who murdered her,' Hester said.

'Or who's *about* to murder her,' Otis added darkly. 'The Pembervilles are in the clear.'

It wasn't evidence that would stand up in court, but it was enough to satisfy me. 'Exactly.' I tried another car door; it was also locked. 'We need to follow Athair and find out where he's going.'

Behind the hulking silver body of a Rolls Royce that I knew Hugo wouldn't be caught dead in, I spotted a motorbike. Excellent: I had form with motorbikes. While old and battered, this one had clearly been well-cared for. There was an interesting collection of stickers plastered to its body, and I snorted mildly at the one that proclaimed proudly: *Elves Do It With Magic*.

'Are you crazy?' Otis shrieked. 'Follow a fiend? Follow *that* fiend? Do you have a death wish?'

'We need to find out what he's up to if we're going to stop him hurting Lady Rose,' I said. 'The hunter needs to become the hunted. Now, help me find the keys for this thing.'

As Otis flapped his wings and glared at me, Hester grinned. 'Steal the bike! Catch the fiend who we think is your dad! Brilliant. I think I know where the keys are – there's a small table beside the stairs with several keys on it.'

'Go get them!' I urged. 'We don't have much time to catch up to him.'

She was already zipping towards the castle. Otis stared at me with a morose expression. 'It's alright,' I tried to reassure him. 'He won't kill us.'

'He's a fiend, Daisy. Killing is what his kind does best. He obviously doesn't know that you're probably his daughter.'

I shook my head. 'If he'd killed us in 1994, he'd have mentioned it when we met him in the future.'

'Only if the future is immutable. We still don't know what effect our time travel will have on future events.'

I met his anxious gaze. 'We can't let him go, Otis. We can't pretend we don't know what will happen.'

He folded his arms. 'We don't *know* what will happen, Daisy. That's the point.'

'We know enough.'

Hester reappeared, flapping towards us and clutching a key that was almost the same size as she was. 'Here!' she shouted. 'I've got it!'

I sucked in a breath. Yahtzee. I grinned. 'Then let's go.'

I was sure that it was as illegal to ride a motorbike without a helmet in 1994 as it was in 2024, but there wasn't one on the bike and I possessed neither the time nor the opportunity to find one. I had to throw caution – and my hair – to the wind.

I revved hard and set off in pursuit of Athair's car. Unfortunately, although I reached the end of the drive in record time, there was no way of telling whether he had turned left or right.

'Go left,' Otis urged.

'No,' Hester said. 'Go right.'

Left led to the Assigney mansion and the rural realm of Perthshire; right led to the A9 motorway to Glasgow, Edinburgh and beyond. I took a gamble based on the assumption that Athair wasn't heading for Lady Rose at that particular moment and swung right. *Please let it be the right choice*, I prayed. I needed a lucky break.

I pushed the bike as hard as I could until the wheels were all but swallowing up the Tarmac. We passed signs for several familiar towns – Auchterarder. Blackford. Dunblane – but there was nothing to indicate Athair was ahead of us. When I saw the turn off for Bridge of Allan, my stomach clenched with disappointment. Stirling was just ahead, and if Athair had driven into that large town I'd have lost him for good.

I scowled as the road curved and the distant turrets of Stirling Castle appeared in all their familiar, commanding majesty. I was pulling back on the throttle, preparing to slow down and admit defeat, when I caught a glimpse of Athair's black car less than fifty metres in front of us. There: he was right there.

I forced myself not to get too excited; I had to maintain a good distance between us because the last thing I could risk was Athair spotting me. I dropped back and let a trundling lorry stay between us; it would be more than enough to block the sight of me in Athair's rear-view mirror.

He appeared to be bypassing Stirling, and I hoped he was on his way to Edinburgh rather than Glasgow. My years as a delivery driver meant that I knew Edinburgh like the back of my hand, whether the year was 1994 or 2024; Glasgow, however, wasn't my home – not now and not in the future. I'd have a much better chance of tracking Athair if he was in the Scottish capital. I crossed my fingers tightly.

When his indicator light suddenly flashed on, I blinked in surprise. He wasn't heading to either city: he was turning deeper into the countryside.

As I followed him off the motorway, I knew I was at risk. There was far less traffic here and certainly no handy heavy-goods vehicles to hide behind. The one thing in my favour was that the road was narrow with far more bends, which made it easier to keep out of Athair's sight. But I didn't know this part of the country at all, so I'd have to keep my wits about me if I didn't want to lose him.

'There are too many insects!' Hester yelled in my ear, raising her voice above the whipping wind. 'They keep splatting me in the face!'

'Then get into my pocket and stay out of their way!' I shouted back at her.

Hester shouted something else but I didn't catch it; my focus was on Athair's car.

He turned onto a single-lane road to the left. I slowed down until I could pull into a small gap on the side of the road and watch his progress. His car continued for some distance before finally disappearing around a corner hidden by a line of carefully planted fir trees. I stood up and tried to see what lay beyond, but it was no good. We needed to get closer.

'You're not planning to fight him, are you Daisy?' Otis's voice was quivering.

I smiled gently. 'You don't think I can beat him?'

He hugged himself. 'No,' he whispered. 'I don't think you can.'

Neither did I. I pointed down the road. 'If Athair has created a lair for himself down there, I want to know about it. But I won't try and fight him.' Not yet. 'If we find out where he's living, perhaps we can use that information later.'

Hester nodded enthusiastically. 'We can set his house on fire while he's sleeping.'

'Fire doesn't affect fiends,' Otis reminded her.

She shrugged. 'We could send in a swarm of angry bees to sting him to death.'

He snorted. 'Because that'll be easy.'

'Daisy can raise an army of zombies and—'

This was getting out of hand. 'Let's just find out where he's staying and what he's up to. Reconnaissance, nothing more.' Then, before my fear of Athair got the better of me and I turned tail and ran away, I lowered myself onto the bike seat, revved the engine and headed after him.

The lane wasn't well maintained and I had to swerve several times to avoid nasty potholes. I kept my eyes peeled, worried that Athair's black car would reappear or that someone else would show up, but the lane remained empty.

When we reached the tree line, I stopped the bike and took a moment to conceal it behind a bush. Given how quiet the lane was, I couldn't risk going any further on it; for all I knew, Athair was lurking around the corner.

The brownies buzzed anxiously as I walked towards the last of the trees – even Hester was showing signs of fear. I told myself that it was good to be frightened of Athair; a flicker of complacency where my alleged father was concerned could spell our doom. It was clear that he was by far the strongest of all the fiends in the country; the first time we'd crossed paths, he could have killed me, Hugo, the brownies and Aine the Welsh dragon without breaking sweat.

At the final tree, I paused for a moment to listen. I heard the twittering of birds and the rustle of leaves as a soft breeze gusted through them, but nothing else. I drew in a breath and peered around. As soon as I saw what the small wood was concealing, a whisper of triumph escaped my lips. 'Yes!'

The landscape in front of us was beautiful. There was a small lake glittering in the dappled midday sunlight with several ducks swimming lazily around its centre and a pair of swans in the far corner. The lake was surrounded by a large expanse of grass so verdantly green that it appeared unreal. Behind that, there was a building – and in front of it a black car. Either the doctor was making more house calls, or this was the place that Athair called home.

When Gladys started to hum at my side, I hushed her. The plan was to remain hidden, at least for now, but I was as delighted as she was that we'd located his lair.

Otis gave a low whistle. 'Quite a place,' he said, gazing at the imposing limestone building with its many windows, rectangular tower and parapet. 'It's exactly where I'd expect a nasty fiend to stay. I bet it's got a dungeon,' he added darkly.

'You know,' Hester said thoughtfully, 'if you kill Athair and he really is your dad, you'll be the owner of this place. You can have your own castle, Daisy.'

Property inheritance was the last thing on my mind, and I rolled my eyes at her. 'We should try and get closer,' I said. 'We need to establish that Athair is holed up here.'

Hester started to nod but Otis had frozen in place. 'Uh, Daisy? There's somebody else here.'

I followed his gaze. Cumbubbling bollocks, he was right: the stooped figure of a man was skirting the western edge of the castle-cum-mansion. He was keeping close to the walls, and when he reached the first set of windows, he ducked further so he could crawl beneath the windowsill. He clearly didn't want to be seen.

'We're not the only ones spying on Athair,' I muttered. I squinted harder, trying to catch a glimpse of the man's face.

'But is that a friend or a foe?' Hester asked.

I shielded my eyes from the sun. The man, whoever he was, had a hood pulled up over his head so I couldn't see his features. He hesitated for a moment and then, still bending low, jogged away from the building towards the trees where we were hiding.

'He's coming this way!' Otis flapped his wings in panic. 'Run! We have to run!'

The man jerked his head up as if he'd heard and I gasped aloud. Tears pricked at the back of my eyeballs. 'It can't be,' I whispered. 'It can't be him.'

Gladys hummed again in her sheath, though it wasn't her usual desperate plea for blood. She knew who was coming.

Hester stared. 'Is that ... is that ... is that ... grown-up Hugo?'

A tremulous smile lit up my face. 'Yes, it is.'

NINETEEN

As Hugo jogged towards us, I ran my fingers through my hair, straightened my top and licked my dry lips.

Hester frowned. 'What are you doing, Daisy?'

'She's making herself look pretty for Hugo,' Otis told her.

Hester snorted; when I glared at her, she pulled a face. 'You always look pretty,' she told me, with an expression that suggested just the opposite.

I gave up on my efforts; instead I drew further back into the dense trees and watched and waited. *Act casual*, Daisy, *I told myself.*

When he drew level, I called out softly, 'Well, well, well. Fancy meeting you of all people here.'

Hugo froze for a moment before turning slowly in my direction. A broad smile spread across his face, displaying his dimple in all its glory. 'I thought I heard something,' he grinned.

He smoothed down his tawny hair, stepped off the road and walked through the trees until we were facing each other. He paused, looked at me expectantly – and then lunged forward to pull me into a tight hug. 'I found you,' he breathed into my hair.

'I think,' I said in a muffled voice, 'that *I* found *you.*'

His voice was emotional and he didn't try to argue. 'Daisy Carter, you are a sight for sore eyes.'

I clung to him for several long seconds. I felt wild magic surging deep inside my belly but I did everything I could to tamp it down; Hugo was here and that was what mattered. I burrowed my head against his chest and inhaled his warm, familiar scent. Suddenly I felt certain that everything would be alright.

Eventually we moved apart and gazed at each other like idiots. 'I was planning to play it cool when you finally showed up,' he said. 'So much for that plan.'

'Are you telling me that I make you lose your cool?' I asked archly.

His voice was low and gruff. 'You know you do.'

Hester zipped into the space between us. 'Hello? We're here too, you know. Aren't you pleased to see us as well?'

Hugo smiled at her. 'Of course, I am.'

Otis squeaked and flew towards him, his little arms outstretched. Hugo raised his hand and opened his palm; the brownies landed on it and hugged his fingers. My glow of happiness only increased.

'How did you get here? How long have you been here?' I was still amazed – and I had so many questions. 'Is Gordon alright?'

'Gordon's fine. He was knocked about a bit and had to spend a night in hospital, but there's no lasting damage.' Hugo drew in a long breath. 'It takes a lot to scare me, Daisy, but when that explosion happened and I ran in and you weren't there...' He inhaled deeply. 'I thought you were gone for good. Don't ever do that again.'

I met his blue eyes. 'I didn't plan to vanish,' I whispered. 'What happened to Athair?'

The warmth in Hugo's eyes disappeared. 'It *was* him dressed as a postal worker, then?' I nodded. 'You know he's wearing the same face now, and that he's staying in that damned castle?'

I swallowed and nodded again.

Hugo exhaled. 'He scarpered pretty quickly after the magical explosion in 2024. He'd already gone by the time I was out of the Jeep and at Gordon's front door.'

So nobody else had been hurt. That was good.

'We searched for you,' Hugo continued, 'and got help for Gordon. He couldn't explain what had happened for several hours. It wasn't … nice.' His voice cracked. Hester and Otis tightened their grip on his fingers while I wrapped my arms around him once more.

'Gordon recovered enough to talk and told us what the golden skull does,' he went on. 'I'll admit I took some convincing.' He gave a baffled shrug. 'Time travel? It's crazy.'

I smiled faintly. 'Imagine how we felt.'

Hugo gently nudged the brownies away and cupped my face in both hands. 'It must have been awful.' He paused and a teasing glint lit his eyes. 'Especially because I wasn't around to save you.'

I curled my lip and he laughed. 'Once Gordon was discharged from hospital, he reset the skull and sent me to join you. I arrived right after you did, but you'd already run off and there was a very angry woman throwing plates. I figured that you wouldn't be able to resist showing up at Lady Rose's door so I came here to wait for you.' His tone was gently chiding. 'You took longer to get here than I thought you would.'

Hester bristled. 'Daisy was busy killing a posse of vampires, a nasty fiend and then inventing Vamp Spray.'

Hugo blinked. 'Huh?'

'I'll explain later.' I nodded towards the castle. 'How did you know Athair would be holed up here? If he spotted you sneaking around…'

His mouth flattened. 'I followed him here from the Assigney mansion yesterday. This is Culcreuch Castle. It's not far from Pemberville, but I've never been here before – I thought it had been abandoned in the sixties. Apparently I was wrong.'

Oh. I looked again at the imposing building and wondered if Athair was still hiding there thirty years from now. Had he been this close to Pemberville Castle – and me – all this time?

'I waited until Athair left today,' Hugo said, 'then I thought I'd snoop around to see if I could find anything useful. He wasn't away for long, so I couldn't do much. I'm assuming you did the same and followed him from the Assigney mansion?'

'I've not been to see Lady Rose yet.' I eyed him. 'I followed Athair here from Pemberville Castle.'

Hugo stiffened. 'You were at Pemberville?' He pulled back. 'And Athair was there? With my parents?' He scanned my face.

'And you,' Hester chirped cheerfully. 'You're a cute toddler, Hugo.'

He stared first at her and then at me.

'She's not lying.' I tried to smile. 'Athair has told your parents that he's Lady Rose's doctor. He wants them to persuade her to leave her house and take some air.'

A muscle throbbed in Hugo's jaw. 'If he tries to hurt them...'

'I don't think he will. He seemed more concerned about using them to get to Rose.' I gazed at him questioningly. 'You've not been to see your parents? You're not curious to meet them and find out what they were like when they were younger?'

A growl rumbled in his chest. 'Desperately so, but I can't risk it. Even if my father didn't recognise me, Mum would spot me in a heartbeat.'

I was surprised. 'Are you sure she'd recognise you? I could see the resemblance between you, but I know the truth. She wouldn't have a clue.'

'She might not understand it, but she'd know it was me.

Mothers are like that.' He shook his head. 'It would become far too messy, no matter how much I'd like to see them.'

I squeezed his hand. 'What about Lady Rose?' I asked. 'Have you spoken to her?'

'No. She won't answer her door, not to me, not to anyone. And the Assigney mansion is heavily warded against intruders.'

'That must be why Athair wants your parents to encourage Lady Rose to go for a walk – he can't get past her ward.' I hesitated. 'But why does he want to get to her? Why go to all that effort?'

'I honestly have no idea.'

'It doesn't make any sense,' I whispered.

Otis and Hester exchanged glances. 'Well,' Otis said with forced cheeriness, 'not all mysteries can be solved. We're reunited now, so let's get back to 2024 where we belong.'

Hester nodded vigorously. 'I want Google. And cat videos. And avo on toast. Get out the skull so we can go home.'

Hugo frowned. 'I don't have the skull. It's in 2024 with Gordon.'

She stared at him. 'You mean,' she said, her voice rising, 'we're *still* trapped here?'

I hushed her. We were some distance from Culcreuch Castle but Athair still might hear her. 'It'll still be under the Fonaby Stone,' I told her. 'We can get it once we're done here.'

'We don't have to retrieve it, Daisy,' Hugo said. 'The skull's magic will only last for so long. Gordon told me we'll probably stay in this time period for several days, but not for weeks. He couldn't give me an exact time frame but sooner or later we'll be pulled back, whether we want to leave or not. We don't belong here. Natural order will force us to return to our own time.'

Otis somersaulted in mid-air. 'Thank goodness!'

I wasn't so happy. 'So we have limited time to help Lady Rose.'

'Yes,' Hugo said. 'But we *will* help her.'

We exchanged brief smiles then I thought of something else. 'If my time here is limited and I'll soon be pulled forward to 2024, you didn't have to travel here, Hugo. You could have waited until I returned. You didn't need to save me.' I looked at Hester and Otis. 'You didn't need to save any of us.'

He gave me a long look and dropped his voice. 'That's where you're wrong, Daisy. Whether you need me or not, I'll always come and save you. No matter what.'

My mouth went dry; so he *had* heard me when I'd whispered after him after our encounter with Baudi. For a long moment we gazed at each other until Hugo cracked a mischievous grin. 'And I think now you'll find that I'm definitely in the lead. I've rescued you more times than you rescued me.'

I thumped him on the arm. 'Piss off.'

He planted a swift, hard kiss on my mouth. Almost immediately, I lost the tight grip I'd been maintaining on my magic and the ground beneath my feet rumbled. I hissed with irritation and stepped back, fumbling for a spider's silk pill. 'Come on,' I said. 'We need to get away from here before Athair realises I've just set off a mini magical earthquake near his house.'

Hugo grinned. 'As my lady commands.'

TWENTY

Hugo clearly hadn't experienced the same financial worries that I had. With some time to prepare before he arrived in 1994, he'd acquired the right sort of cash to see him through and had already used a chunk of it to rent a nippy little car. I left the stolen motorbike hidden behind the bush, made a mental note to return it to Pemberville Castle later, then hopped in next to him.

For reasons I didn't want to articulate, I didn't want to leave his side even for a short journey down the road. I kept glancing at him to reassure myself that he was definitely there. Although he was driving and focused on the road, his hand kept straying to mine and every time our fingers brushed I felt a frisson of happy delight. Yeah: I wasn't falling for Hugo. I'd already fallen. Hard.

I babbled away in a bid to hide my turbulent thoughts, explaining all that happened since I'd landed in 1994. It was satisfying to see Hugo's growing astonishment at everything I'd achieved; sure, I was still a junkie elf with wayward magic and a fiend for a father, but I also had style.

'Do you think that fiend Vargas was telling the truth about

expelling all your magic in one go to achieve control of it?' he asked when we finally turned into the driveway that led to the Assigney mansion.

'I wouldn't trust a fiend in the slightest, but there's no reason to think he was lying. I've never come close to releasing all my magic because I've always been too worried about the consequences. But it could work.'

'It sort of makes sense,' Hugo said slowly. 'It's like turning your computer off and on again, I suppose. But emptying yourself of all your power in one go isn't easy. I did it once when I was a teenager and experimenting.'

'And?'

He pulled a face. 'It took a long time to expel all my magic, I destroyed several acres of good farmland, was grounded for a month afterwards and spent three days sleeping off the effects. If you do this, you'll be incredibly vulnerable afterwards.' He hesitated. 'There's also no telling what effect the spider's silk in your system will have. You might need to go cold turkey before you try.' He cast me a side glance. 'You don't need me to tell you how dangerous that could be.'

He was right. I didn't dare wean myself off spider's silk until I could control my magic, but I couldn't control my magic without spider's silk. Even under the best of circumstances, any withdrawal had to be carefully managed if I wanted to avoid killing myself in the process. It was a question for another time, however; Lady Rose's impending disappearance took precedence.

In contrast to Pemberville Castle, the Assigney homestead looked markedly different now to how it would in the future. I was stunned when I saw the well-kept gardens and the windows sparkling in the sunlight. This was a much-loved home. I had thought that the building was beautiful the first time I'd seen it but that was nothing compared to this.

Hugo noticed my reaction. 'It's quite something, isn't it? I'm so used to seeing it empty and unloved.'

I gazed ahead. Somewhere within those walls, almost within touching distance, Lady Rose was alive and well. A shiver rippled through me; everything about this venture felt unreal.

We were all silent as we approached the front of the house. I scanned the windows for moving shadows, but if Lady Rose was watching us approach I couldn't see her.

Rather than park at the front and advertise our presence, Hugo headed for a narrow dirt road that led to an old barn. He parked the rental car out of sight around the far side and turned off the engine. 'We have to be ready to hide if Athair reappears.'

I nodded grimly. 'He clearly doesn't know who I am. I'd like to keep it that way.'

'There's still no proof he's your father, Daisy.'

I thought of the DNA test I'd taken; the results were thirty years away, but I had a feeling that they would confirm everything that Athair had told me. 'Even if he is, I'm not the important one here.' I pointed at the huge house. 'She is.'

'Then let's see if we can persuade her to talk to us,' Hugo said.

'You could pretend to be a delivery driver again,' Otis piped up from the back.

'Or take a leaf out of Athair's book and be a postman,' Hester suggested.

I shook my head. 'No. Lady Rose needs the truth.'

'That she's about to vanish forever and we're from the future?' Otis screwed up his face. 'I'm not sure that will engage her trust.'

'Maybe not,' I said. 'But I won't lie to her. Whatever is going on here, we need to show her that there are people she can trust.'

'The truth won't work, Daisy!' Hester spluttered. 'It's too bizarre! She'll never trust us if you tell her who we really are.'

I glanced at Hugo but he merely shrugged. 'It's so far-fetched that she might actually believe it.'

I straightened my shoulders and opened the car door. 'There's only one way to find out.'

We marched around the barn, four abreast as if we were cowboys entering Tombstone for a gunfight. The only thing missing was tumbleweed – and guns. Seeming to sense my thoughts, Gladys buzzed briefly and my fingers lightly brushed her hilt for reassurance. 'You're better than any gun,' I murmured. Confused, Hugo squinted at me but I waved him off and pinned my mouth shut.

The only sound was the crunching of both my and Hugo's footsteps on the gravel and the faint hum as the brownies' wings flapped beside us. If Lady Rose was watching us secretly from behind those vast walls, she'd know that we meant business.

The ward that encircled her home wasn't visible to the naked eye but that didn't detract from its strength. Every time I veered close to the building, I felt it thrum and bristle, all but yelling 'keep away'. Despite my anxiety about its reasons for being there, I had to admire its force: this was a magical barrier that any witch would be proud of. No wonder Athair was having to resort to other methods to get to Lady Rose; even he would find it nigh on impossible to get past this ward.

At the main door, I looked at the others. Hester and Otis nodded while Hugo flashed a tight smile of encouragement. I inhaled deeply and walked to the door, ignoring the screech as the ward tried to shoo me away.

I raised my fist and banged loudly on the wooden frame.

Nothing happened. I knocked again; this time I also shouted, 'Hello? Lady Rose Assigney?' No response. 'My name is

Daisy Carter. This,' I waved behind me, 'believe it or not, is Hugo Pemberville. Beside him are two brownies.'

'I'm Hester!'

Otis cleared his throat. 'My name is Otis!'

I raised my voice to its maximum volume. 'We know you're having trouble with a fiend called Athair, but we're here to help you. We are on your side!'

I waited, hoping that Lady Rose would offer some sign that she'd heard me. When there was nothing but silence, I opened my mouth– but as I drew breath to shout again there was a faint creak from above.

I looked up. One of the second-storey windows was opening. Yahtzee. That had been easier than I'd expected. 'Thank you!' I called. 'All I need is for you to hear me out. You see—'

I didn't get the chance to finish my sentence before Hugo muttered a warning. A gust of warm wind rippled towards us from the east; seconds later, that warm breeze transformed into shooting flames that were coming straight towards us.

I yelped, then reacted as quickly as I could. With a surge of defensive magic, I tempered the fire with a burst of cold water conjured up from the damp, humid atmosphere.

As soon as I'd acted, I realised my mistake. The cold water dousing the flames instantly transformed them into scorching hot steam that hurtled towards me. Hugo barrelled into me, knocked me to the ground and covered my body with his. Hester and Otis screamed and also dived. The hot air rushed past, but even with Hugo on top of me I felt the tips of my ears burning. Damn. Lady Rose was far cannier and more capable than I'd expected. The boiling steam could harm us far more than her fire magic.

A high-pitched voice yelled down from the open window, 'Burn in hell, you bastards!'

I swallowed hard.

'I think that counts as me saving you yet again,' Hugo murmured in my ear.

Yeah, yeah.

'Think before you shoot out any more bloody magic, Daisy!' Hester shouted. She had a point. Unfortunately, they both did.

As soon as the steam dissipated, Hugo rolled off me. His skin was flushed but he was otherwise unharmed. He'd been lucky; we'd all been lucky. 'Thanks,' I said, trying not to sound too grudging.

He grinned. 'Time for Plan B?' he asked.

I picked myself up. 'What's Plan B?'

'I was hoping that you knew.'

I grimaced and looked up. I couldn't see Lady Rose but the window was still open. 'We should move away. We're sitting ducks if we stay here.'

'Back to the barn to regroup?' Hugo asked.

Hester pushed back her hair with an irritated hiss. 'Anything's better than staying here. That stupid elf in there is crazy.'

Otis glared at his sister. 'She's defending herself.'

'From the time-travelling heroes who are here to save her,' Hester snorted. 'This won't work if she doesn't want to be saved – and anyway, we probably can't alter history. Let her get killed. We can watch what happens from a safe distance and report to Gordon when we finally get home.'

I wasn't giving up. 'Let's try the back of the house first,' I suggested. I put my hand in my pocket and fingered my stash of spider's silk. I could always swallow several pills in one go and put my addiction to good use; I'd done that once before when I'd needed to break through a ward. 'There might be some weak points in the ward around the rear.'

Hester pouted, but Hugo nodded. Otis didn't look enthusiastic, but he didn't fly away at top speed in a desperate bid to escape.

We headed around the house, taking considerably more care this time. I racked my brains. There had to be a way to make Lady Rose understand that we weren't a threat but nothing was springing to my mind. Not yet. I grimaced and set my jaw in a tight line. I would find a way to convince her. There was no other choice.

It didn't take long to reach the back door. I knew it led to the kitchen, and I knew both what and who was inside. But I also knew that the air-magic trick I'd pulled in the future wouldn't work here.

I turned to Hugo. 'Can you tell what sort of ward it is? I can't see anything so I'm assuming it's not a typical salt ward.'

'I didn't get much chance to investigate it before Athair showed up,' he said. 'I'm not sure what sort of magic is powering it. And we don't want to break it if it's keeping Rose safe from him.'

I met his eyes. 'She's not safe, though,' I said quietly. 'We already know she's in danger. She will disappear in five days' time, Hugo.'

I squared my shoulders and walked closer to the back door with the invisible barrier pushing against me all the time, then I crouched down to examine the ground. There had to be something here that would give us a clue about what magic Rose had employed. If we could find a way to get past it and speak to her face to face, I was sure I could persuade her of the truth.

Hugo sighed heavily. He started to move forward to join me, but he'd barely taken three steps when he cried out in pain.

I spun around, alarm flashing through my bones. Hester and Otis zipped towards him and a split second later, they both cried out too. Shit, shit, shit. I ran to them. Hugo was one knee, sweat beads forming on his tanned face. Both brownies were groaning loudly.

'What?' I asked anxiously. 'What happened?' I glanced upwards to see if Lady Rose had thrown any more magic at us but the windows on this side of the house were firmly closed.

I darted back, crouched down and gazed at the three of them.

'Uhhhhhh...' Otis rubbed his forehead. 'I feel like I've been hit by a bus.'

'A bus that's on fire, is carrying twenty fat elephants and has spiked wheels,' Hester said. Her skin was pale and, despite the obvious exaggeration, she wasn't well.

Hugo sucked in several sharp gasps of breath before pulling himself upright and staggering away from the house. I hastily scooped up both brownies and joined him. 'So much for a weaker ward,' he said, wiping his brow. 'It's stronger here than at the front.' He sent me a long, worried look.

'What?' I asked.

His expression grew darker and he dropped his gaze.

I stared at him. 'What, Hugo? What is it?'

'That barrier has nothing to do with elvish magic. Neither is it normal witchery.'

I tilted my head, confused. 'Okay.'

'In fact,' Hugo continued, lifting his head to shoot a malevolent glance at the Assigney building, 'there's only one sort of magic that's strong enough to create a ward that has that kind of effect.'

A sudden nervous spasm churned in the pit of my belly. 'And what sort of magic is that?' I asked quietly.

He grimaced. 'Blood magic.'

I stared at him. He stared back at me. 'Using blood magic is the first step to becoming a fiend,' I whispered.

'Yes.'

'Are you saying that you think Lady Rose is using blood magic?' I asked.

'She might have hired someone to create the ward for her,' he said, though he sounded dubious. 'But the most likely scenario is that she magicked it up herself.'

A dozen possibilities rushed through my head. What if Lady Rose wasn't a victim at all? What if she was a villain? I swallowed hard, then I realised that Hester was slowly backing away from me, her wings fluttering quickly in the air. Otis looked genuinely terrified. I clocked Hugo's tight, worried expression again.

'Hang on a minute,' I said.

'It didn't seem to affect you, Daisy. The blood-magic ward didn't hurt you in the way it hurt us.'

'Because I've got fiendish blood,' I whispered. 'Because Athair is my father, I'm half fiend and a mere footstep away from becoming an abhorrent evil creature that cares only for power.' Oh God, *I* was the villain here; I was a vile creature who craved blood and death and horror and...

I gulped in air. As my twisting, terror-driven thoughts coalesced, my hands stopped twitching. 'Wait,' I said slowly. 'That doesn't make any sense. Lady Rose created the ward because Athair is after her. We don't know why he wants her, but the visit he paid to your parents and the request he made prove that he wants her out of that house and away from the ward. It's not my heritage that's making me less susceptible – it can't be. It must be something else.'

I still didn't know what made me react differently, but logic dictated that my alleged birth father had nothing to do with it.

Otis relaxed visibly. 'You're not fiendish, Daisy.' He managed a tiny smile. 'You're certainly not evil.'

Hester was no longer trying to put as much distance between us, but she still looked wary. 'I'm not so sure. Anyone wearing that particular combo,' she waved at my charity-shop ensemble, 'has to be *slightly* evil.'

I threw her a half-irritated, half-amused look. Another thought occurred to me. 'It's the spider's silk. It has to be. Something about all those drugs in my system means I'm less affected by that ward than you are.'

Hugo frowned. 'That doesn't make sense.'

'It's the only material difference between us.' I looked at the house. 'I can feel the ward – I know it's there, pushing against me – but if it's not affecting me in the same way that it's affecting you. I think I can move past it.' Optimism rushed through me. 'I can get inside and speak to Lady Rose.'

Hugo was already shaking his head. 'We already know she's dangerous from the way she attacked us, Daisy. If she's using blood magic, you're putting yourself at risk.'

I winked at him. 'Nothing new about that.' Before I lost my nerve, I spun round and ran straight for the back door, determined to force my way in.

TWENTY-ONE

I was three feet away from the door when the repelling force of the ward pushed against me. I was forced to slow down until I was moving so slowly that it felt like I was swimming through sludgy treacle. It was beyond hard, but despite the massive effort it required there wasn't any pain. That realisation spurred me on.

I clenched my jaw and gave it everything I had, even though my energy was being sapped and sweat was dripping down my face. I would do it; I would get past the ward. I held my breath and, with one final heave, slammed my body through. One second I was pushing with all my strength, and the next I was hitting the wooden door with a thud.

I exhaled all the air in my lungs in one relieved whoosh, then spun around and grinned triumphantly at Hugo, Hester and Otis. They were staring at me, wide-eyed. 'See?' I stretched my arms. 'Easy-peasy! You guys wait here and I—'

I didn't get chance to finish my sentence. Behind me, there was a faint creak as the door opened and I turned my head just in time to see a hand lashing out towards me. Fingers latched around my forearm with a vice-like grip, I was yanked into the house – and the door was slammed shut after me.

Before I could say or do anything, a heavy wave of air magic pinned me against the now-closed door. The face of a young woman with wild eyes swam in front of me. 'Who the *fuck* are you? And how did you get past my ward?'

I tried to speak, but the air magic made it impossible for me to form any coherent syllables. It didn't help that my eyes were streaming with tears, which made the woman's face blurry; even so, there was no doubt about her anger and her fear.

I reached inside myself, searching for my own power and a way to use it without harming her. The best I could do was to conjure up a bucketful of water and send it blindly forward. A second later, when I heard a splash and her sharp cry, I knew I'd hit my target.

The air magic vanished and I dropped with a thud to the kitchen flagstones. I could hear Hugo yelling my name on the other side of the door. I raised my fist and thumped three times on it before shouting as loudly as I could, 'I'm fine! Don't worry!'

The woman gave an unladylike snort. 'You're *not* fine and you *should* worry!'

I heaved myself upright, wiped the tears from my eyes and blinked rapidly until my vision was restored. I was certain this was Lady Rose, although her red hair was messy and her features, which had been glowing in the painting, were grubby and tear stained. Somehow that made her look younger. Her clothes were far from what I expected from an elf in her position: she was wearing a shapeless gown that hung like a sack.

I gazed at her face and felt an odd twinge inside me. Huh. 'You don't look much like your portrait,' I blurted without thinking.

It was clearly the wrong thing to say. Lady Rose's scowl

deepened into a vicious snarl. She picked up an object from the kitchen island and pointed it threateningly at me.

I stared at the shotgun in her hands; I had the distinct impression that she would be more than happy to shoot me in the head and worry about the consequences later. I resisted the temptation to reach for Gladys; I needed to de-escalate this situation, not make it worse.

I raised my palms. 'Please,' I said. 'I need you to listen to me. My name is Daisy—'

Lady Rose flinched. That wasn't a good start. I tried again. 'My name is Daisy and I have been magically transported here from the year 2024.' I tucked my hair behind my ears. 'Strange as it might sound, I'm from the future. As you can see, I'm an elf.' I gestured to my eyes. 'If you look at my irises, they have a ring of silver around them because I'm a spider's silk user. I think the drugs in my system helped me to get past your ward.'

Lady Rose didn't say anything; neither did she lower the shotgun or alter her expression.

'I've seen your portrait,' I said, 'because in thirty years' time, I will break into this house to look around. I do that because in a few days you are going to disappear and you will never be seen again.'

The shotgun jerked slightly. 'Don't threaten me,' Lady Rose whispered. Her bottom lip trembled; I really wasn't sure whether she was about to shoot me or dissolve into a puddle of tears.

'I'm not threatening you, I promise I'm not. I know it sounds far-fetched but it's the truth. I don't know what happens, or why you vanish – nobody does. But I've been here in 1994 for a few days and I know that the fiend called Athair is after you.' I drew in a breath. 'My companion out there worked out that your ward is blood magic. If you're using that kind of power, that might be why—'

'I'm using blood magic because I'm desperate,' she snapped. 'Not that it's any business of someone who decides to break into my home.' She glanced out of the kitchen window. 'When you were outside, you said that Hugo Pemberville was with you. Hugo Pemberville is two years old and an annoying brat.'

'The version outside has time travelled from the future, too.' I hesitated. 'But sometimes he's still an annoying brat.' I tried – failed – to sound light-hearted.

Lady Rose looked me up and down and I felt like an insect under a microscope. She examined me for several long seconds and her expression tightened still more.

'I know what you're going to say next,' I said.

She raised an eyebrow. 'Oh, really?'

'You'll ask me to prove that I'm from the future. There are some world events that will happen soon that I can describe to you.' Probably: I was a bit hazy on some of the dates. 'The trouble is that you might have to wait a few months – uh – years before those events happen. However, I have a phone in my pocket which is from 2024. That should help my case.'

Careful not to make any sudden movements, I reached for it and held it up for Lady Rose to see. There was no signal and certainly no internet access, but I hadn't touched it for a while so it still had some charge. I hoped she would see enough on the screen to believe me.

Unfortunately, she didn't even look at it. 'That's not what I was about to say.' A tear trickled down her cheek, but she didn't remove her hands from the shotgun to brush it away. 'I was going to say that you can trot back to that bastard and tell him that this will not work. Even if you are not a trick, I will not be swayed. Get the fuck out of my house and don't ever return.'

Confusion overtook me. 'Lady Rose—'

She lifted the gun and squeezed the trigger. I ducked instinctively, although that wouldn't have helped if she'd really been aiming at me. The sudden loud crack was followed by a cloud of dust and plaster; she'd shot the wall above the kitchen door.

Hugo, Hester and Otis started yelling from outside again as I turned my head to see the hole the shotgun shell had created. It was exactly the same as the one I would notice when I broke in in thirty years' time.

'Get the fuck out,' Lady Rose said to me, more in sadness than in anger.

I stared at her, then I did exactly as she asked.

THE ONLY ONE of us who seemed happy was Hester. 'She didn't shoot you in the head,' she said. 'I'd take that as a win.'

Hugo's arms were crossed tightly over his chest; he was still annoyed that I'd gone into the house on my own, even though he knew I'd had to try. 'She admitted using blood magic?' he asked.

I nodded.

'Daisy, that's not good.'

'I know,' I said quietly. 'She's so young, Hugo. She looks desperate.'

'She was nineteen years old when she vanished,' he said. 'But youth is no excuse. She's a high elf – she has to know the risks. She has to know what blood magic will lead to.'

I sighed as I thought about everything she'd said. Who was the bastard she'd told me to trot back to? She could only mean Hugo – or Athair. 'She was really upset. There's a lot more going on here than we understand.'

Otis flicked his eyes nervously between us. 'Is Lady Rose a bad guy?' he asked in a small voice.

'No,' I said instantly.

'Maybe,' Hugo muttered.

Otis's wings flapped harder, indicating his growing anxiety. 'What do we do now?'

Hester gave him an irritated look. 'Duh. She won't accept our help and there's been nothing so far that suggests we can change what happens in the past. We get some decent snacks, you lot camp out for a couple of days and watch what happens so you can tell Gordon. Then we go home to 2024 and everyone is happy.' She paused. 'Apart from Lady Rose. But we can only do so much.'

'You won't camp out, too, Hes?' Otis asked.

She pointed to Hugo. 'He's got money. He can book me into the nearest five-star hotel where I will wait until the answers are revealed.' She smiled toothily at her brother. 'You can stay with me, if you like.'

'Hester,' Otis said, 'you—'

Hugo interrupted him. 'Shh. Listen. Someone's coming.'

We all froze as we heard a car approaching from the other side of the vast house. I looked at Hugo. Lines of strain were visible across his face; there was a good chance that the car belonged to his parents. We knew that they were supposedly the last people to see Lady Rose alive before her disappearance – and just this morning Athair had asked them to visit her.

I nodded towards the far side of the house. 'If we go that way, we can see who's out there without them seeing us.'

Hugo hesitated, clearly desperate to glimpse his parents, but there was also fear in his eyes. There was still a flicker of doubt deep inside Hugo that his mum and dad had been involved in Lady Rose's disappearance.

'You can stay here,' I whispered. 'I can go alone.'

He shook his head, as if speaking aloud were suddenly too dangerous. I reached for his hand and squeezed it hard. He squeezed back and mouthed *thank you*. Holding hands, we jogged around the house until we could see what was happening.

There might no longer be any staff at the house, but whoever used to take care of landscaping here had done a sterling job. I was particularly impressed with the massive potted shrub placed handily at the corner of the mansion; it was the perfect size to hide behind and it was angled so that Hugo and I had a clear line of vision to the front door.

I took a quick peek to confirm that it was indeed Lord and Lady Pemberville who had arrived. Hugo was holding his breath, bristling with tension. Most of the time, he brimmed with arrogant confidence – but when it came to family, it was a different story.

We were all bound to family, whether by blood or by other means. Even as adults, it could be hard to accept the idea of your parents as individuals in their own right and not loving superheroes who could do no wrong. Athair's face flashed into my head and my stomach tightened; nobody wanted their mum and dad to be evil.

I stepped aside to give Hugo the best view. I didn't say anything; I didn't need to. He knew I was there for him, no matter what.

Lord and Lady Pemberville looked at each other then walked up to Lady Rose's front door. 'She still has that damned ward in place,' Lord Pemberville muttered. 'She's utterly paranoid.'

'She's a young woman living on her own, Charles,' Lady Pemberville said gently.

'If she hadn't fired all her staff months ago, she wouldn't *be* alone.'

'I'm sure she's got her reasons.' She raised her hand and knocked hard. 'Maybe you should let me do the talking.'

That was a good idea; Hugo's mum clearly had a lot more empathy for Lady Rose than his dad.

I expected that Lady Rose would treat them in the same way as she'd treated everyone else: either ignore them or throw magic to drive them away as quickly as possible. Several long seconds passed, then Lady Pemberville knocked again. I was almost certain that Rose wouldn't respond when Hugo's mum called out loudly, 'Rose? It's Charles and Tash. Please open up. We only want to chat.'

Several more seconds passed then, to my surprise, the front door opened.

We couldn't see Lady Rose from our hiding spot. She obviously wasn't planning to go beyond the house walls because that would mean stepping across the magical blood ward.

She must have known that we were still there because when she spoke, it was obvious that she wasn't only addressing Hugo's parents. 'I don't want anybody here,' she said. 'You must all leave immediately. This is my land and you don't belong, no matter who you are pretending to be.'

Hugo's dad was obviously astonished. 'We're not pretending be anyone.'

His wife's voice was softer. 'You know us, Rose. You know who we are.'

'Where's the boy?' she snapped.

'You mean Hugo? He's at home. It's time for his afternoon nap.'

Lady Rose snorted. 'Because he's a toddler?'

'Well, yes.'

Lord Pemberville was staring at her with an expression that I knew well; it was the same expression Hugo displayed when he was talking to Duchess and his frustration was getting the better of him. 'You don't look very well, Rose. Why don't you come out for some fresh air?'

'You'd like that a lot, wouldn't you?' Her voice dripped with sarcasm. 'You'd love it if I left my house right now.' She spoke more loudly. 'I'm not going anywhere! You hear me? I'm staying right here and there's nothing you can do about it! Get into your time machine and fuck off!'

'Time machine?' Lord Pemberville shook his head. 'What's wrong with you?'

My mouth was dry; all this felt like my fault. If I hadn't forced my way inside and spoken to Rose, she wouldn't be so frightened; she certainly wouldn't be babbling about time machines and giving the distinct impression that she was crazy.

'Oh Rose.' Hugo's mum sighed unhappily. 'Why don't we call your doctor and get him to pop by again?'

Lady Rose roared and followed up with a blast of fire magic that she directed at the couple's feet. 'Fuck *off!*' she screamed. 'Fuck off! All of you!'

Lord Pemberville was already hauling his wife towards the car. 'We'll do that,' he said. 'But you need help, Rose. You know you do.'

'Get out of here and don't ever come back!' she shouted. 'Leave!'

Lady Pemberville wasn't giving up. She pulled away from her husband and spread out her hands in an entreaty. 'You know our phone number. If you need anything, or if you want to talk, all you have to do is call. We're only around the corner. We can help.'

'Nobody can help me!'

'Rose—'

There was another rush of magic. She invoked air this time, sending a surge that was strong enough to lift the Pembervilles' car a foot into the air. 'Leave,' she said, 'before I do something I might regret.'

The car slammed down to the ground and Hugo's parents

jumped aside to avoid being crushed by it. Lady Pemberville stared at Rose with a mixture of fear and concern. Her husband glared and muttered something, then they climbed into the vehicle. The engine spluttered into life, the wheels skidded on the gravel and, with a high-pitched squeal, the car left with the white-faced couple inside it.

As they were driving away, Rose raised her voice again. 'The rest of you need to fuck off, too!' She heaved the door shut and silence reigned again.

'Well,' Hester whispered, 'your mum and dad didn't help her, but they didn't kill her.'

A muscle ticked in Hugo's jaw; there was relief in his eyes but something else was flickering there too. 'They should have done more. She's obviously on the edge – she needs help.'

I thought of my spider's silk addiction: it was incredibly hard to help people who didn't want to be helped. 'We'll find a way to help her.'

He stared at me balefully. 'How exactly will we do that?'

As I sighed and pushed back my hair, I registered the clammy sweat on my forehead. I didn't have a clue. 'Er...'

Otis shot up into the air. 'Somebody else is coming.'

I turned towards the driveway. He was right; yet another vehicle was trundling towards the mansion. For a recluse, Lady Rose certainly received a lot of visitors.

Hester wrung her hands. 'It could be Athair.'

Hugo shook his head. 'That's not his car.'

We stayed where we were and watched a flashy Porsche head smoothly into the space Hugo's parents had just vacated. The windows were tinted so it was impossible to see who was inside.

I licked my lips – and that was when my skin started to itch.

TWENTY-TWO

I knew who it was long before he stepped out of the expensive car. Baltar hadn't used his powers to disguise his body, even though he was more than capable of doing so. That was probably why he was driving a vehicle with tinted windows: anyone seeing a golden-skinned creature with long black hair driving a Porsche would remember him. They might call the police and cause all sorts of problems.

Hugo sucked in a sharp breath and the brownies' eyes were as wide as saucers. In thirty years' time I would encounter Baltar on two separate occasions – and the second time I would kill him.

'Athair is not the only fiendish bastard who wants Lady Rose,' I muttered. But we still didn't know why. Surely it couldn't be because she was using blood magic? Were the fiends truly *that* desperate to recruit her?

Baltar tossed back his hair and gazed at the mansion, a snide smile playing around his thin golden lips. Instead of approaching the building, he walked to the passenger side of the car, opened the door, reached inside and hauled someone out. Whoever it was, it wasn't a fiend.

'Who is that?' Otis whispered.

I shrugged to indicate I had no idea.

'Sorcerer,' Hugo hissed. He was right; Baltar's companion had the lean, gangly look of their kind.

'He looks a bit like Gordon,' Hester said. I was about to disagree when I realised she was right. Although this man's swarthy features were totally dissimilar, his expression mirrored the one I'd frequently seen on Gordon's face.

'He's scared,' I breathed. 'That sorcerer isn't here by choice.' I felt sick to my stomach; there could only be one reason why Baltar had dragged him here.

The fiend gave his companion a gentle look – then back-handed him across the face with such force that the crack echoed. I clamped a hand over my mouth to stifle my cry, than I started to move to confront Baltar.

Hugo reached for me in warning. 'Wait,' he said. 'We need to see what happens. We need to know what's going on, Daisy.'

He was right. Despite my frustration, I nodded and turned back .

Baltar shoved the sorcerer towards the wall of the mansion and forced him to crouch down and examine the blood ward. After a few moments, the sorcerer nodded.

The fiend's answering grin was coldly gleeful. He spread his arms wide and addressed the silent façade in a loud voice. 'Lady Rose Assigney! My name is Baltar! You know what I am, and you know what I am here for!'

I didn't know what he was there for; it would be helpful if he spelled it out so we could all understand.

There was no answer. Gladys, however, buzzed impatiently by my side. She recognised Baltar – of course she did; it was her blade that would kill him in the future.

'You must know that you cannot win against Athair,' Baltar

continued. 'You will have to yield sooner or later. I can smooth the path for you, bring all this to an end.'

I suddenly realised what Baltar was up to: he was hoping to ingratiate himself with Athair by helping him achieve his objective. Fiends were supposed to work alone, but in my experience in the future they didn't. Perhaps this was the turning point when their methods changed.

'Drop your ward and open the door,' Baltar bellowed, 'and I will allow you to walk away unharmed. If you don't let me in, I will break down your defences – and you will not enjoy the consequences.' He ran his tongue across his lips. 'Personally, I'm hoping for that – I enjoy tasting elvish blood.'

I shuddered.

The sorcerer, still kneeling, was etching a series of runes on the ground next to his feet. I reached to my left and grazed the wall of the mansion with my fingertips; it was growing hot. Very hot. Whatever that damned sorcerer was doing to Lady Rose's defensive ward was working.

'We have to act, Hugo. We can't just watch,' I pleaded.

His expression was grim, but he didn't disagree. 'You killed that bastard once,' he said. 'If we fight together, you can do it again.'

'And if you kill him,' Hester whispered, 'you'll also prove that the past can be changed. You can alter history.'

I had my doubts about that but I smiled anyway. 'History was never my favourite subject at school,' I murmured.

A flicker of amusement flashed across Hugo's face. 'What kind of treasure hunter are you?'

I looked at Baltar, who was crooking his finger towards the house as if he could coax Lady Rose out by dint of his crappy personality. 'The kind who wins.' Then I withdrew Gladys from her sheath, threw my head back and roared at the top of my lungs.

Baltar froze as Hugo and I emerged from behind the shrub; he obviously hadn't been expecting company. With surprise on our side, we fired off two powerful blasts of magic before the fiend could react. I directed a wave of earth magic at the space around his feet, opening up a wide trench between us that would buy us space to continue attacking from a safe distance.

Hugo ignored Baltar and focused on the sorcerer, who was arguably the more dangerous of the two where Lady Rose was concerned. He shot a ferocious surge of air magic at the nervous man, yanking him upwards several feet and stopping his attempts to break the ward. The sorcerer squeaked as his arms and legs flailed uselessly in mid-air.

Baltar recovered quickly and his smooth, golden face twisted into a snarl. 'Who the fuck are you?' he spat.

I didn't waste my breath answering him; he'd find out soon enough. Instead, palms tingling as I stretched my magic, I used the same trick Lady Rose had employed against us and sent several scorching fireballs in his direction. Fire didn't really harm fiends but the force of the fireballs certainly could. It was a testament to my training with Hugo's Primes that I no longer required kindling to create a blaze; these days, all I needed was oxygen.

As I had done earlier, Baltar flipped out a stream of water to extinguish the fire. Three seconds later he was howling as scalding steam enveloped his body. 'Impressive,' Hugo said.

I grinned. 'I'm a fast learner.' I nodded at the hovering sorcerer. 'Can you deal with him while I take care of Baltar?' Unlike Hugo, I could kill the fiend. My cursed heritage had to be good for something.

He nodded and darted around the steam cloud to the sorcerer. At the same time, Baltar strode towards me, flicking his wrist to shoot out earth magic and repair the trench I'd created. His face was contorted with anger; it was surprisingly satisfying to see his fury escalate so quickly.

'Go Daisy!' Otis shouted from several metres away.

'Kill that fiend!' Hester screeched.

Baltar's eyes narrowed. 'Your name is Daisy? So that makes you – what? Bosom buddies with Lady Rose?'

I ignored my flash of confusion; there would be time to puzzle over his words later. I licked my lips, tilted my head and tossed out a burst of water magic. A perfect sphere of icy water smacked into his cheekbone. It would do little more than sting, but I wasn't trying to hurt him. I threw out another burst and sent a cricket-ball sized sphere towards his stomach.

'What the fuck are you doing?' he asked.

Making you angry, I answered silently. I launched another watery ball at his groin and smiled when I hit my target. Slim would be very proud of my precision.

Baltar scowled. 'You stupid woman,' he muttered. 'You can't seriously think that will hurt me?'

I ignored him and aimed two balls of water at his eyes, temporarily blinding him. He growled and answered with a jet of fire, but his aim was off and I scarcely needed to sidestep to avoid its searing heat.

I glanced over his shoulder to check on Hugo, who was visible now that the steam cloud had dissipated. He had brought the quaking sorcerer down and was preparing to haul him away from the battleground. Baltar appeared oblivious. Good: my distraction technique was working.

Gladys buzzed repeatedly, her hilt warm in my hand, but Baltar was still several metres away from me. I needed him to drop his guard further and come in closer before I swung her blade towards his heart.

I smirked at him. 'You missed,' I said. I sent him a ripple of earth magic that made the ground rumble and shake. Baltar kept his footing – but only just.

His glistening golden cheeks had turned scarlet with embarrassment or anger; it didn't particularly matter which. He snarled again and took three more steps towards me. Only a few more and I'd have him.

I had a far greater chance of success if he came to me rather than the other way around, so I stepped back, hoping that he'd think I was trying to put more space between us.

He laughed coldly. 'I may have missed but you can't harm me.' He thumped his chest. 'I am a fiend! As a mere elf, you cannot do anything that will affect me.' His red eyes glittered. 'In minutes you will be dead.' He raised his long index finger and a bolt of lightning zapped towards me.

This time he didn't miss.

The lightning slammed into my shoulder. The pain was excruciating, reverberating through my body in snaking, agonising threads. I staggered backwards, barely managing to keep hold of Gladys as my knees gave way, and I fell. Tiny lights danced in front of my eyes and nausea rose in my throat.

I swallowed hard and ignored the faint smell of my burning flesh. My tinnitus made an unwelcome return, buzzing in a way that made me want to screech with irritation, but I did my best to ignore it. I looked up and caught a glimpse of Lady Rose's pale face at one of the windows. I wanted to shout out to her that this was part of my masterplan and that I knew what I was doing, but I couldn't make a sound.

I reached inside myself for the strength I knew I had. I was Daisy fucking Carter and I was strong – I was certainly far stronger than Baltar realised. His lightning attack had knocked me for six but I was recovering quickly. It helped that Hester and Otis were screeching support from a corner of the mansion; every fighter should have a cheerleading squad.

I stayed down, hoping to goad Baltar into coming closer for his kill shot. To encourage him, I flicked out more water magic but made sure it splashed weakly into the ground in front of me. 'I'm not dead yet, you fucker,' I whispered.

I knew from the look in his red eyes that he'd heard me. He took one step in my direction and I tensed, praying he would come close enough for me to thrust Gladys into him. Then he paused and looked over his shoulder.

Oh no.

Hugo and the terrified sorcerer hadn't got as far as I'd hoped. The sorcerer had kept collapsing, and when Hugo tried to haul him up in a fireman's lift he'd resisted for several long moments.

Baltar stared after the departing pair then muttered under his breath. A second later, he threw a blast of air magic at them, expertly curving it around so that it whacked Hugo and his clumsy cargo from the front. Even though I was lying some distance away, I felt the force of Baltar's magic.

Hugo didn't stand a chance.

Hester and Otis screamed as he and the sorcerer were thrown backwards. I sensed Hugo conjuring up magic to counter the attack and I did the same in a vain bid to help him, but my effort was weak and Hugo's attempt was too late. He was thrown against the wall of the Assigney mansion with a sickening crunch while the sorcerer's thin body jerked to a halt in mid-air. Hugo crumpled in a heap while the sorcerer stayed suspended. Fuck, Baltar's magic control was impressive. Far too impressive.

I dragged my eyes away from Hugo's body as the fiend stalked towards the sorcerer. 'Hey!' I called weakly. 'I'm not done with you yet!'

'I'll be back for you shortly,' Baltar grunted. 'Don't you worry.'

The surge of anger I felt at my ploy so nearly coming to fruition helped me force myself upright, but by the time I was on my feet again Baltar had reached the sorcerer. 'Is it done?' he spat.

'N – n – no – no.' The sorcerer blanched. 'Nearly.'

Baltar yanked him down to the ground. 'Then finish it,' he snarled.

The sorcerer's head dropped. He trudged towards the mansion and the blood ward he was attempting to destroy.

Hugo stirred and my breath caught in my throat. My earlier strategy hadn't worked. I stopped thinking rationally and clutched Gladys harder. The only option left was to attack Baltar head on.

Before I could move, the front door swung open. Suddenly Lady Rose was on the doorstep. Her face was still as pale as death but she'd scrubbed away the tearstains and dirty marks, and when she spoke her voice was clear and steady.

'You want me?' she asked. 'I'm right here.' And she stepped across her own ward and walked right up to Baltar.

TWENTY-THREE

M y mouth dropped open and I stared. Hugo, still on the ground but clearly conscious, also raised his head. The sorcerer stopped in mid-rune, while Hester and Otis were astonished enough to fly out from their hiding place and join me.

'What the fuck is she doing?' Hester grabbed hold of my earlobe and tugged it hard. 'Stop her!'

I cleared my throat. 'Rose!' My voice wasn't loud but I knew she had heard me. 'Lady Rose! Get inside!'

Baltar didn't look at me as he flicked out a surge of earth magic that was more than enough to send me flying down to the ground once more. The thud sent a jarring bolt of agony through my bones and finally forced Gladys from my hand. The strength of my fall also meant that the brownies were jolted backwards through the air.

While I fought against the pain, Baltar yelled at the sorcerer. 'Why have you stopped? Get back to work and break that fucking ward!'

I caught a glimpse of the sorcerer gulping hard and turning

to his work again. Lady Rose didn't look at him; her attention was wholly on Baltar.

'You wanted me,' she said. 'So I'm here.'

'I don't want *you*,' Baltar replied. 'You know that.' He raised a hand to strike her.

I surged forward on my hands and knees but Lady Rose was already ahead of me. 'Go on then,' she said. 'Hit me. Let's see how Athair will react when he finds out you hurt me.'

'He doesn't care about you,' Baltar laughed.

Lady Rose raised an eyebrow. 'Why don't you smack me around and we can test that theory?'

Despite the gravity of the situation and my confusion about what was really going on, I was impressed by her attitude. Lady Rose was, without a doubt, utterly terrified but she was standing up to Baltar. In fact, she was looking damned heroic.

An old quote drifted into my head: *Courage is not the absence of fear but the triumph over it.* Lady Rose certainly looked triumphant – apart from the fact that she was confronting a fiend and quite possibly was about to be struck down dead for her efforts.

I looked again at Baltar. To my astonishment, he lowered his hand. 'Very well,' he snarled. He pointed at the open front door. 'But this isn't over until you give me what I came for.'

Lady Rose turned her head towards me, and a strange smile of pure sadness lifted the corners of her mouth. Then she returned her attention to Baltar. 'Take me to Athair first. I want to negotiate with him before this is over.'

'Negotiate?' Baltar threw his head back and laughed. 'You don't negotiate with a fiend. You certainly don't negotiate with Athair!'

Her expression didn't alter. 'If that's true,' she said calmly, 'then why are you here? You're looking to bargain with Athair. So am I.'

She was trying to draw Baltar away. If they left together and I stayed here, I'd be able to get inside the mansion and find whatever it was the fiends were after. But I didn't understand: what was so important that she'd sacrifice her life to protect it?

A fleeting thought flashed into my head but I pushed it away at haste. *No. Not that. It couldn't be that.*

Otis hissed from behind me. 'Daisy, do you think that—?'

'Shut up, Otis!' Hester interrupted him. 'This isn't the time!'

Baltar's mouth pursed, as if were considering Lady Rose's proposal. Whether he'd have taken the bait or not, however, we'd never know because that was the moment that the sorcerer gave a croak of strained delight and stood up. 'I've got it,' he said. 'I've broken it!'

My stomach dropped with sickening velocity. Lady Rose stepped back, her hand rising to her mouth as a beaming grin of triumph spread across Baltar's face.

I looked at the vast mansion. It appeared to be turning blood red. Its walls looked as if they were pulsating and there was a nasty smell of burning. Then the air was filled by a long continuous chiming sound, and I knew the sorcerer was telling the truth.

'I've done what you asked!' the thin man shouted, his success making him bold. 'You promised you would leave my family alone if I did what you wanted!'

Baltar looked from the building to the sorcerer. 'I never keep my promises. Your family are dead. And so are you.' Before anyone could make a sound, he zapped out three lightning bolts in the sorcerer's direction, each one striking him in the heart.

The sorcerer keeled over; he was dead before he hit the ground. Baltar didn't watch his collapse; instead, he glanced at Lady Rose. 'I don't need you now,' he said with considerable glee, and he marched towards the open front door.

A strangled cry of desperation escaped from Lady Rose, then she straightened her back, spread her arms wide and closed her eyes. Almost immediately, intricate red shapes started to spread across her pale skin, her body bulging in several places in a sickening manner. She was conjuring up blood magic – but even if such spells could halt Baltar in his tracks, it would bring her eventual destruction. Using blood magic twisted your psyche – and your body. If she kept this up, before too long Lady Rose would turn into a fiend too.

'Daisy!' Hester yelled. 'Do something!'

I heaved myself upright once more, ignoring the stabbing pains in my body. Then I did exactly as Hester commanded.

I threw out a burst of air magic, making the front door of the Assigney mansion slam shut in Baltar's face just as he reached it. While Lady Rose's body continued to bulge and twist, I followed up with a blast of fire, scorching the ground around the fiend's feet.

Despite his sprawled position, Hugo did the same. Then the idiot called out to Baltar. 'Come and get me, you fucker!'

Genuinely angry, I glared at Hugo. This wasn't his fight; it couldn't be.

Baltar, however, had already realised that. He turned his back on Hugo and faced me. 'Really?' he asked. 'You're really coming back for more?'

I answered him with a blast of water. It wasn't a simple sphere designed to annoy him, not this time. Now I was doing everything I could to harm him. The force of the water made him stagger backwards and drenched Baltar from head to toe.

Before I could do anything else, Lady Rose moaned and flung out her arms towards him. Whatever invisible power she'd invoked slammed into Baltar's body and finally he fell – though his collapse didn't make him defenceless. Far from it.

Even as his golden body thudded down, he sent several

scorching zaps of lightning towards me. Chillingly, I knew that there were two good reasons why he was attacking me and not Rose, although she was the greater threat. He wanted her to use more blood magic, he wanted her to twist herself into the same evil space that he occupied. And if that didn't work, he wanted to hand her over to Athair while she was still in one piece.

I rolled and dodged each bolt but several fell perilously close. I couldn't afford to be struck again. The sorcerer had been dead by the time the second lightning strike had hit him., and the same would probably happen to me if I wasn't careful.

Baltar wasn't my only problem, however.

'Stop it!' I roared at Rose. 'Stop conjuring up blood magic! This is what they want. This is what Athair wants, and this is what Baltar wants!' I gestured to the brownies. 'Get to that bloody woman and force her to see reason!'

I didn't wait for the brownies to react because I knew they would do what was necessary. They zipped past me, their wings beating as fast as they could as they headed straight for Rose. Hugo also picked himself up and, thankfully, made a beeline for her while I focused on Baltar.

He was already standing upright but he was dripping wet, and there was a puddle of water at his feet. His red eyes narrowed. Even from twenty metres away, I felt the full force of his fury. He wasn't used to being challenged – at least by not by complete strangers like me.

He sucked in a breath, clearly gathering his power. I blinked once and then, before I could begin to do anything else, Baltar magicked up a fireball to fling in my direction. This wasn't like any magic fireball I'd seen before; this one was fucking massive. And when I sprang to my right, thinking that I could simply dodge it, the damned thing followed me as if were some sort of heat-seeking missile. Cumbubbling bollocks.

Panic lit through me and I twisted left, aware that the vast ball of flame would do the same. I pumped my arms and legs for all they were worth, but I could still feel the searing heat at my back as the fireball drew closer and closer. Baltar's mocking laughter was audible over its roar and I wished desperately that I'd taken more spider's silk pills when I'd had the chance. If I'd swallowed several of them in one go, I might have had a chance. Now I would end up barbecued instead.

'Daisy!' Hugo yelled. 'Duck!'

I didn't think about it, I simply did as he said and threw myself down, face-planting on the ground and receiving a mouthful of dirt for my efforts. As soon as I did so, a cascade of water appeared and extinguished the ball of fire. I rolled, avoiding the hot splatters of steaming water and twisted my head to look at Rose and Hugo. Lady Rose's skin was no longer writhing with nasty red swirls; it was clear that both of them had sent the water magic in my direction.

Hugo bowed. 'You're welcome! That's another time I've saved your sweet arse, Daisy!'

Yeah, yeah. I yanked myself up and spun. I looked at Baltar's wet body, registering the large puddle at his feet once more, and inhaled deeply – then I gave the cumbubbling bastard a taste of his own medicine.

The second the lightning bolt left my fingertips, he gaped. Creating electrical magic out of thin air was the sort of magic that only a fiend could manage. A fiend – and me. Baltar recovered quickly enough to leap to his right to avoid it, but I wasn't aiming at him; I was aiming at the pool of dirty water he was standing in. He might have jumped away from the lightning, but his feet were immersed in water and that was all I needed. The electrical current conducted instantly through the puddle and into his body.

Baltar's body jerked as his muscles spasmed and he threw back his head, dark veins pulsating beneath his smooth golden skin. He didn't make a sound but I knew he had to be enduring colossal pain. Good. I didn't have a shred of sympathy for him.

I folded my arms and watched until his body gave away entirely and he thudded face first to the ground.

'Yes, Daisy!' Hester pumped the air with her fists.

'You did it,' Lady Rose breathed. 'You killed him.'

I shook my head. He wasn't dead, not in any true sense. Before too long, Baltar would rise again unless I did something about it. I stalked over to Gladys and picked her up, and she hummed happily. Stabbing Baltar in the heart and chopping off his head would do it.

I was more than ready for the grisly task. I lifted my sword – then I froze. *Uh-oh.* I licked my lips. Actually, *uh-oh* would have counted as the understatement of the year.

We'd all been so focused on ourselves and our own predicament that we hadn't noticed the car. Hugo's parents had driven the length of the driveway from the main road and none of us had seen them – but they had certainly seen us. Lord and Lady Pemberville were staring white-faced from the front seats. I couldn't begin to imagine what they thought was happening.

Lady Rose glanced over her shoulder to see what I was looking at. When she caught sight of her neighbours, she went white. Hester and Otis also turned, their bodies going rigid. Finally, Hugo checked to see who was there; as soon as he saw his parents staring at him, he turned such a shade of pale that I was concerned he was about to pass out.

Lord Pemberville wound down his window by three inches. The engine was still running and it was clear he was prepared to make a quick getaway if the situation called for it. 'We were worried, Rose,' he called out. 'We thought we'd come back and give the situation another shot. We wanted to see if we could, uh, help you.'

Lady Rose obviously didn't know what to say. Her mouth twisted and she whispered a strangled answer. 'Thank you.'

Lord Pemberville's gaze drifted to Baltar, who remained prone – at least for now. 'Rose,' he said quietly, 'is that a fiend?'

She swallowed hard. I supposed we all ought to have been grateful that he knew what fiends were; this situation was awkward enough without having to explain that part as well. 'Yes.'

'He won't be dead.'

'No,' she said.

He looked at the body of the still-unnamed sorcerer. 'Is *he* dead?'

Lady Rose sighed. 'Yes.'

He shuddered and pointed at me. 'Who is that woman, Rose?'

Her answer was quiet. 'She's called Daisy.'

'Not Gertrude.'

'No.'

'Or Karen?'

I bit my lip. 'I really am called Daisy.'

Lord Pemberville stared at me for another moment. I couldn't begin to imagine what was going through his head. 'We should leave,' he said finally.

She nodded at him. 'That's a good idea.'

He gestured to the back seats. 'All of us. Get in.'

Hugo's dad might not understand what was happening, but he had enough of a grasp of the situation to know what to do. Before anyone could react, however, the passenger door opened. Lord Pemberville's head whipped around. 'Tash!' he said sharply. 'Stop! What are you—?'

It was too late: she was already out of the car. She wasn't looking at Baltar, at Rose, at me or the brownies; she only had eyes for one person. Hugo had been right: mothers know. 'Hugo?' she whispered.

He shifted uncomfortably then turned his head, seeking me out for support. I bit my lip before nodding. He acknowledged the action and returned his attention to Lady Pemberville.

'Hi, Mum.' His voice cracked.

Everyone stared at him except for Lady Rose, who was staring at me. I cleared my throat pointedly. 'We should all leave,' I said. As if he'd heard me, Baltar started to stir. I raised my voice. 'Now.'

TWENTY-FOUR

Lord Pemberville was lost for words, his jaw working uselessly as he tried to make sense of what was happening. 'But ... but ... but...'

'Your son obviously takes after his mother and not you,' Hester said snippily before flying at full speed to the car and inserting herself through a gap in the window. Otis immediately followed suit, while Lady Pemberville continued to stare at the grown-up version of her son.

'Hugo,' I warned in a low voice.

He shook his head and muttered something under his breath, then vaulted towards the car. He nudged his mother into her seat and opened the rear door.

I twisted Gladys in my hands, preparing to slice at Baltar. 'You too, Lady Rose,' I said firmly. 'Get into the car. I'll deal with him.'

'I can't leave yet,' she whispered. She looked at the house.

'Whatever is in there isn't worth your damned life,' I snapped.

Her eyes narrowed. 'You might be surprised,' she returned with equal irritation.

Her vehemence surprised me. I watched as she took off at high speed, pulled open the front door and disappeared inside.

I cursed and took a step towards Baltar as Gladys buzzed with effervescent joy. Unfortunately the cumbubbling fiend wasn't done with us yet. As soon as I raised the sword and prepared to deliver the blow, his hand lashed out and he struck my calf with clawed fingers that ripped through my jeans and tore at my flesh.

Hugo was already leaping away from the car and running towards me, but Baltar was ready for him, too. He flashed out a wave of magic and whipped the air into a black, smoke-filled typhoon. It swept towards Hugo, swallowing him up and dragging him backwards against his will.

Fury roared through me and I swung Gladys down towards Baltar's neck. I wasn't swift enough: he dodged the blow, then he was up on his feet and facing me yet again.

I hissed under my breath and thrust Gladys towards him once more. He grabbed hold of her blade with his bare fingers, squeezing hard and ignoring his dripping blood. He yanked harder and pulled her out of my grasp – it hadn't even occurred to me that such a thing might be possible. Cumbubbling bollocks. I wasn't remotely proficient with a sword, despite the training I'd put in; if I died here it wouldn't be because Baltar had won the fight, it would be because I lost it.

The car door opened and Lord Pemberville stepped out, grim-faced. He stalked forward, breathing deeply. 'I will help you!' he called to me.

Goddammit. 'No!'

Hugo had finally extricated himself from the magicked wind and was also marching towards me. Then, to add further to the chaos, Lady Rose reappeared in the doorway holding a bundle in her arms. For fuck's sake.

Baltar was grinning at me with the confidence of a man

who knew he would win. There was only one thing left for me to do. I reached inside myself and pulled out everything I had. Air. Water. Fire. Earth. Lightning. I scooped up every inch of my power and threw it at him.

He howled – but it wasn't with pain but with delight. I kept going, dredging up whatever power I could find. Air – more air. Blast him in the damned face and chest and legs. Follow it up with waves of water. Rain fire on him. Attack the earth at his feet. Send lightning towards his head.

Over and over and over again I pulled on every thread of magic that I had and threw it at Baltar. He counter-attacked but I paid no attention and I didn't bother to defend myself. His magic had been weakened thanks to his earlier electrocution, and I was dimly aware that Hugo and his father were using their powers to protect me whenever they could.

I kept going, searching my body for every scrap of energy I could find until I'd grasped it and thrown it in Baltar's face. Air, water, fire, earth, lightning. Air, water, fire, earth, lightning. Air, water, fire, earth, lightning.

Baltar fell to his knees and so did I – but where I was struggling to maintain a grip on my consciousness as dizziness and nausea assailed me, he was smiling. 'Is that all you've got? Is that it?' he sneered.

A dark shape loomed behind him, but I didn't have the strength to look up and see who it was. I was done; I had nothing more to give, no more magic to throw.

'Try this,' Lady Rose hissed.

I caught a glimpse of shining steel as Gladys's blade caught in the sunlight before descending and slicing through Baltar's neck, then my vision diminished to little more than shifting shapes and dark shadows. In truth, I felt like little more than a shadow myself.

Strong hands reached for me: Hugo. He wrapped his arms around me, picked me up and cradled me against his chest.

I dug as deep as I could, summoning up the last of my energy. I had to speak; our lives counted on my words. 'Wait,' I whispered. 'Baltar...'

'I took care of him,' Rose said.

'No. He'll ... he'll ... come back. He's not ... dead.'

'Don't worry,' Hugo hushed. 'We have time to get away before he reanimates. It's fine. It's all fine.'

'Will she be okay?' I heard Lady Rose whisper.

Hugo's response was curt. 'Yes, but we need to get her to hospital. Help me lift her to the car.'

I felt myself being moved, heard a door open and registered the flutter of soft wings as Hester and Otis hovered anxiously over my face.

'I'm driving,' Hugo snapped. 'Everyone get in and fasten your seatbelts.'

'Hang on a minute,' Lord Pemberville began.

'JUST FUCKING GET IN, DAD!'

A strange dreaminess overtook me. Nothing mattered any more. It was all fine. Hunky dory.

'Wait!' Lady Pemberville's sharp cry made me jerk.

'Look! That's the doctor's car – he's on his way. He can help Gertrude – or Daisy – or whoever she is.'

Hugo's answer sounded as if it were coming from a great distance. 'Fuck. *Fuck.* The back road – is it clear, Rose? Can we get out of your estate that way?'

I tried to listen to her answer but a strange caterwauling was ringing in my ears, high-pitched and annoying. It sounded like a small angry cat.

And that was the last thought I had before darkness descended.

Even before I opened my eyes, I knew I felt different. It was difficult to put the sensation into words. There was a calmness deep within me that I'd not felt for a very, very long time. I was … centred.

Or I was until I remembered what had happened before I blacked out.

I sat bolt upright. 'Athair,' I said aloud, as a surge of panic overtook me.

'It's alright.' Hugo was holding my hand. 'We got away. We took a back road and drove off before he reached us. We're safe, Daisy.'

I blinked rapidly and gazed into his velvet-blue eyes, which were shining with a heartening mixture of warmth and relief. I reached for him and pulled him close, and he wrapped his arms tightly around me. 'We should add falling unconscious to the list of things you should never ever do,' he said in my ear,

I smiled into his shoulder – then I made the mistake of breathing in. Whoa. 'You, Hugo Pemberville, are very smelly.' Usually he exuded a spicy aroma that made me slightly weak at the knees but right now he reeked of acrid sweat and dirt.

'Is that your way of saying I should let you go?' he murmured.

'Never,' I whispered.

He grunted. 'Just as well.' His arms tightened a fraction.

There were several sharp jabs on the back of my head. 'You're awake!' More jabs. 'I'm so happy.' Several more jabs. 'Can I have a hug, too?'

I reluctantly released my hold on Hugo and smiled at

Hester. She hovered in front of my face for a few seconds then flew to my collarbone and burrowed against my skin. 'I'm so glad you're okay, Daisy. You've been out for a whole day.'

Otis piped up from the corner of the bedstead. 'We were really worried.'

'I'm fine,' I said. 'A bit shaky but fine.' I looked around. Wherever we were, it wasn't a hospital, not unless high-elf medical institutions in the nineties favoured baroque interior design.

'We were planning to take you to hospital,' Hugo admitted, 'but our plans changed when Athair showed up. We couldn't risk him finding us. We're in Edinburgh, in a flat belonging to a friend of my parents.'

A very grand flat; I was in a four-poster bed, for heaven's sake. The wallpaper was heavy, flocked damask and there was a lot of dark burnished wood. It was dramatic, overly ornate – and exactly the sort of place where I'd expect the Pembervilles to hide out.

'How *are* your parents?' I asked.

'Shocked.' He paused. 'To say the least.'

I couldn't blame them.

'They've sent my other self down south for a holiday with my nanny to keep him – me – safe.' He scratched his chin. 'It's not something I have any memory of happening.'

'You were two years old, so that's hardly surprising.' I passed a hand over my face. 'Baltar is still alive, just like in the future. I don't think anything we do here can change what will happen in the future. And that means we can't change things for Lady Rose.'

Hugo lowered his eyes and I stared at him, alarmed. 'What? What is it? Is she okay? Is she here with us?'

'She's here.' He still wouldn't look at me. 'She's fine. She wants to talk to you on your own as soon as you're up to it.'

Hester drew in a breath and prepared to speak but Hugo's head snapped up and he glared at her. I folded my arms and switched my gaze between the pair of them. 'What's going on, Hugo? What aren't you telling me?'

'Rose will explain when you're better.'

'Hugo—'

His voice was strained. 'Please, Daisy.'

Goddammit. 'I'm better now,' I said. I was annoyed. Hugo was supposed to be on my side and we'd promised not to keep secrets from each other. What the fuck was going on?

'Okay.' He stood up and ran a hand through his hair. 'I'll get you some food so you can get your strength up.' He picked up a glass of water from the bedside cabinet and handed it to me, then dipped his hand into his pocket and held out two pristine pills of spider's silk. Bless him. I gazed at the pills for a moment, then all-but snatched them from him.

Hugo looked away as I raised them to my mouth. And then I stopped, swallowed hard and handed one of the pills back to him. He stared at me.

'It worked,' I whispered. 'I released all my magic at Baltar and it worked.' I touched the centre of my chest. 'I can feel it inside me – it's different. I can control my magic, Hugo.'

To prove it, I pushed myself up and kissed him full on the lips. My senses swam at the taste of him and my stomach flip-flopped, but no trace of wild magic surged forward. After all these years, I was finally in control.

I drew back and gazed into Hugo's eyes. Hester and Otis were staring at me, their expressions so desperately hopeful that I couldn't look at them directly. 'I can't go cold turkey,' I whispered.

He nodded, understanding immediately. 'It's too dangerous – you'll go into sudden withdrawal.'

'That doesn't mean I can't start weaning myself off it.'

He wrapped his arms tightly around me, and for that one moment nothing mattered except the two of us. Eventually, he moved away. 'I'll get you some food before I'm the one who loses control,' he said gruffly. 'I'll tell Rose she can come in and speak to you, if you want.'

My stomach knotted. 'I do want.' My addiction was not my only problem; I needed to know what else was going on.

Hugo crooked his finger at the brownies. 'You two should come with me.'

'No way.' Otis shook his head firmly.

'We're staying here,' Hester said.

'Please.'

'Go with him,' I told them softly. 'It will be alright.'

There was a mutinous tilt to Hester's chin, but she glanced at Otis and something unspoken passed between them. 'Fine,' she said and pointed to the door. 'But we will be right there waiting if you need us.'

'We're all here for you, Daisy,' Hugo said quietly. 'Whatever you need and however you feel.'

There was definitely no trace of a calm centre inside me now. I clutched the sheet to my chest and scooted against the elaborate mahogany headboard, wide-eyed and nervous. As soon as Hugo and the brownies left the room, I gulped down my single pill of spider's silk. When it hit my system, my heart rate increased and my ears started to ring. I had to stay absolutely still until the wave of light-headedness and nausea passed.

Despite those symptoms, the kernel of hope deep inside me was growing by the second. If I made it out of this mess alive – and I could deal with the risk posed by Athair – I could work on myself. I was worth recovery.

When Lady Rose came in, she looked even more nervous than I felt, though that didn't make me feel any better. Unlike Hugo, she'd cleaned herself up and found a fresh set of clothes.

With a scrubbed face, she appeared younger than before. I knew that legally she was an adult, but she still looked so very young. I was struggling to deal with the situation, and she was at least ten years my junior, so I couldn't imagine how she was coping.

I reminded myself that I still didn't know the full story and vowed to be patient with her; she deserved that much, at least.

Lady Rose sat down on the chair that Hugo had vacated. 'How are you feeling?' she asked.

'I'm pretty good. Surprisingly so.' I tried to grin. 'I guess I just needed a long nap.'

She didn't smile. 'You deserved it after all you did. When I saw how you fought Baltar, I knew I could trust you – I knew you were who you said you were. The way you went up against that fiend...' Her voice trailed off and she shook her head. 'It was impressive.'

'You're the one who took him out at the end, Lady Rose.'

She grimaced. 'Don't call me that.'

I blinked. 'What would you like to be called?'

She stared down at her hands. 'Maybe just Rose,' she said in a small voice. 'For now.'

I nodded slowly. 'Okay.'

She didn't look up but started twisting her fingers over and over again; she had something important to say and I would give her all the time she needed to say it. Seconds ticked by. Eventually she sighed. 'I know you're worried about the blood-magic business. But I'm not a fiend.'

Not yet, I thought.

'I'm not close to becoming a fiend either.' She shuddered. 'I'd kill myself before I let that happen.'

I tried to keep my voice soft. 'You must know how dangerous blood magic is, though.'

'Yeah. But nothing else has worked against Athair. My

elvish magic is strong and I know I'm powerful, but nothing I threw at him affected him – until I tried blood magic.'

'Blood magic won't beat him, Rose. It will only destroy you.'

Her cheeks flushed; she clearly knew that already. I could empathise because I knew that my spider's silk addiction would destroy me – it was already destroying me. Even now, lying in bed with my wild magic finally under control, my pulse remained erratic and I knew my hands would shake if I raised them. I had still swallowed that pill, though. I still wanted to swallow more.

'I will try and stop using it. If I don't meet any more fiends it'll be easy,' she said with a faint smile of self-mockery.

'How did you get involved with Athair in the first place?' I asked.

'I met him at a party. For a long time I didn't know he was a fiend because he looked so normal. He was charming and sweet and—'

Her eyes filled with tears. 'I felt myself falling for him. It didn't occur to me he was only using me. With hindsight, it's easy to see that he knew I could be manipulated. I don't have any close family left. My mum and dad both died a couple of years ago. My great-aunt tries to keep in touch, but she's often busy with her own life. And it's the same with my friends – they're preoccupied with their own concerns.' She sighed and rubbed her eyes. 'I was easy pickings for someone like Athair.'

'I'm so sorry, Rose,' I whispered.

'It's not your fault.' She sniffed. Then she looked up, gave me a direct stare and changed the subject. 'Hugo told me you were adopted.'

'Uh, yeah.'

'What are they like? Your adoptive parents, I mean. Are they nice?'

My face softened. 'They're amazing. They've always been

amazing. They're human, so they don't have any magic and they don't understand a lot of what's inside me, but they've always supported me. They've always loved me. I'm very lucky to have them.'

'It sounds like you had a happy childhood with them.'

'I did. I really did.'

She bit her lip then, without warning, she stood up. 'I'll be back in a minute.'

What? 'Rose,' I began, 'I still don't—'

'There's something I have to show you.' With her head held high and her shoulders pulled back, she marched to the bedroom door and opened it. Hester and Otis tumbled in.

I gave both brownies an exasperated look. 'You were eavesdropping?'

'Of course!' Hester rolled her eyes to indicate that I was an idiot for thinking otherwise.

'Sorry, Daisy,' Otis muttered.

I tutted, just as Rose reappeared in the doorway. I glanced at the bundle in her arms, then at her face, then at the bundle again. Oh. 'That's a baby.'

'Well done, Daisy,' Hester said. 'Your powers of observation are extraordinary.'

Everything was beginning to fit together. 'Athair's baby?'

Rose nodded.

'And yours?'

She nodded again. 'She's ten days old.' She gently tugged the edge of the blanket to show me the baby's face. She was very small, very red and very crumpled. Messy tufts of bright red hair covered her scalp. 'Her name,' Rose added very quietly, 'is Daisy.'

TWENTY-FIVE

There was a tiny part of me that had known from the moment I'd broken into the Assigney mansion and seen Rose's portrait. I hadn't allowed myself to form the thought into words, but I had known deep, deep down. No wonder I'd managed to force my way through the blood ward.

I was of Rose's blood; I was her daughter.

'Lady Daisy,' Hester said several times, smacking her lips with satisfaction. She punched her brother's arm. 'This is more like it. Minor elvish royalty is exactly who we ought to be working for.'

He rolled his eyes, but from the gleam in his expression he was enjoying the news as much as she was.

We were all seated around a massive mahogany dining table – me, Hugo, both his parents, and Lady Rose. Hester and Otis were perched in the centre, slowly spinning around on a Lazy Susan. Otis looked faintly green around the gills but Hester appeared to be enjoying herself.

Baby Me was asleep in Rose's arms. So far I had declined to hold myself – that was far too weird – but I couldn't stop looking at Rose's face. She was my birth mother. *My birth mother*. Finally I knew where I came from. I had never expected answers about who I was, and to receive even one was extraordinary. To know the whole truth was mindboggling.

I was a high elf – me, Daisy Carter. If I was honest, I wasn't convinced I liked that part because I had been proud of my low-elf status. It was also distinctly odd to be seated across from my birth mother when she was a decade younger than I was because in some ways I felt more like her parent than the other way around. But despite those misgivings, I couldn't feel anything but happiness.

I smiled at Rose. I couldn't call her Mum, I wasn't there yet, but she still smiled back at me.

'Well,' said Hugo's dad, who was now insisting I call him Charles. 'A lot of things are making more sense.' He raised his eyebrows at Rose. 'The way you've been hiding yourself away, firing all your staff ... you could have come to us for help, you know.'

'Gone to the neighbours who the Assigneys have been in dispute with for generations and told them that I'd been seduced by a fiend pretending to be a human and that I was pregnant with his child?' Rose asked with a considerable edge of sarcasm. 'Sure. That would have been a great idea.'

Hugo drummed his fingers on the table. 'It's more credible than time travel,' he said. True.

Tash, Hugo's mum, gave him a tearful smile. 'You've grown up to be such a wonderful man,' she said. 'I'm so proud of you.'

He smiled at her before turning to me with a glint in his eye. 'I'm a wonderful man, Daisy,' he repeated pointedly.

'He's not as wonderful as Daisy,' Rose sniped. 'Without her, we'd all be dead now.' It was my turn to smirk.

'That's fair,' Tash said.

'Mother!' Hugo protested.

She shrugged. 'It's true.' My smirk grew.

'I'm also particularly pleased that now Daisy is awake you finally left her side to take a shower, Hugo,' Tash added. 'Your smell was becoming quite unsavoury.'

The smile left my face and I stared at Hugo. He met my gaze head on. 'I wanted to be there for you when you woke up,' he said simply. My breath caught. 'And I have to say,' he continued, with a touch of smugness, 'that I always knew you weren't a low elf. Deep down, you knew it too.'

I opened my mouth to argue then closed it again. He was right.

'Revelations upon revelations,' Charles murmured. He looked at his son proudly. 'You're obviously a good judge of character.'

I couldn't help myself: I snorted aloud.

Hugo cleared his throat with at least a smidgen of self-awareness. 'Yes, well,' he said awkwardly, 'now that we all know who we are, we have to decide what we will do. Even if it takes weeks for Baltar to recover properly, Athair will be hunting for us. We can't rest on our laurels for long. We have to come up with a plan.'

My lingering amusement died a sudden death. Usually I could come up with a plan, even if it was a bad one, but this time I had nothing. Everyone else was silent too, until Rose licked her lips and spoke up.

'Athair is only hunting for me and Daisy.' She nodded at the sleeping baby. 'This Daisy, not the other Daisy. It's safest if the rest of you leave.'

Hugo shook his head. 'He saw all of us in front of your house, so we're all in danger.'

'And we're not abandoning you,' Charles said firmly. 'We're in this together.'

Rose straightened her shoulders. When she spoke again, her voice was quiet but firm. 'Daisy, I talked to the brownies quite a lot when you were sleeping. You don't believe the past can be altered, do you? You don't believe that the future you know in 2024 can be changed in any way.'

Oh God. I swallowed hard, my mouth suddenly as dry as sandpaper. I couldn't avoid the question, but I had to choose my words very, very carefully. 'I haven't seen any evidence yet that we can change what's to come. However, that doesn't mean it can't be done.'

She gave me a shaky smile. 'You will be adopted by a beautiful couple who will love you very much. They will help you grow into the wonderful woman you are now, someone I admire. Someone who is brave and thoughtful and kind.' She paused. 'And I will disappear forever.'

'We don't know that for certain,' I said.

Charles and Tash nodded in unison. 'It's pure conjecture,' Tash told her. 'None of us can tell how this time-travel business works. There are still lots of avenues left open to us.'

'Definitely,' Hugo added. 'Let's not forget that although Daisy isn't a fiend, she has enough fiendish blood in her to destroy one who crosses her path. She's done it before and she can do it again.'

I gulped. Yes, I killed Baltar in the future, but that had been blind luck. My more recent encounter with Vargas had ended in success – but Vargas wasn't Athair. I wasn't convinced I'd ever be strong enough to kill my birth father. He was the most powerful fiend in existence, and he'd already proved himself to be a lot smarter than Vargas.

Otis possessed none of my doubts, quite the opposite in fact. He agreed vigorously with Hugo, 'There are all sorts of ways this can go. Nothing is a foregone conclusion.'

Hester dropped her feet and brought the spinning Lazy Susan to a halt. She angled her head up at Rose. 'You're nice,' she said. 'I like you. But, yes, you will disappear. Athair will kill you in the next few days.' She pursed her lips. 'Sorry.'

Everyone stared at her in horror except for Rose, who smiled faintly. 'The hard, unvarnished truth,' she said. 'This is what I need.'

There were several burbles of protest but Rose drew in a deep breath. 'I know that Daisy will be fine – more than fine. That's enough for me.'

No. I shook my head. 'Well, it's not enough for me. We're not at a disadvantage here. We're from the future and we know what happens, so we're in a position to change it. Athair won't win. I don't care who or what he is.'

I spoke every word with conviction – but I also felt certain that I was lying.

WE SPENT several hours discussing possible actions and outcomes but unfortunately we couldn't come to any conclusion. Then Baby Daisy woke up and started to squawk loudly in a manner that grated because I couldn't believe I was capable of such a horrendous noise.

I excused myself to go in search of food. The Pembervilles' friends who owned the flat had been absent for some time and the cupboards were bare; if I wanted to eat, I'd have to do some shopping. It was almost a relief; a bit of space and some fresh air would do me the world of good.

Borrowing a long coat that smelled faintly musty but looked clean enough, I slipped out before anyone noticed and padded down the communal stairs towards the front door of the building. A clean-shaven man, who appeared to be human, was standing by the row of mailboxes and perusing the letters. I walked past him and glanced at his face. A second later I glanced again.

The words were out of my mouth before I could stop them. 'Sir Nigel?'

The man turned and blinked at me. He didn't have a perfectly waxed handlebar moustache, and he wasn't wearing a crisp suit and he was incredibly young, but it was definitely him. 'Hello. Do I know you?' he asked.

'Uh, sorry. I mistook you for someone else.' I was useless at time-travelling.

'My name is actually Nigel, although I can't remember ever being called sir.' He smiled with the genuine warmth and ease that I knew from his older self. 'Apart from when my mother decides I'm being too uppity and calls me out for it.'

Flustered, I tried to explain myself. I hadn't ever questioned when Sir Nigel had been knighted; clearly it wasn't a hereditary title. 'That's an incredible coincidence. I should have realised. The Nigel I know is much older than you.' I forced a smile. 'Have a good day.'

'You, too.'

I turned and headed for the door but I'd barely touched the handle when Sir Nigel – or Nigel as he was at that moment – called out again. 'You should take care out there,' he said. 'The sun is going down and there are a couple of vampires hanging about in the shadows over the road. They ignored me, so they're probably not hungry.' He grimaced. 'But you can't be too careful when bloodsuckers are around.'

I turned around slowly. 'Vampires?' I asked, trying to sound casual.

He was still smiling but his eyes were serious. 'Yes. I spotted them on my way home. I'll call it into the police and hopefully they'll send a team out to take care of them.' He sounded doubtful; he was obviously as aware as I now was of how the police dealt with the hordes of Edinburgh-based bloodsuckers.

I kept my voice even. 'Do you often get vampires in this part of town?'

'Very rarely,' he admitted. 'If ever. They tend to lurk in the less salubrious parts of the city where they're more likely to come across hapless victims who can't defend themselves.'

That figured; it was a sad fact of life that in both prosaic and supernatural matters, affluent neighbourhoods were safer. I rubbed the back of my neck, aware of the chill descending through my bones, then I thanked Nigel and returned at high speed to the flat. There would be no casual shopping now.

I burst through the door and it thudded loudly against the wall. Before I could say anything, Hugo marched out of the dining room and glared at me. 'You left without me.' He folded his arms.

'I was gone for less than a minute. And it's just as well that I was.' He caught something in my voice and frowned. I raised my head and met his eyes. 'We have to get out of here, Hugo. Athair is on his way.'

He didn't ask if I was sure, demand an explanation or request more details; he believed me instantly. 'Okay.' His voice was low. 'Let's go.'

CHAPTER

TWENTY-SIX

It took far longer than I liked to gather everyone up and leave because apparently babies came with a great deal of paraphernalia. I still wasn't entirely sure how I felt about hanging around with this tiny version of myself, but at least Baby Daisy's age meant I didn't have to hold a conversation with myself. That would have been far too strange, even for me.

Although Rose was moving fast and collecting everything Baby Daisy needed, I was aware that the news about Athair had unsettled her deeply. I recognised the way she masked the tremors in her hands because I often tried to do the same. I understood why her face was so pale, but it was the occasional flashes of writhing red marks appearing and disappearing across her skin that caused me the most concern. She was trying to keep her blood magic at bay but her anxiety was making it difficult to force down. For the first time in a very long time, I wasn't the person whose unruly powers were problematic, and it was unsettling to be on the other side for a change.

Several minutes after I'd burst back into the flat, we were on our way out. Thankfully, the stairwell was empty and silent. Hugo went ahead to check that nobody was lurking around any corners. Sir Nigel had vanished, no doubt into his own home. I silently – and fervently – urged both him and all the other residents nearby to stay inside. We had enough problems as it was.

We re-grouped at the main entrance. There were only a few pale glimmers of light left in the sky, which didn't bode well. Hugo was peering out of the door, frowning at the gloomy side streets. 'There's no sign of activity out there,' he said. 'But that's not necessarily good news.'

I nodded grimly. I'd have felt considerably less worried if it had just been him and me; the presence of his parents, Rose and Baby Daisy meant that our group was much more vulnerable. 'Where's the car parked?' I asked.

Charles answered. 'To the right, about twenty metres away.' His voice was low and firm, and for the first time I spotted similarities with Hugo that went beyond the physical resemblance.

'Okay. That's not far. That's good.' I met Hugo's eyes. 'You should bring it here to the door.'

He was already ahead of me and taking the keys from his father. 'Athair has met everyone else, but he's only seen me from a distance so he might not recognise me. If he's out there watching this building, there's a good chance that me on my own won't raise his suspicions.'

I crossed my fingers tightly. 'If you do see him, don't do anything stupid.'

'Please.' He rolled his eyes. 'This is me we're talking about. I never do anything stupid.' He paused and something deeper flared in his blue eyes. 'Apart from falling for you.'

Tash gasped, and my mouth dropped at his sudden open display of emotion. There was no time to say anything, however; he was already out of the door, his hands in his pockets as he turned right to retrieve the vehicle and tried to look casual.

I checked on Rose; there were beads of sweat on her forehead, but the signs of impending blood magic across her skin had gone. She was concentrating hard, as if it were taking all her energy not to give in to her darker impulses. 'Have you got this?' I asked quietly. 'Are you alright?'

'Yes,' she whispered.

I tried to smile at her. 'There won't be time to clip Daisy into a car seat. We'll have to jump in as soon as Hugo brings the car and get her sorted out once we're on the move.'

Rose looked at Charles and Tash, then all three of them blinked at me. 'We don't have a baby seat in the car.'

'There's not a larger version for Hugo?'

Tash's cheeks coloured. 'Uh, no.'

'We are planning to get one,' Charles said quickly. 'We just haven't got around to it yet.'

Welcome to 1994. Hester popped her head up from her spot on my shoulder. 'What's wrong with you? Get a proper seat for your kid!'

Otis nodded solemnly. 'Safety first. Always.'

'Tell that to that damned fiend and those vampires,' Charles said. Fair point.

There was a flash of headlights and the sound of an engine as Hugo arrived outside the door. I handed the bag stuffed full of nappies and sweet-smelling baby equipment to Tash. 'Wait here,' I said. 'Don't come out until I say.'

I opened the door, sucked in a deep breath of chilly evening air and stepped out. The street was quiet and I paused for a moment, swinging my head first to the left and then to the right. Everything was clear: there was no sign of the vamps that Nigel had described.

I glanced through the car window at Hugo. His hands were gripping the steering wheel and he was ready to make a quick getaway. Our eyes met, then I reached for both front and back passenger doors and opened them. We had to make this quick.

I spun on my heels and beckoned to Rose, Charles and Tash. They immediately followed me onto the pavement. As we'd already decided, Tash slid into the rear seat first, then Rose handed Baby Daisy – who was thankfully fast asleep – to me before following Tash.

I glanced down at the baby's face. Although her weight in my arms was unfamiliar, I didn't feel as nervous holding her as I'd thought I would. I leaned down and prepared to pass her to Rose now she was inside the car. Charles climbed into the front passenger seat and clipped in his seatbelt.

Rose took Baby Daisy so I could get in, but before I could manoeuvre myself onto the seat a hard voice rang out. 'Give me my daughter.'

'Athair!' Hester squeaked shrilly in my ear.

I raised my head in time to see him stride from the shadows on the other side of the street flanked by two gaunt vampires. Athair wasn't wearing another body this time because he no longer needed to hide his true self. His golden skin glittered in the light from the street lamps, and his red eyes were shining with purpose and intent. But the road was clear: if Hugo reversed quickly we could still get away.

I briefly regretted not taking more spider's silk when I'd had the chance; alas, there was nothing I could do about it right now.

Suddenly a hand slammed into my chest: Rose had shoved me – hard. I staggered as she threw herself out of the car. Tash was staring wide-eyed from her seat as she held Baby Daisy in her arms.

I choked out a cry as Rose stormed past the vehicle towards Athair. Her back was ramrod straight and her head was high. Oh no. 'She's not yours!' she screamed. 'She'll never be yours!'

There was no mistaking the delight on Athair's face. The two vamps started forward, hunger throbbing in their undead eyes, but when Athair lifted his right hand they stopped immediately. He might not command the same numbers of vampires as Vargas, but his mastery over the undead creatures was clearly just as strong.

'Rosie, darling,' he purred. 'I'm so glad we can finally talk face to face again.'

I didn't know what to do. My immediate instinct was to rush forward and either join Rose to face Athair or drag her to the car, whether she liked it or not. In fact, I'd already taken several steps forward to do just that when I faltered. My presence by Rose's side would probably only panic her further. I couldn't rush into this without thinking, I had to come up with a plan first.

Unfortunately, while my mind was racing, it appeared that Rose had come up with a plan all of her own. And it wasn't a good one.

The blood magic she'd been trying so hard to keep at bay flared up, and the now familiar – and horrifying – red shapes danced across her skin once more. She threw her head back and a strange keening sound unlike anything I'd ever heard before escaped her lips. Then she thrust her hands out in front of her and spewed black flame in Athair's direction.

Athair reacted quickly, stepping back and directing the two vampires to form a barrier in front of him. They did as they were commanded, but as soon as Rose's black fire smashed into their bodies they started to writhe and scream, their agony plain to see.

'Daisy!' Hester hissed. 'Get into the car! She's giving us the chance we need to make our escape! This is how it's supposed to be! This is how we save the baby.'

But I was the baby. I would not allow Rose to die for my sake. I looked at Hugo. His jaw was tight, but he nodded at me; he understood.

He opened his door and stepped out to join me, ignoring his parents' cries. Charles fiddled with his seatbelt, clearly prepared to attach himself to our small group of terrified fighters.

I spun around and snarled at him with such ferocity that he blanched. 'No! Slide into the driver's seat and be ready to leave when it's time. You will know when that time is!' I pushed Hester and Otis off my shoulder. 'You two need to get inside that car.'

They hovered in the air then looked at each other. 'Nah,' Hester said. 'The vamps are already goners. There's only Athair left. This time we're with you.'

'Till the bitter end,' Otis agreed.

There wasn't any time to get into an argument; the vampires were already ash and Rose was getting ready to throw more blood magic at Athair. His attention was wholly on her.

'I knew the moment I saw you that you were the right person to be the mother of my child,' he breathed. 'Look at you. You're magnificent.' He spread his arms wide. 'Come on, Rosie. Attack me again. Hit me with everything you've got.'

I gazed at his face. He genuinely wanted her to attack him and the thought was chilling. Athair wanted Rose to give herself up to blood magic entirely. The more of those foul powers that she called upon, the closer she would be to becoming a fiend herself. Perhaps he had visions of creating a happy fiend family – himself, Rose and me. Three fiends together.

A growl rumbled deep in my chest. That wasn't going to happen. I wouldn't let it.

Rose didn't have the same qualms that I did. As Hugo and I ran towards her with both brownies keeping pace in the air, she released another blast of power, conjuring up clouds of pitch-black smoke that billowed in Athair's direction and obscured him from view. I could still hear his laughter as it enveloped him.

I grabbed Rose's right arm while Hugo took her left. 'Enough!' I snarled at her. 'We are leaving!'

'No,' she muttered, resisting. 'I will kill him. I *have* to kill him. It's the only way to keep you safe.'

'You can't kill him, Rose. The only way you can achieve that is if you become a fiend yourself.'

She turned her wild eyes to me. 'So be it.'

I hissed. Hugo looked over her head towards me. 'Do it,' he told me. He was right.

I inhaled deeply. 'Sorry, Mum,' I said. Then I curled my hand into a fist and hit her in the head. She crumpled immediately.

Hugo caught her before she fell to the ground and scooped her up. She moaned briefly. She'd be pissed off when she came round, but she'd recover.

Unfortunately, that was when the smoke started to clear and Athair's figure reappeared. 'Go,' I urged Hugo. 'Get her to the car!'

'Daisy—'

'Please, Hugo!'

His expression twisted but he did as I asked. I turned and faced my father. Any doubt I'd had about our shared identity had long since faded away.

Athair's maniacal grin had been wiped from his face. 'You again.' He stared at me. 'You shouldn't have involved yourself in this. Your death will not be pretty – but it will be well-deserved.'

Otis zipped towards him. 'If you didn't want her involved, you shouldn't have left that letter for her in Rose's bedroom!'

Genuine confusion crossed Athair's face.

Before I could stop her, Hester joined her brother. 'Yeah!' she yelled. 'And you shouldn't appear at Gordon Mackenzie's house in thirty years' time and force her to release her magic and set off the stupid magic skull that sent us here! This is all your fault!'

'What?' Athair asked. 'What the fuck are you on about?' His eyes flicked to mine. 'Why am I being harangued by two brownies with a death wish? What are they talking about?'

My voice was soft. 'You haven't worked it out yet? I thought you were smart.'

Athair's head tilted – and that was when I sent out two blasts of air magic that snagged the cars parked on either side of the road and flung them forward. The hunks of metal crashed down on top of him, squashing him flat beneath their heavy weight.

I knew they wouldn't keep him down for long and I only had seconds to escape. I reached out, snatched a brownie in each hand and ran for all I was worth.

TWENTY-SEVEN

'You know,' Charles said, as we drove away at high speed, 'Edinburgh Council will bill you for that mess if they ever track you down.'

'I've heard they do that,' I said drily, raising my voice to be heard over the cries coming from Baby Daisy, who was now wide awake and making sure we all knew it. Rose was slumped against Tash, Hugo was white faced, and Charles was ignoring every red light. We were in a mess – although Hester and Otis appeared exultant.

'You showed him,' Hester crowed. 'You showed Athair who's in charge!'

Otis added, 'He'll think twice before he tries to come at us again!'

I wished I shared their enthusiasm. 'He won't allow himself to be distracted in that way again. We got lucky this time, but those cars I dropped on him won't hold him for more than a few minutes. He'll already be back on our tail.'

Charles put his foot down harder on the accelerator.

Hester squinted at me. 'What's happened to your usual

sunny optimism? We encountered Athair and lived to tell the tale!'

I looked at her flatly. 'That's not the only tale you've been telling.'

'Huh?'

'It was never clear how Athair knew to leave that letter for me in the Assigney mansion.' I paused. 'But now we know.' I raised my eyebrows at Otis.

'What?' he asked, puzzlement clouding his face. Then his expression altered as he realised what he'd yelled at Athair and his shoulders dropped. 'Oh.' Guilt filled his eyes. 'Oops.'

'Otis!' Hester shrieked. 'You absolute idiot! You told Athair about the letter! You told him what to do! Why did you do that? You nincompoop!'

I glanced at her. 'He's not the only one with a big mouth.'

'I didn't say anything! Apart from the bit about turning up at Gordon's house and...' She stopped mid-sentence; now she looked as guilty as her brother.

'There we go. Now you're both starting to understand.' I turned away from them and checked on Rose. Her pulse was strong but her eyes remained closed. Perhaps that was a good thing, although I was still awash with guilt for hitting her.

I returned my attention to the brownies; their hangdog faces tugged at my heartstrings. 'It's not all bad,' I told them.

They still looked mournful.

'Daisy is right,' Hugo said. 'We know more than we did before. In fact, it's a relief to know that in the future Athair won't be magically listening into conversations or tracking Daisy's movements minute by minute. He's a powerful fiend but he's not omnipotent. He's not a god.'

I thought of Vargas, who had wanted to be worshipped like a deity. Fiends could be defeated, they could be banished by a decent witch and they could be killed by me. Our situation was dire – but it wasn't rock bottom, and we weren't the losing team. This fight was far from over. I straightened my shoulders and grinned.

Hugo, who was watching me in the rear-view mirror, clocked my expression. 'You've got a plan?'

'Not yet,' I said. Baby Daisy gave another loud cry. When I winced, she stopped and blinked at me. I smiled at her. 'But I'm working on it.'

OUR RUSHED ESCAPE meant we didn't have a destination in mind so, as we left Edinburgh, we discussed our options. Hugo's parents were keen on a city. 'We know a lot of high elves who can find us accommodation. We won't be alone next time Athair comes after us,' Tash said earnestly.

Charles nodded. 'There are more places to hide in a city, and a busy place will give us time to re-group and prepare before that fiend finds us again.'

'But the vampires are in the cities,' Hugo pointed out. 'It's safe to assume that Athair can call upon a whole network of the undead. It only takes one to spot us and he'll know exactly where we are. We arrived in Edinburgh last night under cover of darkness, and that darkness is exactly why Athair found us.'

'Also,' I added, 'if we hole up in a city there's more chance that innocent bystanders will be caught in the crossfire. Athair is determined to grab Baby Daisy and he won't care who gets hurt. Quite the opposite – he'll kill anyone who gets in his way.'

Rose twitched.

'But you survive,' Hester said to me. 'He doesn't get you. Not baby you, anyway.'

Otis nodded. 'We know that because you're here now. You're fine.'

I looked at Rose, whose eyes remained closed. Tash glanced at her too, and Hugo. She might be my mother but she looked like a kid – she *was* practically a kid – and her fate was far from sealed. 'Uh-huh.'

In the end we compromised and decided to head for the mid-sized town of Berwick-upon-Tweed. Its location, just across the border with England, meant we had considerable options if we suddenly needed to flee. It wasn't a huge place, and recent reports of vampire culls in the area suggested that we might go unnoticed by the denizens of the undead.

Tash had a cousin who owned a large property there, so we'd have somewhere to stay; even better, a large contingent of talented witches lived nearby. Charles was certain that they had experience with banishing fiends; in fact, he was sure they'd banished one recently, albeit a far younger and weaker fiend than Athair.

'It won't take long to get there,' he said. He seemed happier now we had the beginnings of a plan. His eyes met Tash's in the rear-view mirror and they looked at each other for a long moment before he continued. 'An hour and a half, depending on traffic. I'll have to fill up with petrol soon, though.'

Tash pointed to a sign on the side of the road. 'There's a service station a few miles ahead.'

Rose twitched again.

'Perfect.'

A red car had been behind us for some distance now, but it was too far away for me to see who was inside it. I watched it nervously until Charles slowed down as he prepared to turn into the service station. Almost immediately, the red car indicated to overtake and speeded past. I released the breath I'd been holding.

We had pulled up to the nearest petrol pump when Rose finally stirred and sat up. She looked around, blinked then rubbed her head. I winced and tried to tell myself that hitting her so hard had been the right thing. It didn't help. 'Hey,' I said, wishing I sounded brighter. 'You're awake.'

Her brief smile didn't reach her eyes. She turned to Tash, took Baby Daisy from her and held her close. 'Yes,' she whispered. 'I'm awake.' She looked at me. 'I'm sorry, Daisy. I'm so sorry. There's no choice.'

'It's okay,' I said, doing my best to reassure her. 'We got away. But no more blood magic, eh? You can't risk it. And I'm the one who should be sorry. I shouldn't have hit you like that.'

'You did what you had to,' Rose mumbled and dropped her gaze. Baby Daisy gurgled and she hugged her closer. 'She needs to be changed,' she said quietly, then she rubbed her head again and groaned.

'I'll do it,' Tash said. 'There must be changing facilities here. Besides, I've changed enough of your nappies recently, Hugo. I can do it in record time.'

He groaned in mock horror and, I suspected, genuine embarrassment. Rose paid him no attention and grabbed Tash's arm. 'No. Don't leave me.'

Tash looked surprised, but her eyes were filled with compassion. Her gaze flicked to Charles again, then she bit her lip and nodded. 'If that's what you want, Rose.'

'It is.' Rose straightened up and thrust Baby Daisy into my arms – who immediately started to cry again. Of course she did. 'Can you do it?' my mother asked.

Change my own nappy? 'I've never...'

'Please, Daisy. She needs it.' Rose gave an awkward smile. '*You* need it.' She leaned forward. 'I could do with some paracetamol as well. Hugo, could you get me some?'

'No problem. We should pick up some other supplies if we're camping out in Berwick for the next few days. I'll grab some food.'

Charles delved into his pocket, took out his wallet and withdrew a bank card. 'Can you take some money out and pay for the petrol? The pin is 8749.' Hugo nodded.

I shifted Daisy in my arms. Her face was screwed up and her soft cries were turning into loud squawks. Great. But I could hardly gainsay Rose after thumping her so hard. 'Are you two coming?' I asked the brownies.

Hester flicked a glance at the baby and pulled a face. 'Nah.'

'You've got this, Daisy,' Otis agreed. 'We'll wait here.'

I couldn't blame them.

Charles went to the pump and picked up the refuelling hose while Hugo and I walked across the forecourt. 'I'll get what we need while you change nappies,' Hugo said.

No way. 'I'm not doing this on my own – you're not leaving me alone with myself, Hugo. Anything might happen.'

'You've faced down vampires, fiends and dragons, Daisy. I think you can manage a baby.' I gave him a long look. 'Fine,' he said. 'I'll help.' He leaned over and sniffed. 'I can't smell anything. How bad can it be?'

'Look at the pair of us,' I muttered. 'We're both afraid of a tiny baby.'

'She's not just *any* baby.'

That didn't make it any better. I adjusted my hold on her. 'Come on. I can see a baby-changing sign over there.'

Thankfully the little room was empty, although it was a tight squeeze when all three of us were inside. Hugo rummaged around in the baby bag. 'I don't understand what half of this stuff is for.' He looked at me for guidance.

'What?' I asked. 'You think because I'm a woman I should know? I don't spend time around babies. I'm as clueless as you are.'

He eyed me. 'In this current form,' he gestured to himself,

'I'm four years older than my mum and six months older than my dad.'

'I'm ten years older than Rose,' I reminded him.

'And they can do this stuff without thinking about it.' Hugo straightened his shoulders and did his best to look confident. 'It can't be that hard. If our parents can do it and they're younger than us, then we can do it too.'

'Sure. Although you've gotta wonder why they didn't come and do it themselves to begin with.' I froze, and so did Hugo. I looked down at Baby Daisy who stared up at me with huge, tear-filled eyes. She didn't want me, she wanted her mum. 'Hugo,' I whispered.

He came to the exact same conclusion at the exact same time. Cumbubbling bollocks.

He dropped the bag of baby things and ran outside with me following on his heels. As soon as I saw the car with Charles, Tash and Rose inside it driving across the forecourt and out of the service station, I cried out, 'No!'

Hugo cursed loudly. 'I cannot fucking believe they're doing this!' He drew in a breath, preparing to throw magic after them and somehow stop them in their tracks.

'Don't, Hugo,' Otis said in a tiny, sad voice. He and Hester were hovering anxiously a few metres away. 'They don't want you to stop them.'

Hester sniffed tearfully. 'They've given us a message for you that we have to deliver word for word.'

Hugo growled as I stared at the brownies in growing horror.

'"You don't know what it's like to be a parent",' Otis recited. '"You'd do anything for your child. You'd move heaven and earth to keep them safe. We are leaving. We will draw Athair away in the hope that he follows us and not you. You know what you have to do for Baby Daisy. You know what has to happen. We will find somewhere safe for Rose to stay. When

Athair realises she no longer has Daisy, he might leave her alone".'

I clenched my teeth in a vain bid to stop my tears from falling.

Hester took up the thread. 'This message is from Rose.' She swallowed hard. '"My darling Daisy. We both know this is for the best. I can't stop myself from using blood magic when Athair is near, and I can't protect you if I keep using it. If I stay, I could cost you everything. You will be loved and you will have a happy childhood with wonderful parents. You will grow into an amazing woman with more heart and bravery than I could ever hope for. I will always love you, and I will think of you, every single day".' Hester's voice shook. 'I'm so sorry,' she mumbled. 'We couldn't stop them.'

I stared down the busy road and thought about some of the last words Rose had said to me: *I'm so sorry. There's no choice.* She'd been speaking in the present tense. She had already known she would do this.

Hugo cursed loudly. 'Fuck!'

The car was no longer in sight. My shoulders dropped. 'They've gone. They've really gone.'

And we'd been left holding the baby. Literally.

CHAPTER
TWENTY-EIGHT

I didn't know what to feel. In the space of a few minutes, I ran through the full gamut of emotions from shock to burning rage, which didn't do my drug-addled body any favours. My hands shook and my heart missed several beats.

Then desperation took over and my mind flitted to panicked ideas about how we could steal a car and catch up with our departing parents. Once I got my breathing under control, I felt myself yielding to deep sadness. We were supposed to save Rose, not cause her disappearance.

I dropped my head and stared at my shoes, while Hester sniffed, Otis hugged himself, and Hugo paced up and down the forecourt.

Several vehicles had arrived, filled their tanks and left by the time I realised that my turbulent emotions were twisting into something more positive. A flicker of pride was spreading through me, and there was admiration, too. Rose had analysed the problem, considered all the facts and chosen the path she believed was best. Despite the ongoing churning in my belly, I suspected that I'd have made the same decision.

I sighed and looked up. 'They trust us,' I said finally.

Hugo stopped his furious pacing. 'What?'

'Our parents trust us,' I repeated and drew in a shuddering breath. 'That's pretty amazing when you think that we've arrived from the future, waged a bloody battle on their doorstep and presented ourselves as their adult children, all in the space of a couple of days.'

I rocked Baby Daisy in my arms. Her cries had subsided and she was now producing little more than an occasional hiccupping sob. 'Rose gave me her *child*.'

'You *are* her child,' Hugo said pointedly.

'You know what I mean.' I kept my gaze on him. 'It's the same with your mum and dad. They trust both of us to do the right thing by Baby Daisy and Older Daisy.'

'We're not children,' he muttered. 'We're older than them.'

'But we're still *their* children. Could we do the same if this happened to us? If our children appeared out of the blue as adults?'

A muscle jerked in his cheek, then something flared deep in his blue eyes and I caught a glimpse of old, arrogant Hugo. 'Well, Daisy, there's one way to find out,' he drawled. He stepped towards me. 'Let's have a baby of our own and see what happens. In fact,' he said, 'let's have several babies.'

I didn't get the impression that he was joking, not in the least. With no immediate response to offer, I pretended he'd not said that last part. Yeah: that was the sort of kick-ass, ball-busting, brave heroine I was. Go me.

'Let's find a way to get out of here,' I told him.

'And do what?' he asked.

I looked again at Baby Daisy. 'What we're supposed to,' I said simply. 'Take me to hospital and leave me there so that I can be adopted by Michael and Alison Carter.' I lowered my head and whispered to the baby, 'I know it's scary. But they will love you so much. Everything will work out. I promise.'

She reached up a chubby hand and grabbed a fistful of my hair. 'Yeah,' I said. 'You'll need a lot of expensive conditioner to keep that under control when you're older.'

'But your hair will always be beautiful,' Hugo said to her. 'And you'll be a beautiful soul.' He crouched down until he was face to face with Baby Daisy and gently brushed her cheek with the tip of his finger. 'When you're an adult and you finally meet Hugo Pemberville for the first time, remember that he's also a wonderful, charming man despite your first impression of him.'

I rolled my eyes and Hugo gave me a smirk that was an open challenge. Fine. Two could play this game. 'Trust your gut when you meet him,' I told her. 'He's not as bad as he first appears. But remember that it won't take long before you're a far better treasure hunter than he is.'

A gasp of mock horror escaped Hugo's lips. 'Sorry, Baby Daisy,' he said. 'That'll never happen.'

'Oh, it will,' I smiled.

Then I inhaled deeply. Fuck it, I was going to say it. I would take that leap. 'It also won't be long,' I said, trying to keep my voice steady, 'before you fall head over heels in love with him.'

Hugo became very, very still.

I was dimly aware of Otis and Hester clutching each other and staring at me with wide eyes, but I was more aware of Hugo. Painfully aware. 'Goddamnit,' he muttered under his breath.

Oh no. I'd made a mistake; I should have kept my big mouth shut.

He shook his head with dismay. 'You always have to get one up on me, Daisy.'

Huh?

'I wanted to say the words first.' He brushed Baby Daisy's cheek again. 'Let me say it first next time,' he whispered to her, 'because I'm in love with you, and I always will be.' He lifted his head and we stared at each other.

'For fuck's sake,' Hester said loudly. 'Really? *Really?*' She threw her hands up in exasperation. 'We're stuck in 1994. We've been abandoned at a petrol station without any transportation. We're surrounded by petrol fumes and skid marks. We're fleeing a maniacal fiend. And *this* is when you choose to tell each other that you're in love?'

Otis added his voice. 'Who said romance was dead? All we need now is some stirring music.'

As if on cue, a taxi pulled up at the nearest petrol pump, music blaring from its windows: 'Whatta Man' by Salt n Pepa. Hugo grinned and took a bow. 'What a man I am. You know that has to be our song from now on?'

'That is *not* our song.' Baby Daisy lifted her arms to Hugo and gave a happy gurgle. I frowned at her. 'Whose side are you on?'

'We could take our chance now and escape from these two,' Hester said to Otis. 'If their parents can run away from them, we can do it too.'

Otis pursed his lips and considered it seriously. 'Yeah, but if we leave them on their own they'll only mess everything up. They need us to save them from themselves.'

She sighed. 'Sad, but true.'

Hugo leaned across and brushed my mouth with his. A wave of light-headedness assailed me and my breath caught in my throat. It wasn't drug-induced or fiend-induced or anything to do with my magic; this, I realised, was love. Love that gave me the sudden knowledge that everything would work out fine.

I smiled at Hugo, then glanced across and caught the eye of

the taxi driver. 'Are you free?' I called out. He looked surprised but nodded.

'It's clearly meant to be,' Hugo murmured.

I couldn't argue.

~

WE TOOK the taxi back to Edinburgh since there appeared little point now in avoiding the city. We didn't take any risks or waste any time with diversions but travelled straight to Freemark Hospital, where I knew I'd been left as a baby.

The building loomed large in front of us. Although I was doing the right thing, it still felt awful – and this was only a flavour of what Rose must be feeling. I adjusted the slight weight of Baby Daisy in my arms while Hugo wrote the note.

'Are you sure that you want me to write that she is – that *you* are – a low elf?' he asked.

I nodded. 'Yes. My identity has to stay hidden. It's the only way I can avoid Athair and keep everyone safe. And you have to include that my mother is dead. The police and my parents will still do a search to begin with, but anything we can add that will keep them at bay in the future will help. Include my first name, though – it's the only thing of my real self and of Rose that I've got. We know it'll be fine. It will probably never occur to Athair to check on his own doorstep for any babies left in local hospitals.'

Hugo did as I asked. Once he'd finished, he gave me the letter to look over.

I hadn't expected to start crying. He was alarmed. 'Daisy? We don't have to do this. We can think of another way.'

'No.' I wiped my eyes and tried to smile. 'This is how it has to be. It's just that...' My voice trailed off.

He touched my arm. 'What?'

I sniffed wetly. 'My parents kept everything from this time because they knew I'd want to have as much information as possible.' I pointed to the note. 'They still have this letter – I've read it a million times. This is the letter that was left with me – it was *always* the letter that was left with me. You always wrote it, Hugo.'

He stared at me. 'Then your theory is right and the past can't be changed. That much is clear.'

I wasn't sure if that made me feel better or worse. I sighed heavily and held Baby Daisy a little tighter for a few more moments. Perhaps babies weren't that terrifying after all.

Hester sniffed and nuzzled the top of her fuzzy red head. 'Take care, sweetheart. I'll see you soon when you're much bigger and much less cute.'

I scowled.

'I don't have to tell you to be good, Daisy,' Otis told her. 'I already know you will be.' He patted Baby Daisy's cheek with his tiny hand, then he and Hester stood back.

I handed Daisy to Hugo and swallowed the lump in my throat. He waited until I nodded, then turned and walked into the hospital. I already knew that he'd leave her in the emergency waiting room, in the blind spot in the corner where the fuzzy old CCTV wouldn't pick him up. And anyway, nobody would ever find Hugo; he didn't belong in this time period and he wouldn't be here for much longer, not as a thirty-two-year-old man.

I turned my back on the hospital and wrapped my arms around my body. This was how it was supposed to be; this was the best thing for me. I gazed across the busy car park at the horizon and stared, unseeing, at the familiar Edinburgh skyline.

Hester landed on my left shoulder and Otis flapped his way to my right. 'Are you alright, Daisy?' he asked anxiously.

'I will be.'

'Of course you will,' Hester said briskly. 'And now all that yucky business stuff is out of the way, we can finally start having some fun. There must still be a few days left before we get magically yanked back to 2024. Let's enjoy ourselves! I want to party!'

'We could do that,' I said. 'Or—'

Hester was already shaking her head. 'Oh no. Don't say it. Don't you dare!'

I smiled, but there was no humour in it. 'Or we could take advantage of the time we have left and make sure that Rose and Hugo's parents have the best head start possible.'

'We don't know where they've gone,' Otis said. 'So how on earth can we do that?'

Hugo came up behind me and put his arm around my waist. I searched his face, and his expression told me that everything had gone as planned. Baby Daisy was safe, at least for now. She would be looked after.

'Simple,' he said. 'We go after Athair ourselves. It's always better to be the hunter rather than the hunted.'

'No. Oh no.' Otis shook his head vigorously. 'We've agreed that it's impossible to change the past, and we know that Athair is alive in the future. You don't kill him. You probably *can't* kill him, now or later. He's too strong. There's no point in going after him! This is a terrible idea! You can't change anything.'

'We're heroes,' I told him. 'This is what we do.'

'Besides,' Hugo added, 'my parents survive this. We don't know for certain what happens to Rose, but there's a chance she survives unscathed, too.'

'*You* might still die! *You* might not survive this!' Hester screeched.

His response was matter of fact. 'I've got Daisy to protect me. I'll be fine.' I kissed his cheek.

'Who will protect Daisy?' Otis asked, arms flailing.

Hugo's dimple appeared. 'I will.'

'You're as bad as each other.' Hester clicked her tongue in mock derision. 'Ridiculous. Honestly, you idiots deserve each other.'

Our eyes met. Yep. I grinned – and this time my smile reached my eyes.

TWENTY-NINE

It didn't take long to agree a plan; truth be told, it would have been even faster if Hugo and I hadn't kept pausing to touch each other. There was nothing kinky in it – we didn't have time for anything like that – but his fingers repeatedly brushed the back of my hand, and I found several opportunities to touch his knee. We sat as close as we could; the presence of fiends made me itch, but the presence of Hugo made me shiver. Deliciously.

We rested and refuelled our bodies then, as soon as the sun slid down across the Edinburgh rooftops, we started. We would only get one shot at this so we had to make every second count. Athair was stronger, possessed better magic and was much, much more experienced than we were. I couldn't begin to fathom how old he was – but all those details that made us the obvious underdogs would drive us to success.

'David beat Goliath,' I said to Hugo.

He grinned. 'In 480AD, three hundred Spartans held off thousands of Persian soldiers.'

Otis squinted. 'Didn't they all die in the end?'

Hugo shrugged. 'Yeah, but I'd argue they still won.'

The brownies frowned, clearly still dubious about our plans.

'What about that cat video?' I suggested to them. 'Where the cat fends off an alligator?'

'Or Liverpool versus AC Milan in the 2005 UEFA Champions League final?' Hugo added. All three of us turned to stare at him. 'What?' he asked. 'They were the underdogs. They pulled off an amazing victory.'

'Do you know any football results from 1994?' Hester asked, speaking in a deliberately casual tone.

Hugo's brow creased. 'Brazil won the World Cup.' He paused. 'Actually, I think the FA Cup Final is tomorrow.'

'Who wins?'

'Manchester United, of course.'

Hester examined his face. 'Uh-huh.'

'What about horse racing in 1994?' Otis asked.

Hugo didn't hesitate. 'Miinehoma won the Grand National. Go For Gin won the Kentucky Derby.'

'And tennis?' Hester demanded with a side look in my direction.

'It's not my sport,' Hugo admitted. 'But I'm sure that Pete Sampras and Conchita Martinez won their respective Wimbledon finals.'

Hester folded her arms and glared at me; even Otis looked slightly put out.

'How on earth do you know all this?' I asked.

Hugo suddenly seemed faintly embarrassed. 'I like sport. When I was younger and had more time on my hands, I used to study past sporting events. I wanted to learn about form and history so I could hold my own with the old guys down the pub on a Saturday afternoon. And you know I love competition of any sort.'

Hester shook her head mournfully. 'What could have been,'

she muttered to herself. 'I wish you'd had a misspent youth, Daisy.'

'I did,' I retorted. 'It's just that mine involved drugs.'

I looked to the right and spotted an unnatural looking shadow loitering down a side street. Thank goodness: now I could change the subject. 'There's one,' I said with overly bright cheeriness. It was probably the first time anyone had been pleased to see a vampire.

I glanced down at the glassy eyes of the plastic doll in my arms. She was missing an arm and some enterprising child with an artistic bent had drawn all over her face with permanent marker, but that didn't present a problem to our plans.

'We *are* running away, right?' Hester asked.

'Yep.' I swung my head away from the lurking vamp. 'Act casual. And get ready.'

I cradled the doll. We were all tense, but even if the blood-sucker noticed our simmering anxiety it wouldn't make a difference. Anyone would be tense in our situation. I licked my lips, tugged at the blanket covering the doll, and snapped irritably and loudly at Hugo. 'We have to find shelter. It's already dark – it's far too risky to stay out here.'

He responded in kind. 'That damned fiend won't still be in Edinburgh. He thinks we've left, remember? He won't find us.'

'It's not only Athair we have to worry about! There will be vampires all over the place!'

Hugo hissed, 'Relax, will you? I know where we're going. It's not that far. Now stop yelling. If that baby starts crying...'

'She won't.'

'She's a baby. Crying is what they do.'

We exchanged glances and moved faster down the cobbled street. I had no idea how Athair communicated with the vampires or how powerful his control was over them, but I hoped his link with them was strong; in fact, I was counting on it.

I didn't look behind us, I left that to the brownies who were perched on my shoulders. I held my breath and waited, exhaling only when Otis whispered in my ear, 'She's following us.'

I kept my voice low. 'How many?'

'Just the one.'

That was both good and bad. I nodded, rocked the doll and kept moving quickly. *Come on, you cumbubbling bitch, come after us. Don't stop.*

As soon as we got to the bottom of Calton Road, with the grand shape of Holyrood Palace in front of us, I heard heavy breathing. There was more than one vamp behind us now.

I tapped my fingers on the doll.

Hester murmured, 'Four now.' She sounded scared. 'They're keeping their distance but they're definitely on our trail.'

Satisfaction flickered in my chest. Good; that was very good. 'Which way?' I asked Hugo loudly.

'Right,' he said.

'How much further?'

'Fifteen minutes. Stop stressing.' He still sounded annoyed. Damn: he was a far better actor than me.

We continued on our way. It was strange to pass the site of the Scottish Parliament when the proposals for its construction were a few years away. Most of Edinburgh city centre was old and the buildings had been erected long before Hugo and I had ever been thought of. They'd exist long after we were remembered, but it was good to realise that there would be innovation.

Nothing was set in stone, not even the existence of Athair. Whether he beat us or not, one day he would also cease to exist because not even a fiend could last forever. It was a minor epiphany, for sure, but it was more than enough to buoy my spirits.

It was just as well, because I needed something to keep me going. The gnawing hunger inside my belly was getting worse, though it wasn't for food: my body was craving spider's silk. I was already on half the dose I'd allowed myself a week ago, but I dared not reduce it any further – not without professional help. I didn't want to give into the temptation to swallow down more pills, either. It would be easy to use our plans as an excuse to take as much spider's silk as possible but I refused to do that. I could be strong in more ways than one.

My footsteps slowed as we drew closer to our destination. We didn't know where Athair was; if he was miles away, it could be hours before he got here, assuming he chose to take our bait. But that wasn't the only reason I was no longer hurrying. I didn't have a vast, all-encompassing desire to enter the five-hundred-metre tunnel that ran underneath Arthur's Seat. It wasn't as bad as venturing into a network of deep, dark caves, but it was far from my ideal hangout.

'Are you sure that this is a good idea?' Otis asked, not for the first time.

Hester tapped my cheek with taunting insistence. 'It'll be very easy to get trapped.'

'Can we agree not to use words like trapped?' I whispered.

'How about darker than a seemingly bottomless chasm inside Smoo Cave? How about those words?'

Hugo sprang to my defence. 'Enough, Hester. There are lights inside the tunnel. You know that.'

She stuck out her tongue at him, but at least she stopped baiting me. Now all I had to do was not think about the many tonnes of rock that would soon be above me. Perhaps she was right: perhaps walking blithely into the Innocent Railway Tunnel was a truly terrible idea.

Originally built to haul coal, the tunnel had been underneath Arthur's Seat for almost two hundred years. Even in 1994 it was decades since the railway was last operational; as in the future, the tunnel was used by walkers and cyclists seeking a quick route past the extinct volcano that overlooked the city.

I'd wandered through it many times but always during the day when daylight had been visible at either end. I'd never walked through it at night time – and I'd certainly never walked through it while being followed by a posse of thirsty vampires desperate to guzzle on my blood.

Hugo sensed my thoughts. 'If they weren't under Athair's control, they'd already have attacked. This will work, Daisy. I'll be right by your side all the way.'

It wasn't the vampires that worried me; at that point, it wasn't even Athair.

Hugo recognised my fear. 'Arthur's Seat won't collapse on top of us,' he added. 'Neither will the tunnel. In thirty years' time it'll be completely unchanged.'

If only phobias could be vanquished through rational thinking. I nodded. 'I'm fine. We've got this.'

He took my hand. 'We definitely do.'

I stared at the gaping hole in front of us. Hugo had been right about the lights: they lined the roof of the tunnel, illuminating it from one end to the other. The sight of them made me feel considerably better.

'It's not too late to back out,' Hester said.

A smile curved my mouth. This was for Rose, wherever she was. 'Yes, it is,' I said.

I released Hugo's hand and unsheathed Gladys; we didn't know what else might be lurking in the tunnel and I had to be ready for anything. From the expressions on Hugo and Otis's face, and the sudden, determined tilt to Hester's chin, we were all ready.

'At least I'll die a hero,' she said.

'Nobody's dying,' I told her firmly. Then we plunged inside.

Although the engineering and the history of the Innocent Railway Tunnel was impressive, in 1994 it wasn't a particularly pleasant place. Graffiti, none of which was artistically impressive, lined the walls; a stale stench of urine combined with damp earthiness tickled my nostrils.

And there were rats. Not hundreds – this wasn't an infestation of plague proportions – but enough to make Otis squeal aloud several times. The sound echoed down the long tunnel. Even Hugo looked queasy at the sight of the sleek, furry bodies darting along the edges of the tunnel. I couldn't recall spotting any rats here in the future, so Edinburgh Council must have conducted a thorough clean-up at some point, probably around the time Tracey's vamp spray took off and people were no longer afraid to walk around at night. Still, I was thankful that the rats were the only other creatures inside the tunnel besides us.

About fifty metres in, I turned and checked on the bloodsuckers who were following us. What I saw gave me further hope: not a single one of them had entered the tunnel. Their shifting, twitching silhouettes were clustered at the entrance, hungrily watching us, but they weren't taking a step inside. They were waiting, and we all knew who they were waiting for.

I smiled coldly, then I turned and kept walking.

The tunnel led to Holyrood Park, which we already knew wouldn't contain many lurking vampires. It was a calculated risk on our part that any would appear at the other end because if the bloodsuckers were acting on their own impulses, it wouldn't occur to them to block both ends of the tunnel. Undead creatures weren't capable of thinking strategically. However, we needed to give every indication that we were trapped, so Hester and Otis zipped ahead. When they returned, they were bobbing their heads in fearful unison.

Less than a minute later, I saw several of the fanged fuckers hovering outside. Now there were vampires to the left of us and vampires to the right. Everything was in place, and the sooner Athair also showed up the better. The wait had begun.

An hour passed, then two. Although it was early summer and I was wrapped in warm clothes and a good coat, I still felt cold. It didn't help that every minute ticked by with an inexorable lack of speed: every second felt like a minute, and every minute felt like an hour.

I huddled next to Hugo, trying to ignore my deep craving for more spider's silk, while Hester and Otis dozed on my shoulders. The vampires stayed where they were.

'It's gone midnight,' Hugo eventually whispered. 'No sign of him yet.'

I glanced up and nodded. Time for a little nudge.

I pulled out my mobile phone; there was very little battery life left but it had been turned off for almost the entire time I'd spent in 1994 so there was enough charge to serve our purposes.

I pressed the button to bring it to life and shielded the screen so that its glare wasn't obvious. The recording was ready and waiting to go; without ceremony, I pressed play and made sure it was on repeat.

Within seconds the sound of a baby crying filled the tunnel, amplified by the low ceiling and curved walls. It wasn't Baby Daisy because the plan hadn't occurred to us until after we'd left her at Freemark Hospital, but we reckoned that one baby's cry sounded much like another's. It hadn't taken long to find another baby to record so that our bait was well and truly on the hook.

I put my phone on top of the one-armed plastic doll and

tucked it into the blankets. Then I crossed my fingers very tightly.

Less than ten minutes later, all my fiendish wishes came true.

THIRTY

We heard Athair before we saw him and, even though I'd been praying for it, the sound of his booming, harsh voice still made me jump. 'Where the fuck is my daughter?'

The recorded cries of the anonymous baby continued to echo out from my dying phone. It would shut down for good in the next few minutes but that no longer mattered because the twenty-first century technology had already served its purpose.

I recovered from my jolt and cricked my neck, watching as the crowd of vampires at the far end of the tunnel parted. It was impossible to make out Athair's features from this distance but it was unmistakably him. His broad shoulders, combined with the way he held himself, were instantly recognisable, and when he walked into the tunnel the dim electric lights bounced off his golden skin.

At least, I thought darkly, *he's not bothered to conceal his true self again.* I preferred it when he was honest about what he was – and this would be much easier if we were the only ones playing games.

'Get back, you fucking fiend!' Hugo roared.

I gave him an approving nod and he grinned, then we gave our full attention to Athair who was striding towards us.

'For the record, can I just say that is the worst idea anyone has ever had in the history of all ideas ever?' Hester muttered.

Gladys buzzed loudly by my side in disagreement. She was hungry for Athair's blood – and so was I.

'Hand over Daisy,' Athair called, 'and I will consider letting you go.'

Yeah, yeah. If he truly thought we'd believe that, he was a complete idiot. He still didn't appear to have made the final connection and worked out who I was to him, although he surely had to have his suspicions by now. Still, it was a big fat tick on our list of things that we needed to survive this encounter.

I called back with a counter-demand. 'Come any closer and we will kill her!' Athair burst out laughing and my blood turned to ice. Dread that he'd already deciphered our plans filled every inch of my soul.

Then Hugo nudged me; Athair had slowed his steps. When he stopped and stretched his arms out wide, my tension eased. Maybe we had him.

'Kill a baby?' He laughed even harder. 'You honestly think you're capable of that? How do you plan to do it? Cut her throat and watch her blood spill out while the life drains from her innocent eyes? Perhaps you'll smother her, or break her neck. *I've* done all those things to other children in the past and it was easy – enjoyable, in fact. I doubt you could say the same.'

The thought that Athair might have actually killed babies with his bare hands sickened me, but I couldn't pretend to be surprised. 'Better that she's dead,' I answered, 'than that she becomes a fiend.'

'Really?' he asked sardonically. 'You don't believe in free will, then? You don't believe she's capable of making up her own mind as to what her future holds? I can't force anyone, not even my own progeny, into becoming one of the most powerful beings this world has ever seen because that decision has to come from them. But if you harm her, that will be wholly on you. You will have to live with what you've done.'

Then he added, 'Not that you will live for very long if you hurt her. It's taken me far too long to find a woman capable of bearing my child and far too long to bring that child into existence. I won't walk away, no matter how much you shake your fists or how many empty threats you throw out. That baby belongs with me.'

With that, he started to stride towards us once again. 'There's no way out of this for you. You're already trapped and your fate is already drawn.'

That's what he thought, but there was more than one reason why we'd chosen this tunnel as the venue for our showdown. It was damp, with a lot of moisture clinging to both the walls and the air, and that made it easier to pull on water magic and create the effect we required.

With Hugo still at my shoulder and the plastic doll and my phone in my arms, I yanked on every aspect of water magic that I could find. It was extraordinary how much easier it was to control my powers now; if I hadn't killed Vargas, I'd have owed him a big favour.

I pulled my mouth into a smile and jerked my head at the brownies to move behind us, then muttered to Hugo. 'Three,' I said, 'Two...'

He flicked his wrists. 'One.'

The resulting cascade of rushing water was phenomenal.

The conjuration started in front of us, then we pushed it out, slamming our tsunami-like creation towards Athair. I didn't waste time watching Athair being knocked off his feet and sent tumbling back towards the entrance of the tunnel; instead, I grabbed Gladys.

While she buzzed an alarmed protest, I twisted her blade and cut through my own skin. I winced at the pain, but I needed plenty of fresh blood for this to work. I thrust the doll at Hugo and he held it up while I smeared blood across her cold, plastic body and the blanket. Then I sucked in a breath and threw the doll after the gushing torrent.

The doll joined the swirl of water and the debris that had been caught up in the flood. As soon as it was sucked away, Hugo and I ran – heading towards Athair rather than away from him.

There was only so much water we could magick up in one go. By the time we started sprinting towards him, Athair had recovered enough to regain his footing, although he'd been forced back to the tunnel's entrance.

He roared with fury, somehow managing to make more racket than the water had achieved. I answered him with a high-pitched scream, timing it to the very moment that the doll tumbled past his feet into the crowd of watching vampires.

Athair's head jerked as he spotted it, but it was already too late. Although the water would have washed away most of my smeared blood, there was enough on the blanket to send the bloodsuckers into a frenzy. Athair had great control over them – but in the end their bloodlust was greater.

As if they were one amorphous group, they descended on the doll, screaming and chomping their teeth. Athair bellowed a command, but the vampires had been waiting for too long and they were starving.

My fiendish father spun and plunged towards the vampires, using his magic to send them flying in all directions. I could hear the delighted screams of the vampires at the other end of the tunnel as they whooped and raced after us.

I bit my lip, concentrated hard and threw a jet of hot fire over my shoulder in their direction. I didn't check to see if I'd hit my targets.

WHILE HE BLASTED AWAY the last of the crazed vampires and bent down to reach for whatever remained of the doll, we reached the end of the tunnel. I couldn't allow a second's delay; it wouldn't take Athair long to discover our trick.

When his body jerked with belated comprehension that he was desperately trying to save a doll, I thrust Gladys at him, swiping her blade at his exposed back. She hummed loudly in anticipation as I slashed at his flesh. His skin was tougher than I'd expected, but she still managed to slice an inch deep into his body.

Hugo followed up my heavy swipe with a burst of air magic. Athair let out a strangled cry and pitched forward face first. I leapt forward, more than prepared to finish him off with a single killing blow, but my father wasn't done yet. Without so much as a twitch, power rocketed out of him, and Hugo, both brownies and I were sent crashing backwards. Cumbubbling bollocks.

I tried to get to my feet, but my brain wasn't sending the right messages to my body and my limbs wouldn't obey. Gulping for air sent scalding pain through my chest. I hadn't lost my grip on Gladys, but when I tried to lift her blade towards me for close defence I couldn't manage it. Athair had sent no more than a single flare of air magic towards us and it had almost destroyed us.

A shadow fell across my body. I dimly registered the blood dripping from his side. From the way he was acting it was nothing more than a scratch, although his face was contorted with rage. He leaned over my useless body, grabbed my throat with one hand and hauled me up until we were face to face.

'You're brave,' he snarled. 'And that was a clever feint.' He bared his teeth and his scarlet eyes burned into me. 'But it wasn't close to being clever enough.' He turned his head to stare at Hugo. 'Tell me where my daughter is or your girlfriend dies.'

I choked and spluttered – it felt like my eyes were bulging out of their sockets. My legs were kicking uselessly in the air. I could hear Hester and Otis shouting at Athair but their words barely registered. 'Let her go! Let her go!'

Athair tightened his fingers. My vision was all but gone and I could no longer see him, even though he was right in front of me. I had seconds left – at best.

Hugo muttered something. Hester cried out again, 'Let Daisy go!'

And then Athair released me and I landed on the tunnel floor with a heavy thump.

Arms reached around me, but this time it was Hugo who was holding me. He pulled me back and wrapped himself around me as I swallowed repeatedly, trying to regain control of my bruised throat and trembling vocal chords.

'My name,' I croaked eventually, 'is Daisy.'

Athair spat on the ground. 'That means nothing.'

'We weren't lying before, you wanker,' Hester yelled.

'We're from the future!' Otis shouted. 'We've travelled back from 2024 because you made Daisy trip a magical golden skull into action. It sent us here!'

'We can prove who we are,' Hugo added. 'Manchester United will win the FA Cup this weekend.'

Athair snorted. 'Which proves nothing.'

I gave a mocking smile. With the last of my energy, I tossed out a flicker of lightning; it wasn't enough to hurt Athair, but it sizzled when it hit the damp ground at his feet.

'When was the last time you saw an ordinary elf do that?' I whispered.

He stared at me as the penny finally dropped. I took advantage of the moment and struggled to my feet with Hugo's help. It seemed to take an age, but eventually we were both looking directly into Athair's face.

'I have to say that when you come to me in the future and tell me I'm your daughter, I deal with the information far better than you're doing right now.'

His red eyes remained narrowed. 'I don't believe you.'

I felt incredibly calm. 'Yes, you do. You know who I am.' I paused, actually enjoying the moment. 'Haven't you wondered where Vargas has been for the last few days?'

Athair jerked.

I was only getting warmed up; any trace of fear had melted away.

I touched my hair. 'I have this from Lady Rose.' I pointed at my face. 'I suspect most of this is from you, not that you'd be able to tell nowadays with all your fiend shit. My skin isn't golden and it never will be. You might as well carry on strangling me, Athair. I might be your daughter by blood but I'll never be your daughter in reality. I'll never be *yours*.'

Athair reached out and for a moment I thought he'd follow through and continue with his bid to kill me. Instead, he extended a finger and swiped a bead of blood from the wound I'd sliced on my arm. He raised it to his lips and licked it, he blinked once and stared at me again.

I squinted. 'Really?' I asked. 'Can you tell we share a few genes from *that*?'

Athair didn't answer.

I tried to shrug, but unfortunately I mostly just winced. 'I can't tell you what will happen beyond May of 2024,' I said.

'But I do know that you won't find me for another twenty-nine years. I'm gone, and so is Rose. You won't see her ever again.'

I waited, holding my breath. Hugo's body also tightened.

Athair's expression cleared, although this time there was a definite hint of awe in his face. So he did believe me; he knew I was telling the truth.

His eyes swept me up and down and he nodded. 'Yes,' he whispered. '*Yes*. You're scrawnier than I'd envisaged – and yet you are her. You are my daughter. And from what you say, I *do* find you eventually.' He released a low whistle. 'Time travel. What an extraordinary feat. I should have expected nothing less from a child of my own loins.'

Ick. 'I think I just threw up a little in my mouth,' I said to Hugo.

A slow smile spread across Athair's face. 'I've found you, Daisy. You're right here. And you're mine.'

I smirked. 'Not for long. The magic that brought us here is temporary. No matter what you might try to do, all four of us will be hauled back to where we belong.' I glanced at Hugo. 'In a day, do you think?'

'Less, I imagine,' Hugo replied.

'Rose is no longer in your clutches,' I sneered. 'And soon I will be far away too.'

Athair chuckled. 'Oh, Daisy, not that far away. Twenty-nine years is little more than a breath for me.' He exhaled with satisfaction. 'You and I will do great things together.'

Wanker. 'I will never become a fiend. I'll never be like you.'

He was still smiling. 'We'll have to see about that.' He leaned closer. 'I can show you the world. It will be ours for the taking, just wait and see.'

'Never going to happen.' There was an odd crackling sound in my ears as I tossed his own words at him. 'You don't believe in free will? I promise you now, Daddy Dearest, I will never be like you.'

My stomach lurched suddenly. 'The apple has fallen much further from the tree than you might think,' I hissed.

Athair's lips were moving but I couldn't hear what he was saying. I swayed from side to side, feeling very light-headed, and the crackling sound morphed into a high-pitched ringing.

My eyes widened. *No. Not yet.* I wasn't done yet. Cumbubbling bollocks. 'See you in twenty-nine years or so,' I said, and as soon as the last word left my mouth there was a flash of blinding white light.

I fell onto my hands and knees, retching uncontrollably. There was a loud expletive from behind me and I raised my head in time to see a cyclist veer past me. 'Watch out, you fucking muppet!' he yelled. 'You can't appear out of nowhere like that!' I retched again.

Hester grabbed a curl of my hair. 'Daisy!' she shrieked. 'Are you alright?'

Otis flitted in front of my face. 'It's daylight! We're back. We did it, Daisy!'

'Hugo,' I groaned. He wasn't here: he was still in 1994 with Athair. 'Hugo,' I said again. 'Where—?'

The air popped. A second later there was a loud thump and Hugo's body hit the ground next to me. I lurched towards him, my fingers scrabbling at his skin to check if he was alright.

He moaned and raised his blue eyes to mine. 'We were brought back far sooner than I expected,' he whispered. 'But I think it worked. I think we gave Athair enough reason to leave Rose alone. He knows he'll catch up to you again, no matter what happens. He doesn't need her any more.'

He sagged forward into my arms and we clung onto each other for dear life.

THIRTY-ONE

J une 10*th*, 2024

We spent a warm June night at the French château where Charles and Tash spent most of their time. After a nervous breakfast of croissants, cold cuts and creamy cheese, we clambered into their car to make the short journey to the cottage on the other side of the river. It was a tight squeeze to fit everybody in, but we couldn't leave anyone out.

'It's pretty here,' Hester commented. 'Maybe you should move to France, too, Daisy.'

I nodded, although it was to indicate that I'd heard her rather than to imply I had any intention of living abroad. It *was* beautiful, though. The more I saw of the gently rolling hills, lush vineyards and quaint farm buildings nestled comfortably in the landscape, the more I understood why someone would want to live here. The sunshine and warm weather certainly helped, too. But unfortunately nothing about the stunning location eased the nervous churn in my stomach. My hands were shaking, though whether that was from nerves or the spider's silk I'd swallowed before I'd left the house, I couldn't have said for sure.

'You should have told me, you know,' Hugo said to his parents. 'I can't believe you knew the truth all these years and you didn't tell me.'

I glanced at Gordon. He was squeezed into the corner of the car, his gangly frame folded over in a position that looked incredibly uncomfortable. He flushed slightly and nodded. 'If you'd at least spoken to Grace Assigney and told her the truth, it would have saved a lot of the unpleasantness you've experienced over the years.'

Tash's face was now lined but it still held the same twinkling kindness as it had thirty years ago. She smiled gently. 'It wouldn't have changed anything. We knew what we were letting ourselves in for. Our silence helped to keep both Rose and Daisy safe for all these years. We knew the truth and that was enough for us.'

Hugo's voice was tight. 'I didn't know, although I suspected there was something you were keeping from me.' It was better he didn't mention that those suspicions had included wondering if they really had killed Rose. That particular revelation wouldn't help anyone.

Tash patted his hand. 'It was safer for you not to know. And look at what has happened with you and Daisy *because* you didn't know. It's all worked out for the best.'

Except that Athair was still out there, and he would move heaven and earth to bring me to his fiendish side. He had surely worked out that my friends and family made me vulnerable; while he still breathed, he presented the gravest danger to all of us.

'What happened to the skull?' Tash asked. 'Do you have it? I'd love to see the object that started all of this.'

Hugo snorted. 'The British Museum snatched it within hours of our return from 1994. I expect it'll be safely buried in a deep vault for the rest of time. We'll never see it again.'

His mother looked disappointed, but I was relieved they'd taken it off our hands. Time travelling was an unsettling business – not to mention incredibly dangerous.

Charles indicated left, then turned onto a narrow gravel-lined driveway with leafy trees planted along one side of it. Within moments the trees gave way to a pretty cottage, and I realised that it looked exactly like the painting that still hung in the Assigney mansion. There were the same roses in pink, red and dusky-orange hues, though the daisies, planted in beds all along the side of the house, were new. They certainly weren't in the old portrait.

I gazed at them and a lump caught in my throat.

'Are you okay?' Hugo asked gruffly.

I nodded; I still felt shaky and anxious, but I was okay. Everything was okay.

Charles parked in front of the cottage. 'You should go in first, Daisy,' he said. 'When you're ready, the rest of us will join you.'

'I'm not waiting in the car!' Hester protested.

Otis flapped towards her, cupped his hands and whispered something in her ear. She pouted then her shoulders dropped. 'Fine,' she muttered. 'I'll wait.'

I didn't want to go in alone; this meeting wasn't only about me. I looked at my mum and dad, my beautiful, loving, adoptive parents, whose expressions reflected my own nerves. 'Come with me,' I whispered. They started to shake their heads and I raised my voice. 'Please,' I said. 'Come with me.'

Mum's bottom lip trembled and so did Dad's. 'Are you sure, Daisy?' he asked.

'You're my family,' I told them. 'I need you there.'

Preparing to speak, Hester drew in a breath but Otis jabbed her sharply in her ribs and she subsided. I smiled at them. 'You're my family as well. Just give us a bit of time first, then you're welcome to come in too. We only need a moment.'

Hugo planted a brief kiss on my cheek. 'You've got this, Daisy. It'll be great.'

I wiped my sweaty palms down the fabric of my trousers. 'Yep. It'll be wonderful.' Then, before I could chicken out, I opened the car door and stepped out.

Rose was waiting for us, and she opened the cottage door long before we reached it. Her fingers were twisting together in front of her as she waited for us on the doorstep.

Her red hair was shorter and there were fine lines around her tear-filled eyes. I could tell she was scared, but there was calmness and wisdom there too, even though deep down she was the same steely, bright-eyed, brave woman I'd met thirty years ago. She was older but she looked happier.

I stepped towards her and her arms went around me. 'I shouldn't be surprised,' she whispered in my ear. 'And yet I am. You look exactly the same.'

A soft laugh escaped my lips. It had only been days since I had seen her, but it had been half a lifetime for her since she'd seen me.

'I'm sorry I ran away like that, Daisy.' Her voice cracked. 'It was done with the best of intentions. There's not been a single day when I haven't thought of you. You have to know that I didn't want to abandon you. Please, please forgive me.'

I swallowed the painful knot in my throat. 'There's nothing to forgive. *Nothing*. You did nothing wrong.' I hugged her tightly then stepped back and gestured to my mum and dad, who were standing awkwardly behind me.

'This is Alison and Mike,' I told her. 'My mum and dad.'

Rose brushed away a tear from her cheek then she embraced them tightly, too. 'Your daughter is a wonderful person,' she said.

My mum sniffed. '*Your* daughter is a wonderful person.'

I bit my lip hard. 'We're all wonderful people,' I told them. And I meant it whole-heartedly.

THERE WERE MORE TEARS, more introductions and many more hugs; in fact, it was a full hour before our group was seated comfortably in Rose's garden with enough tea and cake to satisfy an army.

'Alain is a great cook,' Rose told us, waving a hand at her husband.

I smiled at the good-looking, genial, Frenchman whose salt-and-pepper hair caught the sunlight and whose warm gaze whenever he looked at Rose displayed his love for her. Despite all the turmoil and the trauma, my birth mother had found her way in life and she was happy. That knowledge meant more than I could have anticipated.

Hester, whose cheeks were stuffed full of chocolatey crumbs, nodded vigorously. 'Mmmmph.'

'She likes your brownies,' Otis translated.

'*Merci*,' Alain said with a bow. 'Thank you.'

Gordon, who was also looking happier than I'd ever seen him before, took a sip from his cup then laid it on the small table in front of us. He cleared his throat and glanced at all of us before his gaze settled on Rose. 'I'm very glad you're alive.'

Rose laughed. 'So am I.'

He coughed again. 'What's next?'

The crinkle around her eyes deepened. 'I'm hoping to get to know my daughter a little better.' She looked at my parents. 'And her mum and dad. If that's alright with all of you.'

My mum leaned forward and took Rose's hand. 'We're all family now.'

Dad bobbed his head. 'The more the merrier.' He grinned happily and raised his cup to her.

Gordon smiled but he wasn't giving up. 'Will you come back? To Scotland?'

Rose exchanged glances with Alain. 'I sincerely doubt that Athair has any lingering interest in me.' She flicked a worried glance in my direction. 'He only ever wanted a child. While I might have been the first woman who could give him one, I'm now fifty years old and my time to have more children has passed. I've not attempted to wield blood magic since 1994. Any vestige of that dark power that remains inside me is buried so deep I think it's highly unlikely it could ever return. I'm neither a danger nor a temptation to him.'

She shrugged. 'That's not to say he wouldn't approach me to take his revenge, but I suspect it would be nothing more than pettiness. And,' she added pointedly, 'it wouldn't encourage Daisy to his side, which I'm sure we all know is what he wants.'

A discomfiting stiffness spread through my body, even though I accepted the truth of what she was saying. 'Nothing will encourage me to his side,' I said. '*Nothing.*'

'He's more manipulative than you know,' she said softly. A grim silence descended but then Rose offered me a half-smile. 'But you're stronger than he knows, too.'

I fiddled with my cuffs. My initial response was to refute her words but deep down I knew that I was strong. I hadn't survived my wild magic and my drug addiction for this many years through sheer luck – even if my greatest challenges were yet to come.

'So you could come back, Rose?' Hugo asked. 'You could return to the Assigney mansion?'

She took a few moments to respond, though it was clear from her expression that she'd been expecting the question. 'I've spent more of my life here than I have in Scotland. This is my home now. I don't want to be Lady Rose.' She touched the centre of her chest. 'I am glad that I'm still alive, but the Lady Rose that people knew has been dead for a long time. It's Lady Daisy's turn to shine now.'

Oh God. I gulped.

'I hear that you took a DNA test recently,' Rose added. 'That will be more than enough to prove you are my daughter without my sudden reappearance.'

Hester looked up from the pile of cakes. 'Don't worry, my lady,' she said to me with an airy, albeit chocolate-smeared, hand. 'I'll show you how to act. We can begin your elocution and deportment training immediately. We can practise tomorrow when we go shopping.'

'Shopping?'

She smirked. 'For all those dripping diamonds you'll soon be wearing.'

As if. Otis looked at her and snorted. 'Do you know Daisy at all?' he asked.

With a deliberately casual movement, Hester reached forward and scooped up some ganache then flung it at Otis's face. He dodged it with ease.

Aware this could quickly descend into all-out war between them, I snagged him in the palm of my hand while Hugo did the same to Hester. 'Enough,' I said.

I turned my head and gazed at Hugo and he gave a gentle smile in return. There was no pressure in his expression, and no judgement. I knew from the bottom of my soul that he was prepared to support me whatever I did next. All I could offer was the truth in return.

'I don't know what will come of that,' I said simply. I looked from my birth mother, Rose, to my adoptive parents. 'There's a lot to navigate and a lot to consider. I don't want to rush into anything. And there's something that I have to take care of first.'

My dad's eyes narrowed. 'This Athair fellow.' His cheeks stained red. 'He's not your father, Daisy. He never will be, no matter what story your blood may tell.'

'I know that, Dad.' I licked my lips, wishing I didn't feel so nervous. 'But there's something else I've got to do that's more important than Athair and whatever he wants of me. It's more important than the Assigney mansion or titles.'

'Is it more important than diamonds?' Hester asked sceptically, but her eyes were twinkling. She knew what I was going to say next.

I grinned at her. 'Much more important.' I reached across and used my free hand to clasp Hugo's.

Mum gasped. 'Has Hugo proposed?'

I stared at her. 'Mother! Seriously? We're not even in a real relationship!'

Hugo leaned into my ear. 'I'm not so sure about that,' he murmured. His thumb rubbed my ring finger.

Now it was my cheeks that were growing hot. 'It's not that,' I said stiffly. I resolutely refused to look at him and focused on my shoes. 'There's something else I haven't told you.' I held my breath for a moment and then plunged ahead, ripping off the metaphorical plaster as quickly as I could.

'I'm a drug addict. I've been addicted to spider's silk since I was fifteen years old.' The words were tripping over each other. 'I'm finally in a position to do something about it so I'm planning to start rehabilitation. Getting clean has to be my main focus and it will be awful. The thought of it terrifies me but I know I can do it. I *know* I can.'

I continued to stare at my shoes as Hugo's fingers tightened around mine.

I couldn't hear any sharp intakes of breath so eventually I raised my head, terrified of what I might see but unable to hide from the truth any longer.

Gordon and Hugo were watching me carefully, as were Hester and Otis – but they already knew. It was Rose, my parents, Hugo's parents and even Alain who were all looking at me with genuine concern but also unexpected warmth. Huh. It was obvious that they were deeply worried, but they weren't disgusted. They weren't running away.

'Oh, Daisy, this is our fault. We knew there was something going on,' my mum said. 'I didn't realise it was drugs. I never imagined...' She swallowed. 'I'm so sorry.'

I was absolutely adamant. 'It is *not* your fault. There are a million and one reasons why I'm a drug addict and you are not one of them.'

'Why didn't you tell us?' my dad whispered.

I still felt shaky. 'I was scared. I didn't want to hurt you or worry you. It was better this way.'

'Oh, my poor girl.' Mum reached for one of my hands and Rose took the other. 'We should have done something. We should have helped you, Daisy.'

I met her eyes. 'Believe me, there is nothing you could have said or done that would have made a difference.'

'Since you were fifteen?' Dad asked in a small voice.

I bit my lip and nodded.

'The fire,' my mum said as realisation dawned. 'When the house burnt down.'

'Yeah.' My fingers twitched nervously. 'That was my fault. I couldn't control my magic and it flared up during the night when we were sleeping. After that, I started taking spider's silk because it helped me to control my powers.'

'Oh, Daisy.'

I gave a tremulous smile. 'It's okay. I'm okay. And soon I'll be better than okay because I *will* get clean.'

'You have our support all the way,' Rose said.

'All our support,' my mum agreed.

As I looked at both of my mothers, a wellspring of happiness bubbled up inside me. With their help, I could do this. Suddenly I knew that nothing else mattered. Athair didn't matter because he didn't have people like this around him. These people were mine and I was theirs, and drug addiction would soon be nothing more than a note in Daisy Carter Assigney's history book .

'You also have all our love,' my dad added. 'Always.'

'Yes, Daisy,' Hugo murmured by my side. 'You have all my love, too.'

'But you don't have diamonds,' Hester muttered.

A huge grin flashed across my face. 'We'll set up a treasure hunt for some as soon as I've recovered.' I glanced at Hugo. 'If you're in?'

His dimple appeared in his cheek. 'Always.'

AUTHOR'S NOTES

Author's notes

The Fonaby Sack Stone does indeed exist near Caistor in Lincolnshire, England. According to legend, a seventh-century missionary named St Paulinus was passing through the area when he stopped to ask a local farmer for some grain from a nearby sack to feed his mule. The farmer, unwilling to give away any of his produce, lied and told Paulinus that it was a stone and not a sack. The missionary, unimpressed at the farmer's lack of charity, duly turned it into a stone in revenge.

Many stories about the curse are now attached to the stone, including one about a poor stonemason in the nineteenth century who cut a piece from it and died in an accident shortly afterwards.

While I've not visited the site myself, there are numerous anecdotes online about the unnatural and eerie atmosphere around the stone.

Culcreuch Castle, where Athair hides out, is located near Fintry, near Stirling in central Scotland, although mostly it has been used is as a hotel and wedding destination rather than a fiend's lair. Parts of the castle date from the thirteenth century – and it does indeed have a dungeon.

The Innocent Railway Tunnel is a frequently-used passageway beneath Arthur's Seat which nowadays forms part of the national cycle network. I have never seen any rats or fiends inside it.

Helen x

ACKNOWLEDGMENTS

There have been so many people involved in the creation of this book and I owe a huge thank to them all. Firstly, Clarissa Yeo and JoY Cover Designs created the gorgeous cover in all its magical glory. Karen Holmes has not only been a fabulous editor but has also been a great cheerleader all the way alone. Thanks must also go to Ruth Urquhart for her wonderful audio-book narration and help with all the errant typos along the way.

There are also many ARC readers whose contribution has been invaluable. Their support means the world. I'd also like to drop in a special mention to those readers who have been in touch to discuss Daisy's drug addiction and the personal impact on them. You know who you are and your honesty and openness with your messages has been truly treasured.

Finally, thank to you, my fabulous readers. It might sound like a cliche but it's the absolute truth. I wouldn't be able to do any of this without you.

Helen x

Also by Helen Harper

The *FireBrand* series

A werewolf killer. A paranormal murder. How many times can Emma Bellamy cheat death?

I'm one placement away from becoming a fully fledged London detective. It's bad enough that my last assignment before I qualify is with Supernatural Squad. But that's nothing compared to what happens next.

Brutally murdered by an unknown assailant, I wake up twelve hours later in the morgue – and I'm very much alive. I don't know how or why it happened. I don't know who killed me. All I know is that they might try again.

Werewolves are disappearing right, left and centre.

A mysterious vampire seems intent on following me everywhere I go.

And I have to solve my own vicious killing. Preferably before death comes for me again.

adopted family by hiding her apparent humanity, she also has to seek the blood-soaked vengeance that she craves.

Book One - Bloodfire

Book Two - Bloodmagic

Book Three - Bloodrage

Book Four - Blood Politics

Book Five - Bloodlust

Also

Corrigan Fire

Corrigan Magic

Corrigan Rage

Corrigan Politics

Corrigan Lust

The complete *Bo Blackman* series

A half-dead daemon, a massacre at her London based PI firm and evidence that suggests she's the main suspect for both ... Bo Blackman is having a very bad week.

She might be naive and inexperienced but she's determined to get to the bottom of the crimes, even if it means involving herself with one of London's most powerful vampire Families and their enigmatic leader.

It's pretty much going to be impossible for Bo to ever escape unscathed.

Book One - Dire Straits

Book Two - New Order

Book Three - High Stakes

Book Four - Red Angel

Book Five - Vigilante Vampire

Book Six - Dark Tomorrow

The complete *Highland Magic* series

Integrity Taylor walked away from the Sidhe when she was a child. Orphaned and bullied, she simply had no reason to stay, especially not when the sins of her father were going to remain on her shoulders. She found a new family - a group of thieves who proved that blood was less important than loyalty and love.

But the Sidhe aren't going to let Integrity stay away forever. They need her more than anyone realises - besides, there are prophecies to be fulfilled, people to be saved and hearts to be won over. If anyone can do it, Integrity can.

Book One - Gifted Thief

Book Two - Honour Bound

Book Three - Veiled Threat

Book Four - Last Wish

The complete *Dreamweaver* series

"I have special coping mechanisms for the times I need to open the front door. They're even often successful..."

Zoe Lydon knows there's often nothing logical or rational about fear. It doesn't change the fact that she's too terrified to step outside her own house, however.

What Zoe doesn't realise is that she's also a dreamweaver - able to access other people's subconscious minds. When she finds herself in the Dreamlands and up against its sinister Mayor, she'll need to use all of her wits - and overcome all of her fears - if she's ever going to come out alive.

Book One - Night Shade

Book Two - Night Terrors

Book Three - Night Lights

Stand alone novels

Eros

William Shakespeare once wrote that, "Cupid is a knavish lad, thus to make poor females mad." The trouble is that Cupid himself would probably agree...

As probably the last person in the world who'd appreciate hearts, flowers and romance, Coop is convinced that true love doesn't exist – which is rather unfortunate considering he's also known as Cupid, the God of Love. He'd rather spend his days drinking, womanising and generally having as much fun as he possible can. As far as he's concerned, shooting people with bolts of pure love is a waste of his time...but then his path crosses with that of shy and retiring Skye Sawyer and nothing will ever be quite the same again.

Wraith

Magic. Shadows. Adventure. Romance.

Saiya Buchanan is a wraith, able to detach her shadow from her body and send it off to do her bidding. But, unlike most of her kin, Saiya doesn't deal in death. Instead, she trades secrets - and in the goblin besieged city of Stirling in Scotland, they're a highly prized commodity. It might just be, however, that the goblins have been hiding the greatest secret of them all. When Gabriel de Florinville, a Dark Elf, is sent as royal envoy into Stirling and takes her prisoner, Saiya is not only going to uncover the sinister truth. She's also going to realise that sometimes the deepest secrets are the ones locked within your own heart.

The complete *Lazy Girl's Guide To Magic* series

Hard Work Will Pay Off Later. Laziness Pays Off Now.

Let's get one thing straight - Ivy Wilde is not a heroine. In fact, she's probably the last witch in the world who you'd call if you needed a magical helping hand. If it were down to Ivy, she'd spend all day every day on her sofa where she could watch TV, munch junk food and talk to her feline familiar to her heart's content.

However, when a bureaucratic disaster ends up with Ivy as the victim of a case of mistaken identity, she's yanked very unwillingly into Arcane Branch, the investigative department of the Hallowed Order of Magical Enlightenment. Her problems are quadrupled when a valuable object is stolen right from under the Order's noses.

It doesn't exactly help that she's been magically bound to Adeptus Exemptus Raphael Winter. He might have piercing sapphire eyes and a body which a cover model would be proud of but, as far as Ivy's concerned, he's a walking advertisement for the joyless perils of too much witch-work.

And if he makes her go to the gym again, she's definitely going to turn him into a frog.

Book One - Slouch Witch

Book Two - Star Witch

Book Three - Spirit Witch

Sparkle Witch (Christmas short story)

The complete *Fractured Faery* series

One corpse. Several bizarre looking attackers. Some very strange magical powers. And a severe bout of amnesia.

It's one thing to wake up outside in the middle of the night with a decapitated man for company. It's another to have no memory of how you got there - or who you are.

She might not know her own name but she knows that several people are out to get her. It could be because she has strange magical powers seemingly at her fingertips and is some kind of fabulous hero. But then why does she appear to inspire fear in so many? And who on earth is the sexy, green-eyed barman who apparently despises her? So many questions ... and so few answers.

At least one thing is for sure - the streets of Manchester have never met someone quite as mad as Madrona...

Book One - Box of Frogs

SHORTLISTED FOR THE KINDLE STORYTELLER AWARD 2018

Book Two - Quiver of Cobras

Book Three - Skulk of Foxes

The complete *City Of Magic* series

Charley is a cleaner by day and a professional gambler by night. She might be haunted by her tragic past but she's never thought of herself as anything or anyone special. Until, that is, things start to go terribly wrong all across the city of Manchester. Between plagues of rats, firestorms and the gleaming blue eyes of a sexy Scottish werewolf, she might just have landed herself in the middle of a magical apocalypse. She might also be the only person who has the ability to bring order to an utterly chaotic new world.

Book One - Shrill Dusk

Book Two - Brittle Midnight

Book Three - Furtive Dawn

Printed in Great Britain
by Amazon

62688506R00170

THE NEW PRAGMATISM

Also by Alan Malachowski and published by Acumen

Richard Rorty

THE NEW PRAGMATISM

Alan Malachowski

ACUMEN

For Jannie and Sophie

First published in 2010 by Acumen

Acumen Publishing Limited
4 Saddler Street
Durham
DH1 3NP
www.acumenpublishing.co.uk

ISBN: 978-1-84465-072-9 (hardcover)
ISBN: 978-1-84465-073-6 (paperback)

British Library Cataloguing-in-Publication Data
A catalogue record for this book is available from the British Library.

Typeset in Warnock Pro.
Printed and bound in Great Britain by
Cromwell Press Group, Trowbridge, Wiltshire